A
TALE
OF
TRANSFORMATION

A
TALE
OF
TRANSFORMATION

THE LIGHT BEYOND THE SHADOWS

BOOK 2

PETER SANTOS

Spirit Speaks Publishing

A Tale of Transformation: The Light Beyond the Shadows, Book 2

Published by Spirit Speaks Publishing
www.spiritspeakspublishing.com
Berlin, Vermont

ISBN-13: 978-1945705120

Library of Congress Control Number: 2024917272

Cover design by Peter Santos. Cover tree by powensby on Pixabay.

. . . I had no choice but to flow with the circumstances around me, but that was going to change. In due course, I was going to have the ultimate test put before me, one that would entail risk, sacrifice, and death, and my decision would determine not only my future but the future of the entire world.

BOOK 2

A TALE OF
TRANSFORMATION

Anna

Anna returned to her cabin, trembling with emotions. Her teacher had been detained in the Territories and was to be put on trial for subversion, a very serious offense that came with the penalty of death if found guilty.

She sat on her bed and fought back anxious tears. It was her fault. He had taken her aside a week ago and had asked if she would do something for him. Of course she had said yes. Then he told her what it was.

Her ensuing refusal was emphatic; she would not, could not, fulfill his request. How could she be a part of something that would bring him harm? And why would he even ask, knowing what would happen?

After explaining why he had asked *her*, of all people, and describing the repercussions of her accepting the task, he had told her to think carefully on it and to not answer right away. She had done so, taking several days to find a certain level of comfort with her answer. Once she had made her decision and the implications of it sank in, however, her feeling of disloyalty brought about doubt and guilt, and she now bore the cross of that betrayal.

As he had instructed, Anna had told no one of their plans except for her father, a constable in the Territories. Her teacher—"Teacher" to all who knew him—had said that her father would tell another government official, who would understand what was to happen and would put things in motion.

That official had done what was necessary, and now all of it was coming to fruition, just as Teacher had said it would.

It wasn't just hearing the news of Teacher's charge that was affecting her; it was noticing that others had begun looking at her with suspicion, even with anger. Just before returning to her cabin, she had received several disapproving looks and had recognized what they meant: people were blaming *her* for Teacher's predicament. They were upset because he was more than just *her* teacher, he was *everyone's* teacher, both within the Territories and in all the villages outside the Grand Wall, as well as a friend and mentor to many.

He warned me about this, she thought, sitting uneasily with one knee jiggling up and down. Although he had told her what was going to happen to him—and to her—it didn't lessen the impact of knowing that everyone would soon know about her role, as what had been prophesized had now become very real. And despite knowing this was coming, she had underestimated the influence her doubts and fears would have on her emotions and ability to think straight.

Putting a hand on her leg to stop it from moving, she thought, *No, this is not what he would want me to do.* She took a deep breath and let it out slowly, trying to remember his teachings through her emotional turmoil.

She closed her eyes and tried to center herself as best she could, going within to find the peace she knew she possessed. Over the last ten years, she had been trained in this contemplation practice, and she now felt herself expand into that center to find the comfortable stillness she knew so well.

But there were limits to it this time. Her mind and emotions continued to reach for her attention, preventing her from settling into the clear wellspring of lightness she knew was within.

Distracted, she blinked herself back to full awareness of the world around her and stood up. Walking to the window at the back of her home, she stared out at the nearby trees.

She knew what lay before her, as she had felt it for some time now. The short stories she had written the past few years about what she had learned had prepared her well, and Teacher had confirmed that it was time. Strangely, now, amid her agitation, looking out the window and seeing and connecting with the natural world she lived in the midst of, she started to feel the inspiration that had been missing. As a knowingness began to infuse her, she smiled, feeling a small sense of the peace she had pursued just moments before. It was time to begin what had been foretold.

She turned to the shelf on the wall and gathered a quill, a small bottle of ink, and some sheets of paper. Moving to her table, she sat down and stacked the blank sheets to her left except for one page, which she placed before her. She closed her eyes for a moment, trying to become an empty vessel for what needed to be expressed. When she opened them, she took another deep breath, dipped the quill in ink, and in large letters wrote the title she had seen in her mind.

She stared at it for a moment, then nodded in thanks, flipped the page to the side, and put another blank sheet in front of her. The words were coming, and she was ready.

Her story would finally be told.

A Tale of Transformation

Home

I ran away from home the night of my thirteenth birthday. The reasons why aren't as important as knowing that it was the first step toward the life I was meant to live. Suffice it to say that my childhood and family situation left something to be desired. There is one thing, however, that would be helpful to know: without Teacher, my life would be very different.

He came to me on that day I put my childhood behind me and, without knowing it, showed me that no matter what was happening around me, things would turn out okay. I came to learn later that it was his first teaching, and he didn't even know it.

Coincidentally—at least I thought so at the time—it came just after I had read a story that had put me in a frame of mind to recognize what he was and what he represented. That story, an old, handwritten manuscript titled *A Tale of Awakening*, provided me the inspiration I needed at a critical time. However, it wasn't until years later that I was able to truly understand what had transpired that day and the impact the tale had on my life.

When we saw each other for the first time that afternoon on my birthday, we didn't speak; he simply looked at me and I at him and time collapsed to bring me into his world for the briefest of moments, and that was all I needed. The strength I felt from that connection carried me through to when we were finally able to meet years later. Clearly, I had to have my own journey first, and he his.

I left home that fateful night, quietly stuffing a small pack with my meager belongings in the wee hours of the morning and sneaking out of my family's lodging house in the Territories. I didn't know where I was going, but I had a newfound level of self-confidence that had previously eluded me given my childhood upbringing.

It was a cool night, but I had a coat, and I wasn't worried about shelter, as it was a period of generally nice weather before the seasonal rains. I wandered at first, taking my time to meander the empty streets and see more of the city than I had ever seen on my limited routes to school, the marketplace, and the cathedral. Surprisingly, I didn't run into any of the constables who roamed the streets at night. If I had, I would have likely been quickly deposited back home, for I'm not sure I could have credibly explained myself to them as a solitary, adolescent girl with no reason to be out and about at that time. Also, my father was a constable, and he would have gotten the word out to find me as soon as he had noticed my disappearance. I imagined how much angrier he would be with me if I were found away from home, so I remained careful in my exploration.

Wandering by the empty marketplace, I passed one of my favorite shops in the darkness, wondering when I would be able to drop in again. I knew I had to stay mostly anonymous and hidden for a time, and I assumed the antique store would be one of the places people would look for me because of my frequent visits there. Still, I wanted to talk with the shopkeeper because something I had read in the old manuscript led me to believe he could help me somehow.

From what I could see in the dim light of the crescent moon, the square was empty. I looked for one of the characters from that *Tale of Awakening*—a blind panhandler that seemed to often be in the marketplace—but he wasn't there. Mildly disappointed, I wondered if he was off helping someone find deeper meaning in their life like he had done in the story.

With the early morning sun beginning to lighten the sky, soon to illuminate the spire of the cathedral, I found a stairwell next to a bakery a few streets away from the market. There I hid, wanting to avoid all contact from anyone who might be looking for me. It was away from the more trafficked streets, so very few passed by, and even if they did, I could hear them coming and get to a corner where I was invisible from the street.

During the bulk of the day, I stayed there and out of sight. Fortunately, I had brought some food from home so didn't have to risk exposing myself on the streets.

Being in one place gave me time to think about what I had just done and what would come next, which, admittedly, left me a little confused. I didn't know where to go or what to do, only that I needed to be away from my father. For some reason, I didn't worry about it too much because I was still feeling newly empowered by having made such a bold choice, leaving behind what I saw as unsafe and limiting circumstances, and by my first encounter with Teacher.

Sitting on the steep, shady steps, I pulled out from my pack the leather book cover of the aforementioned story, one of the few things I had brought with me when I scurried out of the house into the cool, nighttime air. I had found it on my way out the door, kicked into the corner after being unceremoniously dropped by my father when he last threatened me. Perhaps the cover would help me remember the tale, as the handwritten papers that held the inspiring words had been destroyed. Well, almost all of them.

Looking at the three spirals on the leather cover did indeed bring forth an additional sense of peace, a soft and distant knowing that I had done the right thing despite the unknown future before me. And I continued to hold to the feeling I had received when sharing my first glance with Teacher the previous day, which had imbued me with a confidence that everything would work out fine in the end, whatever was to happen.

The day progressed without incident, except for a few times when the stairwell door opened, and I quickly darted up the steps and onto the street to avoid the encounters, only to return shortly thereafter. But late in the day and out of food, I decided to risk engaging with others. Never underestimate the emotional value of a girl's sad and pleading look, for it served me well that afternoon, and I was able to get small handouts to sufficiently fill my belly.

Afterward, as I scampered back to my hiding spot by the bakery, a tall woman with dark, messy hair grabbed my arm as I passed her on the street. Surprised, I tried to pull away as her intense eyes bored into me, holding me as strongly as her grip on my arm.

"You need to go to the plaza," she said somewhat anxiously.

"Let me go," I said, not too loudly as to attract the attention of others.

She held on for a moment longer with her tattooed hand, then said, "You will find what you are looking for there," and she released my arm and walked away.

I stood unmoving for a minute, watching her leave, unsure of what to make of her words, then continued back to my concealed steps to think about what I would do next.

I wanted to stay hidden, but the woman somehow seemed to know something about my predicament, and it gave me an option I hadn't considered. What she had said somehow resonated with me, so, trusting in the strange encounter, I decided to head toward the plaza as the light continued its descent in the sky.

I cautiously made my way to the city center, being careful to avoid the watchful eyes of the constables, who continued their beats in a rather predictable manner.

Once at the plaza, I kept to the shadows and surveyed the remaining people walking about as storeowners closed their shops, churchgoers left the cathedral, and workers headed home. One figure, however, seemed out of place. She was leaning against the stone wall at the base of the cathedral's grand steps and looking directly at me, unmoving.

Although I didn't know it at the time, she was a monk, one of the elusive figures the Territory Governors were constantly searching for but could never find. She was not dressed as one— or as I expected one to be—rather, she wore relatively plain clothes that were not unlike others who were leaving the plaza. What made her different were the tattoos she revealed when she rolled up her sleeves while walking toward me. They ran up and down her arms and were eerily reminiscent of those in a vivid dream I had recently had. They drew my attention because I had not seen many inked designs on bodies in my young life. As she approached, I saw a quality to her eyes that made them sparkle, like she was in on a grand joke. She carried a bag over one shoulder.

Stopping directly in front of me, she said, "Hi, my name is Shasta."

"Hi, I'm Anna." I couldn't help looking at her arms, so I pointed and asked, "What are those markings?"

She smiled. "They are ancient symbols that have great meaning to me and to many in my village. Do you like them?"

"Yes, they're . . . interesting."

"Why are you here in the plaza?" she asked.

For some reason she engendered trust, and I didn't think she would turn me in to the constables, so I told her the truth.

"I, uh, ran away from home last night," I said. "I spent the day near the marketplace hiding from the constables."

"Oh, I'm sorry to hear that. Are you planning on going home soon?"

I shook my head. "I don't want to go home."

"Why not?"

I hesitated, not knowing how to answer.

"I can walk you back home if you want," she added.

I shook my head again. "No, I don't want to go back."

Is anyone looking for you?"

"Probably."

"Are you sure you don't want to go back?"

"Yes." I was surprised at how firmly I said it. "A tall woman with dark, messy hair told me to come here, so I did. She said I'd find what I'm looking for, but I don't know what that is."

"Hmm, a tall woman with dark hair, you say?" Shasta seemed reflective for a moment. "And you don't know what you're looking for?"

I shook my head. "I just don't want to go home."

I was beginning to feel desperate on one level, not knowing what I should do or where I should go, so I held onto this second, seemingly random encounter that at least might provide me some direction.

"Do you have any place to stay tonight?"

I again shook my head.

"Would you like to come with me back to my village?"

I eagerly nodded. She had a kindness about her, an honesty that made me *know* I could trust her. Also, I had no other options, and it seemed too coincidental that her tattoos reflected the symbols I had seen in my recent dream. It was not an opportunity I could pass up, nor did I want to.

After she rolled down her sleeves, we began walking out of the city heading northeast. On the way, she graciously traded coins for some food with a street vendor so I could eat something: vegetables and cheese wrapped in thin bread and a sweet tea, all of which I consumed quickly. While I did, she closed her eyes and stood as still as a statue. After eating, she checked in with me again.

"Are you sure you don't want to go home? I'm guessing your parents will be missing you."

I shook my head. "I'm sure. I don't think they'll miss me that much." I had made up my mind.

"They might surprise you," Shasta said.

"I can't. I won't. I need to be away from them."

Shasta reflected for a moment, then said, "Okay."

We meandered through the streets, avoiding the constables, eventually clearing the city limits and entering a well-worn, forest path. We spoke little as we walked beneath the trees, and I surprisingly wasn't thinking or worrying as much as I would've thought. Instead, I was acutely aware of being surrounded by nature for longer than I had ever been.

It was glorious! Despite the unknown before me, what I had always suspected, that I would thrive in the middle of the woods, made me accept my circumstances as if I had been there many times before and was simply walking home. It was a far cry from the feeling I had the last time I had gone back to my family's house, which now no longer felt anything like home compared to this.

We continued for a while down the trail that remained wide enough for a cart to pass, then took a small, single-track path to the right where the main trail veered northwest toward the closest section of the Grand Wall, the towering, stone barrier that encircled the Territories. Shasta led the way, and before long we found ourselves in front of the great structure in the dusky light, the barrier's immense height still capturing some sun that peered over the West Wall. The path went right up to the obstacle.

Shasta stopped. I stepped forward and put my hands on the cold stones, feeling the firm surface for the first time in my life. It was as solid and impenetrable as I had heard, which made sense because it had protected the Territories for as long as anyone could remember. I could feel its density, a squeezing, contained feeling that made me want to step back and remove my hands. I didn't, though, because there was something warm and familiar about it as well, not something that I can even now describe.

After a minute, I withdrew my hands, turned, and saw Shasta observing me with a smile on her face. She stepped forward and stood next to me in front of the Wall and said, "Anna, what do you see?"

"Um, a stone wall?" I said tentatively, like I was missing something.

She took my hand and looked down at me. Slowly, a warm, tingling feeling infused my body, and whatever confining feeling I had from touching the Wall evaporated. I felt more expansive than I had ever felt.

Shasta continued to observe me as I tried to wrap my head around what I was experiencing. "Now, what do you see," she said.

I turned to the Wall again, and it didn't seem so solid anymore. It wasn't because what I saw looked different; it was because something inside me *felt* it was different. It felt lighter, less dense.

"What's happening?" I asked.

"Just relax," she said. "I know you can do this." She gripped my hand more firmly and, in what seemed like slow motion, she took an impossible step forward, planting her foot squarely *through* and *into* the Wall.

~

I should take a moment now to mention that Shasta has become one of my dearest friends and mentors. Not only did she shepherd me through my teenage years and early studies, but she was also instrumental in helping me genuinely understand the lessons I received—from her and others—which profoundly altered the course of my life. Her wisdom and guidance prepared me well for Teacher's coming, and I came to realize that without them, I would not have been able to see and experience Teacher for who he truly was. What I had understood about the world before meeting Shasta paled in comparison to my understanding afterward.

Shasta's eyes continued to hold my wide-eyed gaze as the Grand Wall absorbed her body and face with her next step, her arm extending backwards due to my being frozen in place. Her strong grip, however, gently pulled me forward so that I, too, moved *into* the barrier.

Closing my eyes tightly, my body buzzed like it never had before, enhancing the confusion I was already experiencing from her entry into the impassable. When I opened them, I saw, kind of, the path we were on, a continuation of the trail we had walked upon up to the barrier, but the environment was hazy, and I could just make out Shasta's figure in front of me as it continued forward slowly but confidently. The gray of the stone brushed by my face like blowing sand, leaving the slightest tickle. Somehow, I felt it on my insides too, sweeping through my body with countless tiny points of impact that struck gently and then passed by. It would have left me queasy if it wasn't so uplifting, as if I were standing tall and taking a breath of fresh, clean air with my arms outstretched in the sunlight. I walked carefully forward and held her hand in an iron grip in case a misplaced step or letting go would merge me with the Wall and leave me forever trapped within the hard, unforgiving stones.

We continued inside it for at least a dozen of my adolescent-sized paces, emerging on the other side to the dusk that was brighter than what was within the Wall. I exhaled sharply, not realizing I had been holding my breath. Shasta tried to let go of my hand, but I couldn't yet release her.

"I knew you could do it," she said, smiling. She looked down at my anxious, clutching grip. "It's okay. You can let go now."

It took a minute to steady my breathing and loosen my grasp, and the hum and lightness in my body slowly dissipated. I turned around and looked back at where we had come from and took a step back in astonishment. There was no Wall. The trail stretched back like any other trail through the woods. No one would know there was an obstacle there, and there wasn't, at least as it appeared from this side.

Shasta moved a few paces away to the side of the trail. "Do you see this grand red oak?" she said, patting the trunk of a large tree with hefty branches that stretched across the trail. With its wide canopy of flaming red leaves, it was the biggest and most distinct tree I had seen so far on our walk through the woods.

I nodded, trembling slightly due to what I had just been through—literally—not yet able to say anything.

"Remember it. It's a good marker to know when you're about to pass through the Wall, at least on this trail, but once you practice, you'll also be able to feel it, sense it, as you approach."

I nodded again.

She noticed my trembling and came over to give me a hug. "Oh, honey, you'll be okay. The first time is always a bit scary."

I hugged her back. Her warmth was comforting, in more ways than one.

Finally gathering my voice, I asked, "Did we just walk *through* the Grand Wall?"

She freed me from the embrace and smiled. "What did you think?"

"Uh, it was . . . weird. Like I was moving through it, but it was also moving through me at the same time. It's like I actually *felt* the inside of the stones. How is that possible? How did you . . . we . . . do that?"

"You see a wall that is solid, but I know that it isn't, and I brought you into what I was experiencing."

"What? How?"

"It's a combination of seeing, feeling, and knowing. If you believe something strongly enough—if you *know* it through to your bones—and you learn about the true nature of matter, then you'll be able to do wondrous things. What your eyes tell you is just one part of the story, and appearances can be deceiving. You'll learn, and probably fast, too. I believe you have a talent for it. For now, let's just say that the world you think you know isn't everything. There's so much more."

"How will I learn? Are you going to teach me?" I asked.

She smiled warmly. "We've already started."

She sat me down on a fallen log by the side of the trail and continued the lesson on appearances, sharing how she was able to connect with me in a way that allowed me to experience *being* beyond what I saw with my eyes. She also talked about how taking a moment to *feel* what I see or hear would help me understand my environment beyond what is presented on the surface.

When finished, I reached for her hand, which she accepted, and we continued down the trail to her village. My escape from home and luck in finding Shasta, if you could call it that, had helped me crawl through a portal to another world—like the ones in the magical stories I liked to read and the one I had drawn on my bedroom wall when I was a child—but this time it wasn't contained within the pages of a book or in my imagination. This time it was real, and I couldn't wait for the next chapter.

~

When I had looked back at where the Wall was supposed to be, something felt different. I couldn't quite put my finger on it, but there was a clarity to the feeling that reminded me of my first glimpse of Teacher.

From what I knew about the Grand Wall at the time, those who went beyond it most certainly perished in the supposed desolate landscape on the other side or at the hands of the dangerous and depraved foreigners who somehow survived outside the Territories. I was a little apprehensive at this thought because I was now marching boldly forward toward an unknown destination outside the protection of the Wall with someone I barely knew. But there was no feeling of danger at all, and the natural environment seemed to become more and more pleasant as we continued. In fact, I felt more alive and connected to my surroundings than I had ever felt living in the city.

Shasta and I continued up the trail through the forest. About thirty minutes later we came upon a village with a clearing in its center. Small log and earthen houses were scattered about, and adjacent to the clearing was a larger building, which matched a similarly-constructed one up on a knoll away from the other structures. To the side, a stream babbled its way down the hill to the edge of the open area, its small waterfalls creating a pleasant, natural sound that was music to my ears.

About half of the dozen people I could see were dressed in faded, red and orange robes, the others in simple shirts and trousers or unassuming dresses, and most were smiling and laughing and seemed perfectly happy. An older couple was sitting in front of the building on the knoll in what appeared to be deep thought, and three others were doing a slow dance under the trees next to the clearing. I took in the wondrous, magical scene with all my senses. It was like nothing I had ever seen or studied, even in the fictional tales I had read.

We walked toward one of the larger houses near the stream, and I could see and even *feel* the residents of the village looking at me, a stranger amid their utopia. It made me wonder how often they were visited by people from the other side of the Wall, if ever.

As we approached the house, the door opened and a tall woman with dark hair emerged, staring at me with her steady, brown, piercing eyes. I immediately recognized her as the woman in the streets of the Territories who had told me to go to the central plaza where I had met Shasta. I must have looked shocked because she reached out her inked hand, put it warmly on my shoulder, and said, "I know. I'm sure it's a bit of a surprise to see me again."

Her appearance and demeanor were very different from when I had seen her earlier. Her long hair was not at all messy—rather, it was well combed and tied in a ponytail with a fine, blue ribbon—and she was not anxious or agitated as she had been when she had grabbed my arm in the city. In fact, she now seemed very much more composed, exuding a rather serene bearing that, despite her intense gaze, felt warmly welcoming.

Behind her was a large man in dull red and orange robes, a contrast to the woman's modest attire of a white shirt under a long, light brown dress. They both had a regal quality about them, and I couldn't help but get the impression that they were appraising me.

"Anna, this is Kyna," Shasta said, gesturing to the tall woman, "and Caedmon," motioning to the man.

"Nice to meet you, Anna," Kyna said, nodding. Caedmon bowed more deeply but said nothing. "Welcome to our village. You'll be staying with Shasta next door. I hope that's acceptable. It's all set for you." She pointed to a small cabin about twenty paces away.

"Uh, thank you," I said.

Noticing my confusion, Kyna said, "Yes, we were expecting you. I'll explain later. Make yourself at home. You must be hungry after your journey. We'll gather for mealtime soon, but until then, Shasta, take her to the kitchen and get her whatever she wants."

Shasta nodded. "Of course."

I stood there dumbfounded. Maybe it was the feeling of lightness in my head, being tired after a night on the streets and the long walk from the city, my experience of moving through the Wall, or perhaps a combination of all of them, but I certainly was surprised at the idea that they had known I was coming.

"Let's drop our belongings and head to the kitchen," Shasta said, and I followed her to the adjacent cabin in the waning light.

Shasta's place was a simple, wooden dwelling, essentially one large room with two beds along one wall, each covered by a multicolored blanket, and a table and two chairs by the opposite wall. In between the beds was a standing partition, and I could see a washbasin in the corner partially obscured behind another partition. A circular, woven rug lay in the middle of the room, and a small table holding a few candles and what looked like a bunch of dried leaves were in another corner. There was an armoire at the back of the room and a few shelves on the walls that held various items in baskets. I immediately fell in love with its natural simplicity.

"So, this is your home?" I asked my companion.

"Yes. Do you like it?"

"I love it! It's very different from my place in the city, in a good way."

"I'm glad. I hope you don't mind living with me for the time being. When you're ready, you can build your own home if you want to."

"Really? That would be amazing." The prospect of a new beginning, and even having my own place, excited me beyond words. It was more than I could have hoped for when I decided to run away and leave everything I had ever known. And staying with someone with whom I felt increasingly comfortable and could learn from was perfect, not to mention being in what appeared to be a wonderful village community, which was certainly better than living on the streets . . . or with my parents.

We dropped our belongings, left the cabin, and Shasta walked me to the back of the large building by the clearing. Inside was a kitchen being tended by a young, affable couple, who greeted Shasta warmly when we entered.

"Hey there! How was your excursion to the city?" the woman asked.

The two hugged. "It went as expected," Shasta said. Turning to me, she said, "I want to introduce you to Anna. Anna, this is Jamaica and Guri. They do most of the cooking."

"So, this is the one," Guri said, coming over and taking my face in both his hands. "I can see why she's here."

"Um, nice to meet you," I said, wondering what he meant.

"You too," Guri said. He and Jamaica smiled affectionately at me. They clearly were told something about me beforehand, but how could they know anything? I had never been outside the Territories and had never engaged with anyone like Shasta or the other people here. Something strange was happening in this new world I had entered.

The kitchen itself had what looked like a brick oven attached to a large fireplace that held an outsized pot over the fire. Baking in the oven were loaves of bread whose aroma wafted deliciously through the space. A large table in the center of the room was filled with vegetables and fruits in various stages of preparation for cooking and baking. It looked as though they were planning a feast.

"What would you like?" Jamaica asked as she stepped back to the table and began cutting some carrots.

"Uh, I'll just grab an apple, thanks," I said and reached for one in the bushel by the door.

"Take anything you want," she said. "We'll be eating soon enough."

I nodded, and Shasta guided me through double doors into an expansive dining hall with an enormous wooden table in the center and a few smaller tables along the walls.

"This is where we eat," she said.

I walked slowly around the room, taking a bite of the apple and looking about. Shasta sat on one of the benches at the table. I completed my circuit of the space and sat down opposite her.

"How many people live in the village," I asked.

"Close to one hundred," she said.

I nodded. "Are you a monk? Are all of you monks?"

Shasta smiled. "What does it mean to be a monk?"

"Um, I don't know, except that the Territory Governors always said to watch out for you, that you're dangerous."

"Do you think we're dangerous?"

"No," I said, more quickly than I would have thought. The words came from a feeling. "Why do they think you're dangerous?"

"Because they're afraid of losing control and they will do anything they can to retain it," she said, looking me squarely in the eyes.

"Can they get through the Wall?"

"Not with their current thinking."

"What do you mean?"

Shasta took a deep breath. "I wasn't going to get into another lesson just yet, but suffice it to say that their external environment reflects their internal environment."

Strangely, despite the *How?* question that came up in my mind, what she said felt right and made some kind of sense, despite it not really making any sense at all. I must have had a confused look on my face because she laughed and said, "We'll get into details later."

With that, Shasta rose and said, "Come on. I'll show you around the rest of the village while there's still some light."

I followed her out of the great hall and into the clearing, continuing to eat my apple. I pointed to the three people still practicing the slow dance under the trees and asked what it was.

"They're doing an ancient practice that cultivates energy."

I was curious but didn't ask more. There was a lot I was already trying to absorb. I figured the answers would come in time.

We walked past a large boulder at the edge of the clearing and up the slight hill to the larger building on the knoll. It was like the kitchen and dining structure but with wooden steps up to a deck in front of the doors. Two older monks in robes, a man and a woman, sat peacefully on the platform with their eyes closed. We ascended the stairs and Shasta turned around and said softly, "What do you see?"

I turned and from our vantage point on the knoll, we were looking down on the village. In the dusky light, I could now see that the community dwellings were distributed in the approximate shape of three spirals that came together at the clearing in the center. I let out a gasp.

"I know this shape!" I said. "It was on the cover of a book I read just yesterday!"

Shasta looked at me, seemingly confused at first, but then her face relaxed and she broke out in a grin, nodding slowly.

"I see," she said. "Interesting."

"I have it with me, just the cover, though, not the story inside."

She kept nodding slowly, seemingly off in another world, like she was trying to put the pieces of a puzzle together. She didn't explain further, and I didn't ask. I told her I would show it to her when we returned to her cabin.

We turned to the building's entrance and walked through the large double doors into another great hall. Inside, benches lined the sides of the open space leading to a raised platform at the back. There were several symbols carved into the beams and hanging on the walls, lit up by the numerous hanging lanterns. I looked at the arm tattoos of my companion and many of the designs were similar.

"What are the symbols?" I asked.

"They are part of an ancient language we tap into through our practices," she said. "They speak to the world within."

"The world within?" I said. It was a new concept to me, having only been exposed to it through the story with the spiral cover, an idea I hadn't yet had an opportunity to explore.

"Yes," Shasta said, "that part of you that feels beyond feeling, knows beyond knowing . . . the part that gives meaning to why you're here."

Being only thirteen, I hadn't ever given any thought to why I was here. I paused for a moment and then looked at her and asked, "So, why am I here?"

The monk smiled. "That is for you to discover for yourself."

~

It was getting dark quickly, so we went back to Shasta's cabin so I could rest and try to get settled before dinner. Since I didn't have much with me, I just sat on the bed and breathed out what felt like years of pressure and tension. I was spent, but the anticipation of a delicious dinner kept me from falling asleep.

Remembering the leather book cover with the three spirals, I opened my pack, pulled it out, and handed it to Shasta, who took it and turned it over in her hands.

"Yes, this is the one," she said.

"The one what?" I asked.

"Oh, it's just very familiar, almost like I had it in my hands this morning," she said with a grin.

There was something about how she said it that made me think there was more to the cover's story, but I was too tired to follow up.

A short time later a bell echoed across the clearing and into my new home, and I followed Shasta out to the main hall to sit with the other residents at the large table in the center of the room. The welcome I felt was like nothing I had ever experienced. Some tried not to stare at the new stranger in their midst but found it difficult, and everyone I met was exceedingly generous in their acceptance of my presence in the community, almost to the point of being joyful for it. They all seemed thrilled to have me there. It was so different from my previous existence that I indeed felt like I was in another world. It was a lot to take in, as I wasn't used to that kind of attention, but it left me feeling genuinely loved and accepted, a rarity I had only occasionally experienced before.

A few people rose and helped Jamaica and Guri bring out dinner, the most delicious meal I had ever eaten. I savored a depth of flavors I couldn't have even dreamed about before. When I asked what kind of meat was in the wonderful stew, people laughed, and Shasta said it wasn't meat but a vegetable and grain combination, which surprised me because it had the consistency and taste of meat. There also was fish, something I had heard about in the Territories but had never tried, and I found it delightful. Breads, cheeses, fruits, and vegetables filled the rest of the table, and everyone happily passed around and shared the bounty. The freshness and energy of the food was fantastic, and it made the food in the Territories seem bland and empty in comparison. It was perfect.

When I collapsed into my new bed after dinner, the sweet sounds of light and loving conversation still echoing in my ears, I fell asleep almost immediately. The day's activities and events had exhausted me. Any apprehension over what I had experienced melted away during the evening, pulled from my body by the friendliness of the people, the glorious food, and the cool, fresh, night air that sizzled with an energy that the air in the city didn't have, couldn't have. I now realized how much I needed the natural world around me.

I didn't realize it then, but I had felt something I'm not sure I had ever felt so convincingly. Despite having left my childhood home in the Territories and being in a place I had been told was dangerous and deadly, for the first time I truly felt safe.

I was finally home.

Anna

Anna stopped writing, put down the quill, and massaged her hands. The bottle of ink on the table was almost empty. On her left were just a few blank sheets of paper, and on her right was the beginning of her story. She had been writing for hours.

She needed a break, and more writing supplies, but she felt it was too late to bother the bookmaker in the village, even though she was sure he would have gone out of his way to help her. No, it could wait until tomorrow.

There was a knock on the door and Jillian entered. She was about Anna's age, and they were very close. She was clearly checking in on Anna.

"I heard what happened. How are you doing?" she asked.

"I'm okay. What did you hear?"

"That he's being charged with subversion and that," she hesitated, "that people are saying it's your fault." Anna could tell it was hard for her to say.

Word of Anna's betrayal must have traveled fast. Anna knew Jillian wouldn't be upset about it, as she knew Anna well and was aware of the importance of her role, however it played out.

"It was going to get out sooner or later," Anna said.

"Are you really okay?" Jillian said, placing a hand on Anna's shoulder.

Anna nodded and put her hand over Jillian's.

"It's been difficult, as you know," Anna said, "but now everything's in motion. It'll take some time for me to adjust to it all, but I think I'm right where I need to be, even though knowing that doesn't make it any less uncomfortable. I've got to stay centered and remember the teachings."

Jillian removed her hand and leaned down to give Anna a hug, which Anna heartily embraced. She didn't know how badly she needed to feel Jillian's warmth.

Anna eventually let go, and Jillian sat in the other chair at the table, glanced at the stack of handwritten papers, and said, "Looks like you've been busy."

Anna chuckled. "Yes, I can barely keep pace with what's coming through me."

"Is there anything I can do?"

Anna normally wasn't very good at delegating, but this felt like an appropriate opportunity.

"Actually, I need more ink and paper, and perhaps a new quill. Would you mind going to the bookmaker and getting me some? I'm starving and thought I'd run to the kitchen and grab something before everyone gathers for dinner. I don't feel like eating with the group tonight, especially since word's gotten around."

"Absolutely. No problem," Jillian said, standing up.

She grabbed Anna's hand, held it, and looked at her. "You're going to be okay."

It reminded Anna of her first ever interaction with Teacher, and Anna gave her a slight nod, squeezed her hand back, and said, "Yes, thank you."

Anna rose and accompanied Jillian out of the cabin and down the path toward the village center. Just then, the reverberations of the dining bell echoed throughout the forest, signifying mealtime. Anna considered her options. She didn't want to be around people, but she knew she needed nourishment to keep her energy up. After a quick contemplation, she decided to just bring some food back home.

She had always received many glances from the residents of the village due to her anticipated role in the prophecy, but the looks she now received—and felt—were very different. Word had indeed spread about her involvement in Teacher's arrest, because she was now being looked at not with gratitude as before but with various measures of disapproval, and she had to stay centered to protect herself from the sharp points of those energies that stabbed at her through the angry looks. Not all held that view, however.

"Hi, you two," Naveen said as he approached. He must have seen them emerge from the wooded path at the edge of the clearing. His years of cultivating energy with the slow dance had been good to him; it had infused him with a poised composure and graceful expression of movement.

"Hi, Naveen," Jillian said. Anna gave him a quick wave.

"Shall we sit together?" he asked.

"I'm going to grab something and bring it home instead," Anna said.

"Do you want company?" he said.

Anna thought for a moment. She often liked to work through situations on her own, relying on all the teachings she had received, but this time was different. This time she couldn't quite shake the unseen trembling in her core, and spending some time with close friends might help ground her or help her gain some clarity.

"Sure, yes," she said.

"Great! You too?" he asked Jillian.

Jillian looked at Anna, who nodded. "Yes, as soon as I run an errand," and she turned off the path to walk up to the building on the hill.

"Are you doing okay?" Naveen asked Anna as they continued to the kitchen.

Anna gave him a nod. "I'm okay. I'm doing what I need to be doing."

"You know better than to blame yourself."

"I know, but it's tough sometimes. I guess everyone knows by now."

Naveen nodded. "Probably. Anything I can do?"

"No, just having a quiet meal with you and Jillian would be great."

"My pleasure," he said.

They walked to the kitchen at the back of the building where Jamaica and Guri had prepared the evening meal. The two cooks were busy scooping stew into bowls, preparing large dishes of noodles, and cutting hot bread straight out of the brick oven. Several residents entered and left through the doors between the kitchen and the main hall to bring out meals for others. One middle-aged man shot Anna a cross look when he entered. Jamaica observed it, saw that it was directed at Anna, and immediately snapped at the man.

"I will not have that energy in my kitchen!"

The man's expression changed at the scolding, and he slinked back into the dining hall with a few plates and bowls. He didn't come back in.

"Thank you for that," Naveen said to Jamaica.

Anna knew she had her friends to protect her, even though she was fully capable of protecting herself. She felt honored that her friends could see beyond the shadows of the incident in question and stand up for her knowing she might have difficulty finding her center amid the circumstances.

"Do you both want a plate in here?" Jamaica asked, gesturing toward a small table with two chairs in the corner where she and Guri often sat between their meal preparations.

"No, thank you," Anna said. "I want to take it home, if that's okay with you."

"Of course!" Jamaica said. She looked at Naveen. "You too?"

"Yes, please. And Jillian will come in soon for one, too," Naveen said.

Jamaica nodded, and seconds later she was handing them each a plate of bread and a bowl she had filled with hot stew and noodles.

The two thanked her and Guri and slipped out the back door of the kitchen to head back to Anna's cabin.

The First Week

I slept very deeply that first night in my new, unfamiliar living conditions, wrapped in the comfort of dreams that carried me softly to vaguely-remembered places where I felt sheltered and secure. Awakening later than I usually did, I found myself alone in the cabin. Shasta's bed was made and there was a small bowl of fresh fruit and a glass of water on the table. I sat on the bed, yawned, and stretched my arms wide, then emptied the bowl of its delicious contents, sipping the water as I ate. I detected a hint of lemon and something else I couldn't identify in the drink, a subtle flavor that felt like the morning sun making its way to my stomach. After a quick rinse at the washbasin in the corner, I made my way to the door and opened it to reveal the crisp, natural, forest air. I was ready to meet whatever the new day would bring.

Breathing deeply, I stepped out of the cabin and observed my surroundings. One young monk was doing the slow dance under the trees like when I had arrived yesterday, and another was sitting peacefully and silently on a bench on the other side of the clearing with his eyes closed. Two older residents in regular clothes strolled nearby and upon seeing me smiled and bowed in greeting, which I reciprocated. I heard some noises coming from the main hall, which I assumed was a gathering for food and drink, but having had the fruit in the cabin and not feeling like being the object of attention again, I decided to explore.

I went to the edge of the triangular clearing and followed one of the paths to its center where a large, round stone lay buried in the earth. My eyes widened and I gasped when I saw the three spiral carvings on its surface, as the engraving was exactly what I had seen in my morning dream two days before, the day of my birthday, the day that changed my life. In addition, it matched the spiral pattern on the leather book cover I had taken with me, as well as the shape of the village I had glimpsed last evening from the building up on the hill. I bent down and ran my hand over the flat, rough stone, my fingers tracing the swirling grooves to the triangular center. It was real, not just an image from my dream, and it made me think about what else in my dream that morning might be real, or maybe a premonition. I stood up and couldn't suppress an audible laugh at the ongoing coincidences with the symbol.

"Would you care to join me?"

I spun around to find the source of the young, male voice. It was the monk who was practicing the slow dance under the trees at the edge of the clearing. I walked over to him.

"Hi," I said.

"Hi." He paused his movements and extended his hand. "I'm Naveen."

"I'm Anna," I said, shaking his hand. He was extremely handsome, almost distractingly so, with prominent cheekbones, a natural smile, and a glowing energy. He looked to be a few years older.

"Welcome to our village. We're glad you're finally here."

"Thanks, I'm glad to be here. But what do you mean by 'finally'?" I asked.

"Oh, so no one's told you about the prophecy?"

"Um, nooo . . ." I said, looking at him with raised eyebrows. "I only arrived last night."

"Oh no! I probably wasn't supposed to say anything," he said, biting his lip.

"Well, now you're just going to have to tell me," I said. "I'm sure I'm going to find out sooner or later." I felt confident in my new surroundings.

He took a deep breath and looked around, but no one was within earshot. He stepped closer to me, and my skin tingled.

"Okay, so there's been a prophecy for as long as anyone can remember that someone from a different land would come to the village and that their arrival would signal that a teacher will soon be coming."

I stared at him, not saying anything.

"That teacher, it is said, will change the world."

I continued to look at him blankly. It didn't make any sense.

"Then, a few years ago," he continued, "Promeus had a vision that provided more details about it, that the person coming to the village would not only signal this teacher's coming but would also play an important role in the changes to come. He said it would be a girl."

"Wait," I finally said, "are you saying that's me?"

He nodded.

I laughed. "C'mon. Really? Me?"

He looked disappointed, almost hurt by my reaction.

"Okay, so, who is this teacher?" I asked. "What changes are coming? And who is Promeus?" I was undoubtedly skeptical about what he had said, because how could it possibly refer to me, a thirteen-year-old, city-born runaway who knew nothing about this land beyond the Wall until yesterday, not to mention somehow having a connection to an unknown teacher who would change the world? And all this from a *prophecy?* It sounded crazy and defied logic, and it was overwhelming what my young brain was already trying to assimilate in my new surroundings.

He stared at me like I should have known the obvious, which was, of course, not so obvious to me at that point. But I could tell he really believed what he had said.

"I know it's you," he said. "I can feel it."

"And you think *I'm* supposed to play an important role somehow?"

He looked at me matter-of-factly. "Yes, your arrival tells us that the prophecy is beginning, and I'm sure your role will become apparent at some point. I'm just glad it's going to be during my lifetime."

Whatever warm and fuzzy feeling I was having that morning dampened quickly as my initial doubts about his words began to melt away. He seemed so genuine, which made me believe him, or at least made me believe that he and others believed it.

This was the first time I had felt a twinge of my old life since crossing the stone barrier, a harkening back to the pressure to perform. I had left my responsibilities and controlled existence behind in the Territories only to walk into some kind of obligation that I didn't know how I could possibly assume, foretold by someone who had a vision. It sounded crazy, but with recent events, I was beginning to trust that sometimes dreams and visions were more than just whimsical pictures in our heads. Sometimes they were real.

"Who is Promeus?" I asked, wanting to know more about the person who apparently knew more about my fate than I did.

"He's an older monk, the best of us with that sort of thing, better than others anyway. I don't think he's ever been wrong."

I laughed a nervous laugh, and Naveen joined.

"It's probably a lot to take in on your first day. You know what might help?"

"What?"

He took a step back to where he was previously practicing the slow dance and gestured me over.

"Follow what I'm doing," he said. "Try to copy it exactly. I guarantee you'll feel better after."

I don't know how long we practiced, but the time seemed to pass quickly. My sad attempts at mimicking his stance and movements, which were especially graceful, only led to both of us laughing hysterically as I fumbled one position after another. Finally, he said to just sit and watch him for a few minutes.

I sat leaning up against the tree and watched as he performed a stunningly beautiful combination of movements that seemed an embodiment of physical perfection—the balance of his upper body to his lower body as he stepped and turned slowly and softly, his groundedness to the earth, the graceful flow of his arms, hands, and even fingers moving as if there was some invisible energy directing his efforts. With his eyes only slightly open, his movements blended into the natural environment around him like the tree branches above bending with the wind. I felt an energy that I wasn't familiar with, one that linked me to him and to the earth and to the beauty I was beholding. It was hypnotic.

When he finished, after moving his hands up and down slowly in front of his body, then placing them together in front of his chest, I thought I was in love for the first time.

He opened his eyes and rubbed his palms together, then took a deep breath while stretching out his arms. "Nothing like some good, inner energy work to start the day!" he said.

"That was amazing. *I* felt something, too," I said.

"Like what?"

"Just an openness, an inner excitement. I can't really describe it. I feel really awake now, though."

"Just wait until you do it yourself. It's pretty great," he said.

"Will you teach me?" I asked.

He hesitated. "I would love to, but maybe you want to start with someone who can teach the basics better than I can. I can do the movements, but I haven't yet become an official teacher."

He must have read the disappointment on my face, so he added, "But we can practice together though."

That made me feel better. I smiled, thanked him for the lesson and demonstration and said, "I guess I'll see you around." I felt it was time to find Shasta and get something else to eat.

"Looking forward to it," he said.

~

I made my way to the main hall and entered. Shasta was sitting at the large table with several others, chatting amiably.

"There she is!" she exclaimed when she saw me approach. "Come sit and have something to eat. I trust you had a good rest?"

"Yes," I replied. "I slept a bit late."

"Oh, don't you worry about that. You've had a stressful couple of days. Your body needs some time to catch up and adjust."

"Thanks."

I sat down in front of various plates of fruit and a few kettles of what looked like hot tea. I grabbed an empty mug from a collection of them in the middle of the table, poured myself a cup, and took a sip. It was delicious. My face must have registered my delight because Shasta commented.

"Yes, it's really good. It's a particular blend that Guri created, a mix of licorice, mint, and elderberry I think."

"And a few other secret ingredients," Guri said smiling, entering the room from the kitchen with a plate of eggs and sausage, which he placed in front of me. "Eat up. You need to start the day off with some good energy."

"Thank you," I said. Even though I felt energized by my time with Naveen, seeing and smelling the contents on the plate before me made my stomach grumble in anticipation. I took a few bites while the others watched me. The food was delicious, once again far better than the food in the Territories. The sausage tasted different than when I had had it before, with a crunchiness and subtle, peppery flavor, and there were flecks of green and white mixed in with the eggs—I assumed herbs and a type of half-melted cheese I wasn't familiar with. "Mmm, really good. Thank you."

"You're very welcome, my dear," Guri said.

"You know," Shasta said, "there's no meat in the sausage. It's Guri's special recipe of vegetables, grains, and herbs. It's part of why breakfast is my favorite meal of the day."

"Oh, stop," Guri said, smiling.

"Would you like some?" I asked Shasta, offering her my plate.

"Oh, no thank you, but that's sweet of you to ask. I ate before you came in."

Shasta was looking at me and smiling. I think it gave her pleasure to see me so contented, which I was, especially as I was consuming the delightful meal. It was a different feeling than what I had been used to with my family in the Territories. But underneath being comfortable and satisfied, I was also experiencing a little anxiety, for what Naveen had said about the prophecy had left me a bit unsettled. Also, as much as everything in the village seemed to be close to perfect and I eagerly looked forward to learning more about my surroundings, I couldn't help but feel some apprehension at what might come next.

I quickly devoured my plate as Shasta introduced me to the others around the table. There was Leslie and the couple, Joran and Kalisa, who helped tend the gardens and grow the food for the community. Rohn, a man with a strong, wiry build, was a blacksmith, and Tenzin, who had one of the most open expressions I had ever seen, was a teacher. They all looked at me with a kindness that made me feel like I was part of one big family.

After eating, I brought my dish and mug to the kitchen and again thanked Guri and Jamaica for such a wonderful meal. Jamaica said, "Honey, when you make something with love, it's always going to be good," which warmed me even more than what the hot breakfast had done to my stomach.

I walked back into the main room, and Shasta and I left the building. Standing outside in the fresh air, Shasta guided me over to a bench and began to explain how the village operated.

As I came to learn, there didn't seem to be any specific scheduling or allocation of resources for what needed to get done for the proper functioning of the community. The residents merely applied the appropriate resources at the right times and the results took care of themselves, as if an unseen hand were crafting the circumstances, decisions, and actions for the most suitable outcomes. The *how* of it was something I would learn, which would take time, because it just didn't make sense, even after seeing it unfold in front of me many times. I didn't understand at the time how people knew what to do and how to coordinate their efforts, but eventually I learned how to be a part of its flow and how my participation affected the collective.

Shasta had tried to explain it to me that day. In response to my question, "Then how does everyone know what to do?" she took a deep breath before answering.

"I know you're taking in a lot of information, and there are some things that you just won't understand until you're in the moment *doing* them. I know you can grasp these things mentally—you're smart—but *experientially*, you're young and new to our ways. You'll get there, but it will take some time."

I nodded, understanding her but also feeling impatient to get to the experiences that would help me *really* understand.

"Let's start with trying to quiet your mind," she said.

"Okay," I said, wondering why I would want to do that.

"Take a deep breath in slowly, hold it for a moment, and then let it out slowly."

I did and saw that she was doing it with me, while also making a peculiar hand gesture.

"Now do it again and try to relax here—she put her hand in front of my stomach—breathing slowly and fully so that your belly expands with each in-breath."

I realized that my breathing was more in my chest compared to what I saw in Shasta, but after a few cycles, suddenly my stomach relaxed and I was able to take in more air as my belly expanded like hers. She noticed my surprise and chuckled.

"Good! That's a first step, to relax enough to be able to breathe fully. Keep going . . . slowly and deeply."

We sat there breathing together for several minutes. I noticed that my cycle of breathing had slowed down considerably from its normal cadence, surely due to the deeper, more full breaths that brought in more air. At one point, I felt lightheaded, but it passed as I relaxed further into the slowing rhythm of my inhales and exhales.

"What are you thinking?" she asked.

It was an interesting question. With my focus on breathing, I hadn't noticed that my mind had quieted down to simply observing the physical act of it. I was no longer thinking of what the day would bring, the prophecy, or anything about my new living situation.

"Um, not much. I'm just focusing on my breathing," I said.

"Yes, very good," Shasta said. "That's a great start. I told you you'd learn fast. Now, what do you *feel?*" She emphasized the last word.

I took a moment and checked in with my body, and what I found was a level of physical calm that I can't remember ever having felt. It was as if the underlying stress of my previous life had just disappeared, at least for that time. I felt energized like when I was practicing the slow dance with Naveen, but in a different way.

"Peaceful," I said. "It feels amazing."

Shasta smiled. "Yes, it does, doesn't it? And the more you do it, the more consistently amazing you'll feel, and the more you'll understand how everyone knows what to do around here. When you're really in that peaceful, uplifted space, you'll be better able to *listen* to and *feel* what's around you to more clearly find the best course of action, because the noise within has lessened."

Since I was feeling it right then, what she said sort of made sense.

She continued. "When you are really able to quiet your mind, you come to a place where you operate *with* your environment, and your thoughts, words, and actions are in harmony with the world around you—the people, the earth, nature, the community, and what needs to get done. You'll just know. You'll *feel* it."

"What will I feel?" I asked.

"Well, it's like what you're feeling now but quieter and more tranquil, and then you'll get impressions that might take a while to trust, but you'll get there. It's difficult to describe, but you'll feel the peace of not having to think about it, not having to listen to your mind or emotions or anything besides just being in the natural flow of what's occurring around you. And by not *thinking* about it and by allowing yourself to *feel*, any answers simply come to you and you'll know what to do."

"That doesn't make a lot of sense," I said.

The monk laughed. "Yes, you're right. It doesn't make sense, at least not right now based on what you understand. It's almost the opposite of what makes sense." She paused. "When you arrived here yesterday, you saw houses and buildings, right?"

I nodded.

"And when we went up to the contemplation hall, what did you see?"

"I saw that the houses were in the spiral pattern that was on my leather book cover."

"Right," Shasta said. "You looked down upon the village and saw it from a physically higher vantage point, essentially from a higher context."

I nodded.

"It's similar with quieting your mind. When you come to that inner peace that hushes the outside world, you'll see, feel, and understand from a greater vantage point, really an *inner* vantage point."

"But how?" I asked. "If I'm quieting my mind, how does it know what to do?" My young brain, schooled within the Territories, was having difficulty understanding.

"It doesn't. That's the beauty of it. The mind is a useful tool, but when you focus on *not* using it, you can better hear the quiet voice inside that's in harmony with what's around you. And from that place you can better partake in the natural flow of life instead of trying to bend or control your surroundings based on the limited vantage point of the mind."

I just looked at her. It was a lot to take in, and I couldn't process it all. I knew I was smarter than most kids my age, but this lesson went beyond the logical thinking I was familiar with.

"There are many in the village who still struggle with this on various levels," she said, "and they grew up here! It's not a natural way to function based on the appearances the world presents to us, but it makes going through life easier, less stressful, and more joyful. Don't you worry. It might take some time, but I sense you're going to be very good at it. For now, just know that the more you're able to quiet your mind by turning your attention within, the more you'll know what to do, despite the circumstances around you. In the meantime, just ask me."

That seemed to be the end of the lesson because she stood up, and I followed suit. But then she added a teaser.

"And that's when the real fun begins," she said with a mischievous glint in her eyes.

As a new, young inhabitant of the village, that made me incredibly excited, and I couldn't wait for it. Little did I know that it would take years to begin to really understand and experience what she was talking about. In one sense, it sounded like fun, but in another, it felt like the most serious responsibility any person could bear. Either way, I found myself thinking, *I'm really going to like it here.*

~

We spent the rest of the day wandering around the village, meeting people, and getting me acquainted with the rhythms of the community. I recognized most of the residents from the previous evening's dinner where I seemed to be the object of attention, but now I was able to meet them face to face instead of being stared at from afar. They didn't engage much beyond greetings and basic pleasantries, seemingly giving me some space to acclimate to my new surroundings. I think Shasta also managed it well, keeping conversations short so I wouldn't get overwhelmed.

Everyone was exceedingly pleasant and seemed happy to have me around. No one mentioned the reason for their enthusiastic welcome, which I assumed to be what Naveen had told me about the prophecy, that it finally meant that some long-awaited teacher would be coming soon. No one, that is, until I met Promeus.

"Ah, there she is," the old, bearded monk said as Shasta and I approached him where he sat outside the contemplation hall on the hill. From dinner, I remembered his kind, wizened face that had made me feel so welcomed.

He smiled and grasped my hand with both of his while examining me intently. He seemed not to be looking at my physical face as much as beyond it, through it, as if he could see who I was under the surface. I instantly had the feeling that he already knew me better than I knew myself.

"Anna, this is Promeus," Shasta said.

"It is my sincere pleasure to meet you, child," Promeus said, bowing slightly then releasing my hand. "We welcome you to our humble village."

"Nice to meet you, too," I said. His face was even more wise and kind up close.

"So, do you know why you're here?" Promeus asked, his eyes possessing a quality that, as Naveen had said, seemed to perceive beyond what the physical world presented.

"Um," I hesitated. I didn't want to get Naveen in trouble for telling me about the prophecy before I was supposed to learn about it. Thankfully, Promeus quickly broke my awkward pause.

"Ah, yes," he chuckled. "Youth have a way of discovering that which is concealed, don't they?"

He looked at Shasta, who registered surprise and then annoyance. She looked at me.

"Naveen?" she asked.

I sheepishly nodded.

"Oh, leave him be," Promeus said. "He's a good boy and I'm sure quite excited to know that things are now in motion. We're all excited by your arrival. Some of us have been waiting our whole lives for it."

I must have turned red because I suddenly felt overwhelmed by my supposed significance. Me! Someone who had just run away from home and was essentially a stranger in a strange land. In addition, what Naveen had told me about doing something important in the future left me feeling once again burdened by the expectations of others.

Promeus put both his hands on my cheeks and looked me in the eyes. This time, it seemed he was focusing on my actual eyes instead of beyond them.

"It's okay. It's all going to be perfect, and you will fulfill your role and do exactly what's needed. There is no need to worry."

That's easy for you to say, I thought. *You're not in my shoes.*

As if hearing my thoughts, he said, "My dear, we all will play a part in what is to come. The transformation has already begun, and whether you know it or not, you've already played a considerable role."

I was confused upon hearing that I had already done something that related to all this. What had I done? I was just a kid who had never done anything notable in my short life, but something about what he said sat powerfully within me and made some sort of sense. I just didn't know what it was yet.

I also felt some relief hearing that others would be involved in some way. In fact, I eventually came to realize how much we all were in it together. I, on many levels, was beginning to feel that I was no longer alone.

~

The rest of the week was like that first full day—chatting with Naveen and clumsily practicing the slow dance with him in the morning under the trees, meeting more of the residents and learning about what they did, receiving beginning lessons from Shasta, and generally getting a feel for the pace of living in the forest.

I found that nothing was considered *work*. Everyone seemed to be content simply carrying out what needed to be done, as Shasta had indicated when she had talked about flowing with whatever circumstances we found ourselves in. People seemed to gravitate to what they were good at, and many seemed to have particular abilities that lent themselves to those efforts.

Kyna, the tall woman with the dark hair, was essentially the head of the village. She seemed to understand everything that was happening both inside and outside the community. Residents would come to her if they needed help managing or coordinating tasks with others, and she would help them figure out a way for everything to get accomplished.

As much as I had already had my mind blown by experiencing walking through the Wall, what I heard she could do was even more fantastic. She was graced with a very rare ability. It was said she could sit in contemplation and project herself physically to another place, even into the Territories, while also remaining where she originally sat in the village, essentially creating a copy of herself to go where she willed. Perhaps that's why she seemed to always know what was happening in the city and the latest on what the Territory Governors were up to. That must have been how I had first seen her in the city when she had directed me to the plaza, and perhaps why she seemed a little erratic there. I learned that it can be difficult to retain proper functioning when projecting yourself like that. She was very different there than when I had met her upon my arrival here, where her stately composure contrasted to her earlier disordered energy in the city.

I learned that her husband, Caedmon, who always wore monk's robes, was a teacher at the school, and he was in the middle of many days of intense, silent contemplation outside the village that would help guide his teachings. He had broken that self-reflection and had come back to the village to meet me when I had arrived, which, upon learning about it, added to my increasing unease at my popularity. What was I predicted to do that was important enough to pull this venerable man from his admirable and important concentration just to meet me?

I should add now that even though I may express some apprehension at whatever future significant role I was to play, that anxiety and pressure paled in comparison to the stresses I had experienced when living in the Territories. My new life within the village created an elevated backdrop of comfort that allowed these concerns to dissipate most of the time, and even when they were uncomfortably roaring in my ears, they were far less agitating than my previous, anxiety-filled life with family and school pressures.

Banna, a muscular, middle-aged man, was the primary builder of everything structural, really anything that wasn't simply a dirt path. He planned and constructed all the cabins and stone walls in the community, often with a few younger apprentices who hung on his every word. At one point I saw him move an immense stone with virtually no outward effort. I asked Shasta about it later and she said that that was one of his strengths, so to speak, being able to move physical objects easily by connecting with them energetically and working *with* them. I didn't understand, but she reminded me about when we had walked through the Wall and how physical objects really had all this space inside them. Banna just had a unique ability and knowledge of how to influence the space and therefore the object. He would eventually help me build my own cabin.

Joran and Kalisa ran the farm that grew the incredible fruits and vegetables we ate at mealtimes. They and their apprentices worked in the fields outside the village to bring in the harvest, something I hadn't been exposed to before being from the city. At times, though, I witnessed them just sitting in contemplation around the crops. I was quickly getting used to seeing that behavior all over the village, and Shasta told me that they, similar to Banna and others, connected with the fruits and vegetables in a way that encouraged maximum growth and nutritional value. Indeed, the size of some of the apples, tomatoes, squash, and other produce astounded me. They were consistently bigger and more delicious than anything I had ever encountered in the Territory's marketplace.

I met Cassie, a seamstress and loom worker, who created the beautiful fabrics and clothes that most villagers wore. She seemed to revel in her activities, expressing a love and enthusiasm that was reflected in the garments she produced. Her daughter, Jillian, who was about my age, worked alongside her when not studying, often patching up someone's favorite shirt that had become thin or frayed. Jillian and I hit it off immediately, and we came to spend many hours together talking about life in and out of the village and speculating about what important thing I was to do.

Many residents had one or more tattoos whose symbols looked like those I had seen in my dream just before running away from home, like Shasta's and Kyna's tattoos and the images on the walls in the contemplation hall. I was told they were from the sacred language of the Ancients—which I knew was forbidden in the Territories—and that their representations carried power when focused on.

I spoke further with Promeus, who, when pressed, revealed that he hadn't received many details about the next stages of the prophecy, which apparently had surprised him because he usually could see more. But he said that my role would be significant and that it would play a part in bringing a better way of living to many, many people. He said that even though various future details were cloudy to his sight, the power behind his visions was stronger than anything he had ever encountered. This, to him, meant that the teacher from the original prophecy was indeed finally coming.

It was when I was speaking with him on a warm, sunny afternoon, seven days after my arrival, that Kyna came and interrupted us on the steps of the contemplation hall. Seeing me there, she said nothing but just looked at Promeus with a knowing gaze, and both of them seemed to lose themselves in the moment. I could see it in their eyes. Over the week I had continued to practice breathing, cultivating the inner awareness, and performing the slow dance with Naveen, and so was beginning to become familiar with at least the basics of quieting my mind and going within, and I could tell they were definitely checking in on something.

Promeus began to smile, a genuine, warm, and loving smile that became wider and wider until it looked like his face couldn't take it anymore. His eyes became misty and a tear rolled down his cheek. Kyna smiled only slightly, knowingly, but I felt she was experiencing the same thing Promeus was expressing. I felt something, too, but couldn't grasp or define it. It rolled over me slowly with a deep, warm, inspiring power that was very different and more abstract than what I felt with my own beginning inner practices.

With their distant eyes, they both looked at me, which, given the weight of their expressions and the feeling I was experiencing, made me want to curl up inside.

"This is a good day for humankind," Promeus said slowly.

Kyna gave a barely perceptible nod and turned to leave, having said nothing the whole time she was there.

As she walked away, Promeus's expression then turned to a sort of kindly sadness, and another tear dripped down his face. He reached out and put a wrinkled hand on my cheek, and I sensed that there was something about what had just transpired that lent some clarity to his previous vision, but it contained a heavy undercurrent. Despite the uplifting power that even *I* felt, there was a struggle contained within it, and I got the impression that the struggle was going to be mine to bear.

Anna

Sitting across from each other at the table in Anna's house, Naveen and Anna broke bread and slurped their noodle-infused stew, saying nothing. Anna appreciated that Naveen knew not to make idle conversation without prompting, as she was sure he could read her energy that simply wanted his company.

Soon, they heard a thumping knock on the door. Anna rose to open it, and Jillian was standing there holding a basket of papers, ink, and a new quill in one hand and a bowl of stew in the other. She had kicked the door with her foot.

"Come in, come in," Anna said, taking the basket. Thank you so much for getting this. Did you have any trouble?"

"Not at all. I encountered the bookkeeper leaving the building to go to dinner, and we went back inside and he gave me these. Did I get the right things?"

"Yes, perfect!" Anna said. "Thank you. Did he ask you why you needed them?"

Jillian smiled. "No, but I could tell he knew they were for you."

Anna was thankful for those looking out for her, and in the case of the two in her home, supporting her as she dealt with the fallout of her role in the prophecy.

"Come, sit with us," Anna said, pulling out a chair.

Jillian sat with Anna and Naveen, and the three ate in silence for a few minutes. Eventually, Anna's curiosity prompted her to speak.

"What are people saying about me, about Teacher?" she asked.

Naveen stopped eating and put down his spoon.

"Obviously, everyone's upset that Teacher's been arrested, but they're mixed on their view of you. They know you signaled his coming, so that's a positive, but right now, many aren't happy with what just happened and are questioning your motives."

Anna always appreciated his directness, and what he said made sense. She nodded.

"We trust you," Jillian said, putting a hand on Anna's knee.

With that, Anna closed her eyes and brought her attention within. She was checking to see if it would be appropriate to share her secret with her close friends, and she felt the soft, knowing confirmation that it would be okay.

"I have something to tell you," she said, feeling a weight in the air just after she voiced it. She wasn't sure if it was because of what she was about to share or if Naveen and Jillian's energies instantly ramped up because they anticipated her saying something significant. Regardless, she proceeded.

"People are right to blame me. It's my fault that Teacher was found and arrested. What they don't know, though, is that I didn't want to do it."

Naveen and Jillian stared at her, unmoving.

"Teacher *asked* me to tell the constables where he was, to betray him and the group. He knew he would be arrested, and he needed someone to enable it." She paused, and Naveen reached over and put a hand on Anna's arm.

"I fought him. I told him that I couldn't do it, but his explanation of what he says will happen convinced me that the world would be a better place if I did it, even if . . ."

Anna stopped, put her head in her hands, and took a deep breath. When she raised her head, her eyes were moist and glassy.

"Not only did he know this would happen, he knows what's going to happen."

Again, she paused, feeling the emotions in the room rising, despite her best effort to keep them in check.

"Does this mean . . ." Naveen began.

Anna looked at him and nodded, then immediately burst into tears. She had been holding the secret for too long and needed to share it to release what she had been suppressing. Teacher knew he was going to be put to death, and *she* had facilitated it.

Naveen and Jillian both rose, stepped over to Anna, and hugged her in a deep, loving embrace as her tears streamed into her lap. Whatever tools she had learned to rise above her emotions were noticeably absent, and she could feel her friends infusing her with love, which she desperately needed at that moment.

"We understand. We're here for you," Jillian said.

Anna didn't know how long she was in their embrace, but her tears finally stopped, and Naveen and Jillian stepped back and sat down in their chairs. The energy they had surrounded her with, however, lingered in the room.

Wiping her face, Anna shook her head and chuckled. "I didn't know how badly I needed to tell someone, or how badly I needed, need, your support." She looked lovingly at Jillian, then at Naveen.

"Uh, Naveen . . . did you just give me a healing?" she asked. He had put his hand on the back of her neck, and she had felt it had helped.

Naveen smiled sheepishly. "You noticed that?"

Anna nodded, and all three laughed, which helped dissipate some of Anna's remaining emotions.

"Thank you for telling us," Jillian said. "We're here for you, whatever it is and however we can help."

"Yes, whatever you need," Naveen said.

"Thank you," Anna nodded. She took a deep breath. "What am I going to do?"

"Looks like you already know what that is," Naveen said, looking at the stack of written pages on the table.

Anna chuckled. "Yes, I suppose I do, at least right now."

"You've talked about writing something for a long time," Jillian said. "Nice to see it happening."

"Yes, finally," Anna said. "It came on so fast. Just this morning when I heard the news about what Teacher was being charged with, I just knew I had to start. For some reason, I *know* this is the next step on my path."

"Does the prophecy say anything about it, what you're writing?" Naveen asked.

Anna shook her head. "Not that I'm aware of, but I'll check with Promeus tomorrow."

She looked deeply at both of her friends. "Thank you for being here for me. Really."

"We're fulfilling our roles just as you are," Naveen said.

Anna nodded, smiled, and said, "Well, right now, I think our roles are to fill our bellies before the food gets too cold," and the three went back to their meals.

<h1 style="text-align:center">Seven Years Later</h1>

I awoke at first light feeling so refreshed that I wondered if I was a different person. Then I realized that I was.

Seven years had passed since I had first entered the village. The last few years I had been living on my own in a small log cabin located at one of the outside sections of one of the three spiral paths that wound outwards from the center clearing. I had selected its location with the pristine forest as my backyard, as I had come to enjoy the border between the village and the deep woods that gave me easy access to both. The cabin was set back a bit from the path so I could disappear into it if I wanted to, welcoming the option to have distance from others when needed. It enabled me the privacy to practice what I had been taught.

I had received a great deal of assistance building it, especially from Banna, the builder, but also from my friends and teachers who had lent their physical and non-physical abilities to help erect the simple structure. It was nearly identical to the first home I had shared with Shasta near the center of the village where I had lived for five years. She had been my mentor and parental figure throughout that time, even more so than I could have wished for because of her openness and understanding of what I was going through and what I had already endured. She now had her place back to herself, although she often hosted others who visited from neighboring villages, something she seemed continually drawn to do.

I had no such proclivities and so thoroughly enjoyed my own space, not unlike retreating to my childhood room in my parents' apartment in the lodging house in the Territories to escape the external pressures of my early life. But there was no such pressure here other than what was self-imposed. Once I had reached a certain level of basic training and knowledge of the practices in the village—which, granted, took years—for the most part I was left alone to figure out what I wanted to do. I suppose being someone with a key role to play in the prophecy had its advantages.

My progress over the years had been slow but steady. At least *I* thought it was slow, but I was told that I took in the lessons faster than most. Thankfully, I had Shasta as my primary teacher and guide. She had been a classroom teacher before locating me that fateful day in the plaza and so knew how to communicate the lessons well. I was told she had stopped teaching at the school so she could find me in the Territories, which was quite odd to hear but fit into the narrative of my so-called importance. I would later come to learn that there was more to her visit to the city that day.

I hadn't discovered much additional information about the prophecy over the years. Apparently, someone like me was to come to the village and study with the community because that person needed to be ready to fulfill a very important role whose function and timing were still unknown. And, as I had heard years before, the arrival of that person was also supposed to signal the coming of some great teacher, which hadn't yet happened, so I had begun to question if the foretelling had gotten it wrong and had meant to anoint someone else instead. However, Promeus and others with second sight had repeatedly confirmed that I was indeed the person in the prophecy. This is why everyone had become excited at my arrival, for it supposedly portended great things.

At one point, after a few months struggling with some lessons, I remember laughing out loud at the prospect of my significance. How could someone like me—*me!*— be tasked with something noteworthy in the midst of people with such amazing abilities in this magical village?

For someone recently exposed to a new way of living, a new way of *being*, it had been difficult to accept that I would play some kind of notable role in *any* capacity. Over time, though, I began to accept that maybe, *just maybe*, there *was* something important for me to accomplish. There didn't seem to be anyone else who fit the prediction, and no one in the village seemed to think it was anyone other than me. Also, as I began to further understand the ways of the community and its people, my trust in their judgments and beliefs increased, which went a long way toward convincing me that what they believed might indeed be true.

Since I had been quite academically successful at school in the Territories, I was good at focusing, absorbing, and processing information, at least on the mental level. I had a lot to learn, however, about experiencing and understanding my surroundings on the level of *feeling*.

Soon after my arrival in the village, I had quickly fallen into a routine once I settled into the cabin with Shasta. Although she was about twenty years older, as my guide and confidant, I could share anything with her, and I'm certain I would not be who I am today if not for our hearty discussions and her feedback that educated and supported me along the way. Between learning practical tasks necessary for me to understand the functioning of the community and the mystical lessons she imparted that fostered my personal growth and development, she was steadfast in her support of my progress. She, too, must have been a part of the prophecy in some way because without her, I would still be in the Territories.

Most of my first few months had been spent getting familiar with the people, customs, and activities in the village so I could do my best to fit in. Shasta had encouraged my engagement, but she also said to remember that everyone was unique and brought different talents and personalities to the collective, so I should let my personality shine. That was a bit challenging because my personality was rapidly shifting with the drastic change in my surroundings and way of living—from the city to a small, forest community, from being controlled to experiencing some freedom for the first time in my life, and from feeling limited in communicating to being encouraged to express. It took some time for me to integrate my previous existence into the new and wonderful environment I found myself in.

Strangely, I didn't miss the primary activity from my upbringing within the Territories that had made life tolerable there: reading books. I recognized I had used those stories to escape that world around me, and one could even say it was because of reading that I had made it to the village in the first place. With the remarkable environment I now inhabited, I no longer craved reading fiction because it felt like most days I was participating in and even directing myself as a real, living, breathing character in a magical story like those in my favorite tales from the past.

I had, however, recently begun to write some short stories of my own, parables that borrowed heavily from the people in my life who had taught me so much. In the process of composing them, I came to understand the lessons I had received more clearly, and I did my best to infuse the brief tales with that understanding. I told no one of my writing, including Jillian,

Shasta, and Naveen, as I felt the work was for me and me alone to lend clarity to my lessons. In that sense, the parables served as a kind of personal journal that helped me on my path.

With the incredible experiences I had been blessed to witness and take part in, I knew more writing was in my future, like telling the story of my own life and its transformation, but I wasn't yet drawn to do that. Also, I wanted to concentrate on my practices. I felt the time would come when my desire to write more than my short parables would become strong enough to let me know that it was time to act, and I would focus on it then.

There were many books in the village, but they were mostly related to the practice and understanding of the inner world that I would come to learn so much about. The elder monks in the contemplation hall safeguarded and occasionally allowed me to read some of the older, sacred texts. They weren't totally unlike the stories I had previously enjoyed, but they had an otherworldly quality with layers of symbolism that took me out of time and place while conveying grand lessons on living and understanding the extraordinary world I lived in, the one world we *all* truly lived in. Even though they were initially beyond my comprehension, they still carried and somehow imparted something beyond words despite my failure to fully understand them on an intellectual level at that time.

My mornings generally consisted of some kind of study or practice that would cultivate the higher energies, like reading and reflecting on lessons about how to recognize and move past old, unhelpful concepts or performing the slow dance that I had seen on my first day and now practiced consistently with Naveen, an exercise I found to be incredibly energizing to both my body and mind. Whatever it was, most residents did something first thing in the morning that would remind them to be in the flow of life around and within them and to engage the higher purpose for which they were living.

That was also the reason to study something right before going to bed, to keep a lesson foremost in the mind—which occupied the mental state—and allow it to infuse the abstract, twilight sleep, as well as the deeper dreams, with its truth. I did this as best I could in the evenings, but sometimes I was so exhausted from the day's activities that I had no energy for it. The combination of mental, physical, and emotional fatigue was sometimes just too much. But I valued the idea of these morning and evening habits to keep me on task with learning all I could about the world I had been dropped into. And I appreciated how the evening habit, when I did it, even put my sleep time to work for me.

Shasta was good to tolerate my numerous questions, although she sometimes didn't answer directly or at all, allowing me to struggle to figure things out or experience them for myself. I occasionally didn't accept those types of non-answers.

One time, after reading in the morning about how to recognize the subtle voice of intuition, I asked her for some clarification.

"When you feel like you know something, how do you know if it's intuition or if it's your mind justifying the thought or impression?" I asked.

Shasta took a moment and after a long pause said, "You'll come to know the difference."

I wasn't going to let her get away with such a simplistic answer this time, so I pressed.

"If I mentally notice an intuitive feeling, then I'm thinking about it, so my mind is involved, which taints the intuition itself, right?"

She sighed, put down her book, and closed her eyes for a moment. It was clear she was seeking guidance within. She opened her eyes.

"You've learned that what you get from your intuition can be more real than what you get from appearances or your logical thinking," she said. "Mixing those two things is not the only potential pitfall. Just as the mind can make you think that *it* is the only real thing you should be following, your emotions can do the same."

"Right," I said. "You taught me the difference between emotions and intuition, even though they may come across as similar."

"Yes. Feeling is on a continuum, just like the energy of the mind is, with negative, heavier emotions being denser than positive emotions, and both being lower than intuition, which is a higher level of feeling that comes across as a sense of knowingness. Emotions and your lower mind—which is concrete, analytical thinking—can work together to subvert the authenticity of your intuition or co-opt it for its own purposes."

"Can you give me an example?" I asked.

She looked at me, *through* me, as if trying to read a personal example from my history, which she had done a few times before. It usually worked pretty well because I obviously could relate to it as it was already in my experience. That skill of personalizing lessons helped make her one of the better teachers in the community. I was lucky to have her as my personal educator, despite sometimes feeling uncomfortably called out for mistakes.

"Do you remember a few weeks ago when you were agitated because you thought you lost the book you borrowed from Promeus?" she asked.

"Oh, yes!" I replied. "I was a wreck. I thought he would be mad at me for losing it."

"During that experience, did you notice your breath?"

I thought back to the episode, which immediately brought back the feeling of tightness in my core and the shallow breathing I had felt.

"Yes, I can feel it now, a tightness right here," I said, and I pointed to the center of my torso.

"And did you notice what was happening to your mind during that time?" she asked.

"Yes, it was running all over the place, thinking of where the book could be and what I would do if I couldn't find it, as well as what his reaction would be."

"And what did you do?"

"Well, I took your advice and sat in contemplation, but it didn't help me find the book," I said.

"Why not?"

"I assume because my mind and emotions were too distracting."

She looked at me and nodded. "But you found the book," she said.

"Yes, it was later the next day after I had calmed down and practiced breathing and inner work."

"And what did you feel during the contemplation practice?"

"I felt a warmth and a grand sense of peace in my core," I said, again pointing to the center of my body.

"So," I continued, before she could ask another question, "it's only when we go within and settle down our breathing and our mind that the warmth of intuition comes." It was a statement, but I was looking for confirmation.

"Mm hmm. And what do you notice about the location of the anxious emotion and the calmer feeling of peace?" she asked.

"They're in the same place," I said.

She nodded. "That is also where your intuition lies. Sitting quietly and cultivating that peaceful feeling inside fosters intuition, which is a higher energy and the soft undercurrent of *feeling*. In contrast, your worries about the book and Promeus's potential reaction were emotions, which sit directly on top of intuition and shout more loudly to convince you that *it* is more important."

"Is it ever?" I asked.

She looked at me like I should have known better, and indeed I did.

"Anna," she said, "your intuition is always there waiting for you to listen to it, but it's difficult to discern because it speaks so much more softly than your mind and emotions. But *that's* where you will find your answers . . . and your power."

I felt I was actually getting it this time.

"And to go back to your original question," she continued, "when you get an impression and you think it might be your mind, check in to see how it *feels*. If it's warm and peaceful and *knowing*, then it's intuition. If it creates or enhances any emotion—good or bad, depressing or exciting—or starts to make your mind spin, then it's something else, something that you'll want to look at to see why you are reacting in that particular manner."

I took a deep breath and let it out.

"And to go back to my original answer," she said, "You'll know the difference."

I understood, at least I think I did. What she had said consolidated many other lessons I had been given. I could feel myself reflecting, but it wasn't frantic or agitated or rationalizing; rather, it was largely abstract. I noted later that it seemed to be more like an absorbing of the information beyond any type of linear thinking.

I went to bed that night in that same intangible mental and feeling space, somehow processing what she had said without trying to. Upon waking, I found that sleeping on it had helped organize my understanding because it felt like all of it had integrated into my being without any hard, logical, grinding away with my mind, which I tended to be very, very good at. The conversation and its aftereffects were eye-opening, and the experience gave me not only the knowledge of the relationship among emotions, the mind, and intuition, but also how I could receive and process new information with less effort.

I was glad I had pushed her for more than her first, one-sentence answer.

~

What was most exciting for me was learning how to use what I had been taught to transcend the rules of the physical world, like how Shasta and I were able to walk through the Grand Wall so many years before. I had been impatient to learn this particular skill, but Shasta had continued to tell me that I wasn't ready and that I needed to be in a vastly different place to even begin that lesson. Nevertheless, I persisted in pestering her enough that she finally talked about it with me about five years after my arrival. She called it the transit.

I had prepared by studying hard and spending many of my mornings doing the slow dance under the trees with the other monks because Shasta had said that that was one thing that would help cultivate the inner feeling I needed in order to do the transit on my own. Indeed, it did help me feel more in touch with my body, both physically and otherwise, and the energizing effect on my whole being always left me vibrating on the inside, like I was being stimulated by an unseen force. So, I threw myself into that practice and found other studies to help me understand the *what* and the *how* of the improbable, transiting ability in preparation for actually doing it. Shasta continued to caution my zeal, however.

"You can't just study yourself into being able to do it," she had said after I had gown frustrated after many days on a particular lesson with little progress. "It's not just an intellectual exercise."

"I know, I know. I have to *feel* it," I said, repeating what she had told me countless times before. "That's why I've been practicing so much. You know, I did feel it the day you took me through the Wall."

"That's different. You experienced it as a passenger, not as someone who initiated it."

"So, what do I have to do to feel it more so I can do it myself?" I asked.

"Like I've said before, you have to believe it so strongly that there is zero doubt in your mind, and that takes time, sometimes lots of time. This is just the first baby step. You have a long way to go."

I grumbled, reservedly acknowledging her statement. She hadn't been wrong before. I just wanted to progress faster. At that time, I still had the impatience of youth driving me forward yet also likely inhibiting my improvement. As I eventually learned, advanced skills like walking through walls couldn't be rushed.

It would be a few more years before she felt I was ready to attempt it.

~

Over my time in the village, I had developed some good, deep friendships. Besides Shasta, who was a combination mentor, teacher, parental figure, and friend, I had become quite close with Naveen and Jillian.

I saw Naveen most mornings when we practiced under the trees. As good as I thought he was when I had first arrived, his skills had increased to a level that truly transcended the movements alone. He had mastered them with such precision and grace that just being around him while he practiced brought more than just a welcome burst of physical energy. His exceptional gift at executing the dance had allowed him to train so he could teach it, and he had become the youngest by far to take on that role. I think a few of the older teachers welcomed his youth and vigor, not to mention his taking over some of their practice sessions and classes. I was happy to be included as one of his students.

My friend, Jillian, had become more than just a friend. We had such an easy rapport and mutual understanding that it was difficult not to want to spend large portions of my days with her. Even though my background was so very different, she appreciated my past—more so than I did—and liked the fact that I wanted to learn as much as I could about her community, what had become *my* community.

Since I had not experienced or even observed any kind of more-than-friend, same-sex relationship in the Territories, I initially didn't know what to do or if it was accepted here in the village. I had seen some couples that made me think it was okay, but I wasn't sure, and I was too uncomfortable in my uncertainty to ask Shasta about it. My worries were set aside one day after a few years of being there during a fun and playful chat with Jillian.

She and I had come back to the cabin from dinner, the home I still shared with Shasta, who wasn't there, and we both plopped onto my bed, lying on our backs with our feet on the floor.

"So," she said turning to look at me, "I see you're spending more and more time with Naveen."

I must have blushed because she pushed my shoulder and laughed out loud, a very genuine, deep laugh that was contagious to most who heard it. I was not immune to such magic so began laughing along with her.

"He *is* very good looking, don't you think?" she said in between the remaining chuckles.

I did find Naveen quite handsome, and his skill with the slow dance was out of this world, which added to his allure. He and I were very friendly, almost to the point of flirting, but I wasn't really sure where that line was. I wouldn't have known what to do if I was over it anyway. At one point, I thought I might've had romantic feelings for him, but now I wasn't sure.

I smiled and looked at her. "Yes, he is. I'm just enjoying the morning practices with him."

"Oh, I bet you are!" she exclaimed, laughing uncontrollably again. I joined in but then tried to correct her erroneous understanding.

"No, I really am enjoying trying to learn from him." He had just started teaching formally at that time and would correct major faults in my posture and movements when we practiced together. "It's just practice."

"Uh huh. Is that what you call it?" she said. "Oh, let me touch your hip to correct your stance," she said trying to mimic his voice as she sat up and reached over to tickle me near my hip.

I laughed, sat up, and tried to tickle her back.

"And your shoulders should be back further," she continued in his voice, reaching for my shoulders.

We were both laughing hysterically as I tried to playfully fight her off. "And you need to tuck your butt in more," she said mockingly as she reached for my lower back.

We wrestled on the bed, and I wound up on my back with her on top of me tickling my midsection. Snorting with laughter, I eventually got hold of her wrists to stop the torture.

She relaxed, then leaned down and kissed me briefly on the lips before straightening up and looking me in the eyes. We had both stopped laughing.

I was surprised but happy. I smiled, let go of her wrists, and reached up to brush her hair to the side. She leaned in again.

We've been together since that day.

Now, with my own place, she sometimes stays over, but most of her nights are spent at her family's house closer to the center of the village where she continues to work with her mother on fabrics and clothing. Early on, she recognized my desire to frequently have peace and quiet for study and integrating what I had learned, so she knew to leave me alone when I needed it, as well as when *she* felt I needed it. Despite my occasional protests, she stuck to her decision to do that. I think others, like Shasta and perhaps Promeus, may have had a hand in persuading her, not because of our relationship but because of my need to be ready for the important role I had coming, whatever it was, and they knew what was best for me more than I did.

~

There were other villages outside the Grand Wall, most about an hour's walk away, and I had found out that they, like the layout of this triple-spiraled community, also formed particular shapes due to the arrangements of the dwellings. Some of them corresponded to the symbols that adorned the contemplation hall's walls and the tattoos on Shasta's and others' arms, and some were simpler, like in the shape of a crescent moon. What had become apparent over the years was that my new home community was a kind of meeting place for travelers because of its relatively centralized location amid the other villages and its proximity to the Territories.

I had been fortunate that Shasta had taken me to meet some of the inhabitants of several of the other settlements. Although each was a fully-functioning, prosperous community with all that one would expect of such, they each also seemed to have their own collective focus—like industrial, agricultural, or mystical—and therefore presented different proficiencies and energies.

One village was filled with master metalsmiths who produced the hardy tools and long-lasting knives for the area, not to mention the incredible, inventive sculptures that lined the main path that led into the town center. I had never seen such grand artistry. With the metal scales of towering dragons shimmering in the light and the fine, silvery, elfin figures that moved with the wind, it was like walking through one of the fantastical tales I used to read.

Another community, in the shape of a large circle—the ancient symbol for wholeness—specialized in healing and training healers. These skilled practitioners were called upon whenever there was an injury or serious illness, and they would often travel to the surrounding villages to care for those in need. What I had seen them accomplish was astounding to my Territory-schooled brain. Broken arms and debilitating sicknesses were mended or healed in minutes if not seconds. How, I didn't yet know, but I certainly wanted to learn. It was yet another thing that told me I had escaped the city to live in another world.

My adopted community, I found, specialized in higher energetic practices. All the other villages also practiced these ancient traditions to some extent, as they used them in their work such as healing beyond natural, physical means, but the practices I was learning took them to another level. With concentrated study, repetition, and an innate ability, one could eventually be able to transcend aspects of the physical world. Shasta demonstrated this quite clearly when she pulled me through the Grand Wall seven years ago. She was among the more skilled in the village at defying what I thought were the inviolable laws of nature. I did my best to emulate her as the years passed.

I was told of my own natural ability, often referred to as my *gift*, and I began to believe it after numerous residents seemed to marvel at the speed at which I progressed. Apparently, I had learned in my relatively short time there what took most others fifteen or twenty years to learn and master, if they did at all. From my early, awkward movements that first morning with Naveen, I had evolved into a smooth, skilled practitioner of the slow dance, which helped put me in a higher state of contemplation and allowed me to better feel my environment and the flow of energy within and around me. And I was able to reach that state even without moving, by sitting still and sending my thoughts upward until they dissolved into the oneness of the surroundings of which I was a part.

It was now, seven years later, after a year of being able to reach this elevated state, that Shasta came to me with a lesson I would never forget. I was to be taught how to do the impossible.

"Come with me," she said, interrupting my contemplation on a bench outside the great hall on the hill. I heard her, but it took a moment to bring myself back into my body after wiggling my fingers, my preferred manner of re-grounding in the world after sailing high in the ethers. I opened my eyes and saw Shasta on the steps and Promeus on the bench next to me. He opened one eye, raised an eyebrow, and grinned slightly.

I stood up and followed Shasta. It didn't feel right to speak as we made our way back through the village clearing and down the forest trail that led to the Territories. I had traveled the same path a few times before to the big red oak tree that I remembered marked the Grand Wall's location, but I hadn't risked going past it. Instead, I had sat on the log where I had my first lesson with Shasta and had stared down the trail, reflecting on whatever made the stone barrier invisible from this side. On those occasions, I had dared not tempt fate by trying to cross it.

Heading back there now with Shasta, there was a seriousness to our walk. Something felt important, like I was being guided toward something with a sacred significance. Thirty minutes later, we once again stood by the grand oak. The events of my first day there remained vivid in my memory.

I looked further down the trail, essentially through what I assumed was still the magically-invisible wall, and sensed the imposing structure. With all I had practiced over the years, I now knew how to recognize when something was different in my environment, and the squeezing I felt in my chest and head told me that *something* unusual, even unnatural, was close by.

I looked at Shasta and said, "I can feel it."

She smiled. "Good."

"How come we can't see it?" I asked.

"Because we don't need to."

I gave her a look that said that that wasn't enough of an answer.

"The Ancients had abilities far beyond ours," she said. "They were able to do things that we still don't understand."

I nodded.

I had learned more about the Ancients and their revered symbols over the years. It was said they had lived in a manner that made the inner world manifest. But, I was told, just as a light cannot help but extinguish the darkness, the full, true expression of the inner world cannot help but destroy the outer world, so they had to adapt in order to exist here. This, of course, was confusing to someone rooted in the physical realm and just beginning to learn about what was within. Somehow, being in a continual, pure state that enabled *some* expression of the inner world allowed them to influence their environment in miraculous ways.

The Perceiver was one such Ancient, the first really. He had created the Territories and everything in it in the middle of the desert. Others had learned from him, and as a group they came to be called the Ancients by those who followed centuries later. It was said they spoke a sacred language and wrote with sacred symbols that tried to convey the grandeur of their existence, and it was these words and symbols that the current monks revered and protected in the old books found in the great hall and in the inked symbols on their bodies.

I had tried to read some of those books, with Promeus next to me helping me translate, but they were difficult to understand and largely beyond my comprehension. However, simply holding the old texts conveyed a lightness that enabled me to more easily rise up to access the peaceful internal space I practiced every day.

Hearing Shasta mention them again brought a similar light energy to my body, and I felt a soft, distant buzzing like when holding their books. I then realized I had been feeling it during most of the walk to the Wall, an uplifting undercurrent to the squeezing I felt being near the barrier. Perhaps that's why I didn't feel like speaking, as words would have diminished the barely-perceptible feeling. It had a quality to it that made me think that one of the Ancients was somehow there with us and had been with us since the village.

Shasta sat down on the log near the red oak where we had sat previously for my first lesson and picked up a branch about a thumb's width in diameter and as long as her forearm. I joined her on the log, feeling the cool wood beneath me.

"Do you remember going through the Wall?" she asked.

"Of course," I said. "How could I forget it?"

She offered me the branch. I took it and turned it over in my hands.

"And do you remember what I said about it?"

I did. I had seen a wall that was solid whereas she knew that it wasn't. I nodded.

"Is that branch solid?" she asked.

I looked at it. Her lessons had taught me that things are not as solid as they appear and that there was another way to approach seeing and feeling them. Even though I had been practicing raising my energy to see and feel on a higher level, I had not yet brought it to actually feeling something physically, as I was only energetically sensing it before.

"Yes and no," I said. "Yes, because it's solid enough in form to be a branch in the physical world, and no, because I know now that there's a lot of empty space and that its form is held together by some energy, giving it the appearance of solidity."

Shasta smiled. I was a good student. She reached out for the branch, which I handed over.

"Watch," she said, as she closed her eyes, then moved her free hand *through* the branch.

I observed closely, knowing this was a big lesson, and her fingers did indeed pass through the wood. There was a crackling feeling in the air when she did it, as if sunlight were streaming through pinholes in a fine curtain hung by the window, illuminating the true nature of the wood that longed to be released. Even though I had been anticipating a lesson like this for a long time, I still was not prepared to see it happen right in front of me. My eyes widened and I took a deep breath.

Shasta opened her eyes. "So, what did I do?"

"Wow, that was amazing!" I said, before tempering my excitement that this lesson was finally happening. "Um, you raised your vibration and *knew* you could do it."

"Yes. What else?"

I looked at her. I didn't know what else to say. Belief that she could do it was critical, as was going up to a place, a context, where she could make that knowingness become real.

"What about my fingers?" she asked. "What do they have to do with it?"

I looked at her fingers, then at my own.

"Uh, you applied your thinking not just to the branch but to your fingers as well, seeing them as not as solid as they appear."

"Correct, except it's not *thinking* and *seeing* but *feeling* and *knowing*," she reminded me. "It's a very important difference."

"Yes, of course," I said. I had been taught many times about those differences, but it was sometimes difficult to conceptually switch from the denser energies that helped me navigate the external world to those more refined energies of the inner world.

"Try it," she said, handing me the branch.

I took it, looked at her, and froze. This was it, my chance to do something beyond the bounds of natural laws. I took a few slow, deep breaths, closed my eyes, and went within, following my breath to my center. Then I brought my hand down to the branch.

And I touched it. Nothing out of the ordinary happened. I felt the bark with my fingers as if I had simply picked it up off the ground. Even though I thought I was in an elevated space, it apparently wasn't enough. I made a face and looked at Shasta.

"Remember," she said, "*feel* the space."

I didn't know if she meant the space within my fingers and the branch or the inner, peaceful space I had spent years cultivating. Perhaps it was both.

"*Know* that this world is an effect, not a cause," she continued. "*You've already accomplished it.*" She said the last sentence slowly and with intention.

I nodded and closed my eyes, feeling myself begin to escape my form. I was rising up, higher than before, differently than before. I took my time, letting my mind drift into the distance to allow a soft, vacuous center to inflate in its place. As it expanded, it began to crackle with an energized feeling of possibilities, of potentialities, which grew into a light buzzing as I brought my hand down to the branch . . . and through it.

As I registered the excitement of knowing that I did it, I rapidly crashed out of my uplifted state and back to the world around me. My first thought upon opening my eyes, besides the excitement, was that it tickled my fingers. I looked at Shasta with what must have been extreme excitement because she began laughing at my reaction.

"Yes, it's often like that the first time," she said.

I looked down at my fingers and wiggled them. I'm not sure what I expected, but they felt fine, back to normal, no longer tickly. The branch, too, seemed fine.

"Congratulations," she said. "You now have a tangible experience that grounds in the physical world what you've learned over the years. Remember it, the *feeling* of doing it, and it will be easier to repeat."

I nodded.

"You may have questions," she added, "but leave them be for now. Just sit with the *feeling*."

I nodded again, still reveling in the idea that I really did it. Even though I had known this lesson was coming and had played it out in my mind countless times, it was quite surprising to *actually* do it. Going through the Wall with Shasta's aid years before was shocking enough; doing something like it by myself took it to a whole other level.

Shasta said nothing more as I slowly calmed down from my initial excitement. She was right in that I had questions, but I wasn't able to articulate them anyway. We sat in silence as my head spun with the possibilities, eventually quieting down enough so that I was able to rise once again and go within to the higher level of energy of that same, blessed space and repeat the feat.

I was less surprised after doing it again and became even less so as I repeated it a few more times.

Looking mildly surprised, Shasta smiled and said, "I told you you were going to be good at this."

I had brought my emotions under control, as I had been trained to do, which made staying in the open, elevated space that allowed the achievement much easier. I looked at her and handed her the branch.

"So," I said, "that was easy. What's next?" I was only half joking.

She chuckled and shook her head. "Most people stay with the branch for a while, but it looks like you've got it pretty much under control. You must have a good teacher."

We both laughed, but I absolutely knew that I wouldn't have been able to do it without her teaching, guiding, and sometimes annoyingly harassing me to constantly train over the years.

"Is going through the Wall any different?" I asked, hoping she would indulge at least a few questions. Thankfully, after giving me a look, she responded.

"That depends on you. Our minds can believe that stone is more impenetrable than wood because it's harder and heavier.

In truth, they operate on the same principle of having space within. The hardness is due to how bonded together that space is and how that increased binding is expressed in form."

I had learned much, but what she said was a little confusing. I understood the concept of the space within—obviously, I was able to perform the feat—but this was the first I had heard of it being bonded together. She registered my confusion.

"I'm only saying that since you *expect* a rock or stone to be different, it could affect being able to do this. Another example would be *me* instead of the branch. Would you like to try walking through me?"

"What? No!" The idea of it horrified me. "That would be . . . ugh, weird, wrong, whatever." I gave a shudder, trying to get the thought of squishing through her body out of my mind.

Shasta laughed. "Yes, I thought so. It's the same with other objects, too. And that's my point. Our minds and emotions can inhibit this ability. This is why practice is so important, to train ourselves to be able to go past the mind and emotions when we need to, no matter what is happening around us. Just when we think we can do it in any circumstance, the world will give us a distraction to challenge that confidence."

I understood, but I still wanted to try.

"Can we try going through the Wall?" I asked. "I mean, can I?"

"Not yet," she said. "Like I said, you should practice more first."

I grudgingly acknowledged her statement. She had been careful with the pacing of my learning since my first day in the village, despite my youthful distractions and desire to learn faster. It took a few years, but I eventually learned to trust her judgments, because the few times she had indulged my yearnings, it was clear that I hadn't been as ready as I thought I was. So, I trusted that judgment now, as unsatisfying as it was.

We rose and began to walk back up the trail to the village, but not before I took one last, longing glance in the opposite direction past the grand red oak tree to where the Wall stood beyond my vision.

I couldn't wait to come back to test my newfound ability.

~

I practiced incessantly over the next few weeks, moving beyond branches to many other objects and materials—tree trunks, food, tables, chairs, and even rocks, which initially I had difficulty with, exactly as Shasta had predicted. It became a fun challenge to see how quickly I could elevate myself to a high enough space to be successful at each attempt.

It didn't always work, however, as sometimes my fingers simply met the surface of the objects and went no further. I noticed that this happened when I was distracted or had any emotions present, so I knew I needed to be clear of thoughts and emotions to be able to accomplish the feats. Shasta had confirmed this, but it left one thing unaddressed.

"What if you get distracted or emotional in the middle of doing the transit, like when going through the Wall?" I asked her after feeling more confident with the practice. I assumed she would know what would happen. She paused, seeming to carefully consider her words.

"Don't," she said, looking at me seriously.

I waited for more, but that was it. Her answer left me more worried than before I had asked the question.

"Um, has that ever happened to you?" I asked.

She sighed. "As you've experienced during your practicing, to be able to do it in the first place, you have to have at least a minimal level of clarity within and *be* in that space, right?"

"Right," I said.

"But once you're engaged with the other object or material, even if distracted, the combined energy of your inner state and your engagement with the object tends to preserve itself to get you through it."

That was a relief to hear. I was worried there was a possibility to be trapped forever inside the Wall or permanently merged with a branch. I almost chuckled thinking about how awkward it would look walking around with twigs coming out of my fingers.

"However," she continued, "don't get distracted too badly when doing it. It can be very dangerous if you abandon the inner space completely."

That got my attention. She saw my worried look and added, "You'll be okay if you just stay focused and clear. Why do you think I waited so long to show you this? I wasn't going to teach it until I knew there was little chance of that happening. Your years of training have brought you to a good enough place to be ready to do it without a major issue like that."

"Good enough?" I said. "Then there's still a chance though." I desperately wanted to squeeze any last doubt from my mind.

"Well, it's very simple . . . just don't get distracted," she said, giving me a wry smile.

I chuckled nervously in response. I trusted what she said, but as much as I wanted to put any worries about it behind me, our conversation only encouraged my fears. Had I made things worse simply by asking the question? Hopefully not. I told myself not to let my guard down and resolved to continue to concentrate on my practice.

~

One day after our conversation, Shasta took me to see Kyna, who had requested my presence.

I still didn't know that much about her, even after so many years, except that she always seemed to be involved in the higher-level administration of the community and surrounding villages. I understood she spent a fair amount of time in the contemplation hall on the hill, often nestled in one of the enclosed nooks in the back of the large room that protected her from being disturbed. It was during these times that I learned she was traveling, so to speak, given her ability to essentially duplicate herself in a far-off place, like when I had first seen her in the city seven years ago.

I still didn't understand how she was able to do that. I hoped that Shasta, or maybe even Kyna herself, would eventually try to teach me, but I also knew that I was already learning some incredible things that I could never have even dreamed about in my previous life in the Territories. Acquiring more skills would be wonderful, but I continued to trust whatever timeline Shasta had put me on for preparing me for whatever I was to do with the prophecy. In any event, I now had my hands full with practicing my new transiting skill.

Shasta and I went to Kyna's cabin where she welcomed us in to sit and have tea. We sat on the couch and Kyna sat in an older, well-worn chair.

"So," she began, "have you heard the rumors?"

I shook my head and looked at Shasta, who nodded slightly. It surprised me a little that she had heard something that I hadn't. We had shared everything for years, or so I thought, but as I had become more independent in the community over time, she had begun to pull away to allow me the space to develop on my own. Still, since we did still share so much, I felt left out.

"He's coming," Kyna said. "I've seen him in the surrounding villages. That's why I've been away for much of the past month."

I wasn't sure if she meant physically away or in her traveling space away, and I now remembered not seeing her around the village much recently.

"Who's coming?" I asked.

Kyna looked at me with her intense, knowing eyes, but it was Shasta who spoke.

"The teacher from the prophecy," she said.

I felt the blood drain from my face, from my body. Now that I thought about it, something I couldn't describe *had* been percolating in the background for many weeks, but I had attributed it to getting into the uplifted space to practice the transit. But it was there, something subtle that had been poking at my intuition for some time, something sacred and world-changing. Now, being told the likely reason for that feeling, it roared forth in my awareness as I recognized and felt the power behind it. It had been there all along; I had simply dismissed it as something else.

The prophecy was coming true. Knowing that I was an integral part of it made me feel small, embarrassed, and inadequate, not ready for whatever my role was to be. I shifted nervously in my seat.

"I'd like you to meet me in the city tomorrow," Kyna said, looking at both me and Shasta. "There's someone there who can fill us in on the Territory Governors' reactions to his pending arrival."

My eyes widened because I hadn't been back to the Territories since I had run away, and I didn't know what to expect or if it would be dangerous. Shasta answered for both of us.

"We'd be happy to," she said before looking over at me. "You'll be fine. You know enough."

"Good!" Kyna said. "I'll meet you at the store mid-morning tomorrow."

"The store?" I asked. It sounded like a regular meeting place.

"The antique store by the marketplace," Kyna said. "The owner is one of our contacts. He usually knows what's going on around the city."

I could barely contain my excitement. The antique store had been one of my favorite shops in the city when I was younger. I used to love to browse the overstuffed aisles full of history and stories. That's where I found the book with the cover with three spirals on it, the one that in a roundabout way led me to Shasta and the village.

Kyna noticed my reaction. "You know that shop?" she asked.

"Yes, I used to go there as a child."

"Hmmm," she nodded.

"What's he like?" Shasta asked. There was a softness to her question, and it seemed the room went abnormally silent for a moment.

"He's all that we expected and more," Kyna said carefully. "His presence is," she paused, "invigorating, fascinating, otherworldly. You have to experience it yourselves to truly understand."

Now it was Shasta's turn to show her excitement, while I probably exhibited apprehension. For years, whenever the prophecy had come up, I had become anxious at the prospect of wanting to be ready but not knowing how to prepare for what I was fated to do. Today was no different. I could feel worry creep into my body as I didn't know what I was preparing for, when I was to do it, where it was to take place, how I was going to do it, or if I was ready. The pressure to perform something I knew nothing about left me feeling uneasy.

Up to now, I had had some success in dissipating these fears. I had kept telling myself to just take it one step at a time, one day at a time, one practice at a time, and everything would work out. Also, after having discussed the issue with Shasta, I found that my angst was largely a result of not trusting that I would be ready for whatever was to come. I could focus on practicing, personal experiences, or learning new skills, but fundamentally I was still in the dark about what the prophecy entailed. Even Promeus didn't know the details. Shasta had encouraged me to trust in the flow, trust in her guidance of the lessons and training, and place trust most of all in *myself*, something I found difficult to do when these agitating emotions arose. Still, these interventions did have some effect on lessening my worries, and I reached for them now.

Changing topics, Kyna said, "I understand you've learned the jointure."

I gave Shasta a puzzled look, not recognizing the term.

"That's what you've been practicing," Shasta said. "Jointure is an old term for the transit, not used much these days."

"Are you saying I'm old," Kyna said with a slight grin.

"Haha, no!" Shasta said laughing. "Of course not!"

Kyna laughed along. "Well, I *am* old, but I don't look it. That's what these practices can do." She was looking at me. "They keep you looking young."

I smiled, not knowing what to say.

We all had been sipping our teas, which were only half finished, and Kyna stood up and thanked us for coming.

"See you tomorrow in the city," she said.

"We'll be there," Shasta said as she and I made our way out the door.

"Thank you for the tea," I said.

"My pleasure, dear." Kyna closed the door behind us.

Shasta walked me back to my cabin. I had questions, lots of questions, now that the prophetic tales were beginning to come true.

"Who is this teacher?" I asked, wondering if she knew more than what she had let on.

"I don't know much, only that they say listening to his teachings and being in his presence is incredibly mind-opening," she said.

"In what way?"

"I suspect his energy is high enough and powerful enough that it uplifts those around him. Have you felt something in the past few weeks?"

"Yes, but I thought it was because of practicing the transit."

"It feels different than that," Shasta said, "and I understand how you can confuse the two, especially when they're new to you. I've felt it, his exquisite energy, quite strongly at times, even though I've never seen or heard him. I've been drawn to it, but Kyna has directed us not to seek him out because he will come here at the appropriate time." She looked at me and smiled. "I wasn't happy hearing that, but I, and others, trust in her direction and the teacher's timing, and you should as well. But get ready. The prophecy is being fulfilled."

I swallowed nervously. "Do you think I'm ready for whatever my role is?"

Shasta looked at me with a kindness that dispelled my fears, at least in that moment. "Everything you've done, everything you've experienced, has brought you unerringly to this moment, and I have no doubt you will do exactly what is needed when the time comes."

I let out a deep breath, which I had been holding. "Thank you. I needed to hear that."

We had arrived at my cabin. I invited her in, but she shook her head.

"No, thanks. I want to prepare for tomorrow, and you should, too."

"What should I do to prepare?"

She thought for a moment. "Try to relax. You'll do fine." And she turned to go.

"One more question?" I said, and she stopped and faced me. "Why are we going to the city? If he's here, then he's outside the Grand Wall, so why do we need to know what they're thinking inside the Territories?"

"Because the Territory Governors are a danger to him," she said. "Promeus and Kyna have sensed it, as have I. You might discern it, too."

As soon as she said it, I felt it was true. I didn't need to sit in contemplation. It was an instant feeling in the pit of my stomach, a feeling of tightness, of limitation, of being opposite of what the teacher seemed to represent, opposite of what I had been learning all these years. It reminded me of my stifling upbringing, and it almost made me queasy.

"Yes, I can feel it," I said.

"We're just going to gather information tomorrow. We shouldn't be in any danger," she said.

"Danger?"

"We'll be okay. We'll be in a safe place."

I nodded. "Why would Kyna ask me to go? I haven't even gone through the Wall on my own yet."

"Well, then I guess tomorrow is your lucky day," Shasta said, smiling, and she turned and strolled back down the path toward the center of the village.

After years of anticipation, it appeared that my reason for being there had finally arrived. The time for learning and practicing the skills needed for my role in the prophecy were over. I had taken in all I could. I only hoped it was enough. Now, it was time to step into my preordained destiny, whether I was ready or not.

~

Upon waking the next morning, the first thing I did was sit in contemplation to try to feel the energy of the teacher Kyna and Shasta had spoken about. Indeed, as soon as I set my intention to recognize and feel it, I was overcome with its power, *his* power. It was, as Shasta had said, an energy quite different from the feeling of doing the transit. It was soft, pleasant, and loving, as if it were a force only for good, and it had an unwavering strength under the surface that was inconceivably resolute in its fortitude. Anything negative or destructive I felt would crumble in the face of its blessed power.

It was a cool, crisp morning, and I met Shasta at her cabin after getting something to eat in the dining hall. I asked about Kyna, and Shasta said that she was going to meet us in the city. I assumed that meant she would *travel* there while in contemplation.

We proceeded down the trail that led away from the village and toward the great red oak tree. Shasta seemed lost in thought, or perhaps processing the teacher's arrival or our mission to the city, so I didn't pester her with questions. I wasn't even sure what I would ask at this point because I was trying to wrap my head around the new energy I was feeling and what responsibilities might be coming.

When we arrived at the imposing red oak, Shasta stopped.

"We're going to go through the Wall now," she said. "There's nothing to worry about. It's just like you practiced. Remember, the more you clear your thoughts and emotions, the easier it is."

She then proceeded forward on the forest path no differently than walking on any other trail. Any observer wouldn't know there was an invisible barrier there at all. Twenty paces away, she stopped on what I assumed was the other side and looked back at me.

I stood in place, not sure what I was looking for or waiting for. Then I closed my eyes, emptied myself as best I could of the distractions of my mind and emotions, and went within where I quickly found the sweet spot of stillness I had practiced. I took a step forward before opening my eyes.

It took a few more steps to feel the Wall, and when I did, it was only slightly different compared to walking freely on the path. Like with my practice of the transit with the branch, there was just minimal resistance to my movement through it, but not nearly enough to hinder my progress. I felt the familiar tickling, this time on my insides instead of just in my hand, exactly like the feeling of my first passage through the barrier so many years ago.

As I couldn't help observing and mentally analyzing what I was doing, I could feel myself start to drop out of the stillness that enabled the feat, which corresponded to an increase in resistance as I moved forward. The tickling, which was almost a pleasant feeling, became thicker, heavier, and more uncomfortable the more my mind spun, and I began to panic.

With that quick rush of emotion, the resistance became obstructive, and I suddenly didn't know if I could make it through to the other side. Not knowing how many more steps I had, I tried to physically push myself forward by attempting to move faster, but resorting to focusing on my physical body only made it worse, which, of course, increased my fear of becoming trapped. The spiral that had started with a few innocuous thoughts had grown into a full-blown, emotional dread that was quickly suppressing *any* movement.

I felt something on my arm, and the resistance immediately lightened as Shasta pulled me the short remaining distance to the other side. I realized I must have shut my eyes to try to regain my concentration in the middle of my turmoil, as her touch surprised me. I bent over and breathed heavily, physically free, trying to regain my composure.

"Thank you," I said.

Shasta looked at me intently, finally saying, "You can do this. In the face of rising emotions, you can find your center. I know it."

I took a moment to take in her words, then nodded, her serious tone having restored some of my confidence. Even after something like this, she was ever the teacher.

After I collected myself, we continued southwest down the trail that would take us to the city. As we progressed, I noticed there were more dwellings and shops further out from the city center than I remembered. It seemed a lot can happen in seven years.

My previous time in the Territories had instilled a certain level of fear of the authorities, which I considered appropriate given that I knew about my father's work as a constable, so I asked Shasta about how we were going to avoid them.

She replied that we shouldn't have to worry about it because we didn't stand out, but we should be vigilant nonetheless. She was right. Once we arrived in the city, it was clear we were dressed just like the other townsfolk who walked the streets, so we blended in well. I noted that she had already rolled down her sleeves to cover up her tattoos. Still, I was wary of the constable patrols, especially after seeing two of them hassling a man carrying a large sack of goods.

Some of the streets were eerily familiar as we made our way to the marketplace on the southern edge of the city. I was glad, however, that we didn't walk down the avenue I used to live on. I didn't want to encounter my parents or be reminded of my previous life, although it got me thinking about eventually seeing them again. I certainly didn't want the distraction of a reunion right then—good or bad—as we had another objective.

And then there it was before us, the antique store I had spent many hours in as a child. A rush of memories flooded back, including the feeling I had when I had first picked up the book with the spirals on the cover.

Shasta opened the door confidently and I followed, lost in remembrances of things past. Just before entering, however, I felt the need to look to my left, and I saw a beggar sitting on the cobblestones nearby against a shop's wall. He was looking in my general direction but with his eyes closed. There was something about him—a wisdom, a presence, I didn't know what—that immediately brought me back to the present. I wondered if it could possibly be the blind beggar from the lost, forbidden manuscript. I turned back and entered the shop.

The ringing of the old bell above the door was familiar, even after all these years. The rotund man at the counter shifted his gaze from Shasta to me. He was the same shopkeeper I had known in my youth, only with even less hair, more graying, and a few more pounds and wrinkles. His smile was the same though, which immediately lit up when he saw me. I was sure my red hair had given me away.

"It *is* you!" he exclaimed. "Kyna said you would come at some point, but I didn't believe it. He came out from behind the counter and gave me a big hug.

"Look at you. I assume you enjoyed the story?" he said.

After all this time, he remembered our special secret from back then, one that he helped me hide from my parents. I nodded.

"Yes," I said, "it changed my life."

"As I knew it would. Come. Let's go to the back room. Kyna is already here."

He led Shasta and I to a door in the back of the shop, and we entered a small room with a round table in the center surrounded by four chairs. The bookcases on all four walls were filled with old items, the types I used to like to browse in the shop. Another door on the back wall I assumed was a closet. Kyna was sitting at the table.

Her hair was slightly messy, but it was her energy that struck me. It was odd and quite unlike how I knew her in the community. She *felt* very different. Then I remembered . . . she wasn't really there. I had thought she might use her exceptional ability to project herself to the shop—likely from a nook in the contemplation hall in the village—but it was difficult to reconcile that thought with seeing what looked like her physical form right in front of me. I gave Shasta a look about it, and she smiled.

"Any trouble getting here?" Kyna asked as we sat down. Her behavior was almost the same, or maybe it was the same and I just recognized her very different energy. It was almost as if she were an actor playing the role of Kyna. I couldn't help staring at her, trying to figure out—*feel*—the differences.

Shasta said, "Just a minor hiccup at the Wall, but we made it."

Kyna looked at me. "The last time you saw me here I was probably a bit different, a bit more disconnected and agitated," she said.

After running away from home, I remembered her frantically grabbing me to tell me to look for Shasta in the plaza. I nodded.

"I can control it better now," she said.

"We never stop learning," Shasta said.

"Indeed," Kyna said. She turned to the shopkeeper. "So, Quinn, what are you hearing?"

I felt a twinge of guilt for never having learned his name.

"There's a lot more activity in the government buildings," he said, "and the enforcement division is preparing. They don't know for what, though, but they're acting like there's a threat coming."

"Any official warnings?" Kyna asked. I assumed she was referring to the blaring tones and messages that came from the speakers all around the Territories, something I hadn't heard since I had lived in the city.

"No, not yet. It's different this time. Despite rumors of the Governors being overly anxious and unsettled, there's a new head of enforcement who seems to be more of a thinker, and he's slowing the old process down."

Kyna closed her eyes for a moment. The rest of us watched her in silence.

"Yes, he is, and," she paused and looked at me, "he will do what's needed when the time comes."

I didn't know what she meant, but it felt like it was related to me.

"Despite that," Quinn continued, "the constables are harassing people a lot more, often without reason. It's almost like they're doing it to make a show of it."

"Yes," Kyna said, "to keep people on edge."

Quinn nodded.

"Do the Governors have any idea of what the threat is?" she continued.

"I don't think so, but it sounds like they're really feeling vulnerable, like truly in danger this time."

"That'll be a first," Shasta said.

"Well, it's true," Kyna said. "The coming of this teacher may just change everything in the Territories." She glanced at me again when she said it.

"So, the rumors are true?" Quinn asked. "He really is coming?"

"He's already here," Kyna said.

Quinn's eyes opened wide, and he sat back in his chair and took a deep breath. "Wow, I wasn't sure I'd see it in my lifetime. I thought I had felt something, but as you know, it's a little more difficult to recognize it here."

I wondered what he meant for a moment before realizing that my intuition here felt more muted than in the village. In fact, the closer we had gotten to the city, the more constrained it had become. Even when I recognized the difference in Kyna's energy, that recognition had a muffled feeling to it compared to how I had come to perceive and read people's energies.

We all sat quietly for a few minutes digesting what Quinn had told us. Shasta eventually broke the silence.

"So, what do you expect from the Governors? Any idea of their plans or defenses?"

"It's not going to be like that," Kyna said. "He doesn't come to fight, only to teach. But they will see it as a fight for survival."

We all looked at her. She must have known something she wasn't sharing, perhaps from this mysterious teacher, something that made that statement make sense. I, for one, was confused. I looked at Quinn, and he was staring at Kyna, either evaluating what she had said or evaluating whether or not to ask for clarification. He demurred with a slight nod.

"I'll keep my ears open," he said.

Kyna stood up, clearly signaling the end of the meeting. Quinn, Shasta, and I stood and walked back out into the shop. I turned around to see if Kyna was following us, but she had gone to the door at the back of the small room and had opened it. From my vantage point, it looked like a small closet with only a chair inside. She entered, sat down, and looked at me before smiling and closing the door behind her.

A moment later I sensed a shift in energy that I hadn't felt before, or at least I didn't know how to explain it. Then I realized that it was probably that Kyna had left the building . . . from the closet. I shook my head thinking that I'll probably never get used to all the extraordinary abilities I had been exposed to.

I walked to the counter where Quinn held out a small trinket for me.

"I remember you used to like these," he said.

He was right. As a child I used to collect small, unique items like this from his shop.

"Take this with my compliments," he said, handing me the item. It was a small pin with three spirals coming together in the center.

I didn't know what to say except a heartfelt "Thank you!" and gave him a hug.

"But be careful where you show that here in the Territories," he added. "As you know, the government doesn't look kindly upon symbols like this."

I thought of my father's angry reaction to finding the book cover with the same symbol on it.

"Yes, I'll be careful," I said. "Thanks for the warning." I tucked it into an inner pocket at my waist.

"Thanks for the info," Shasta said, "See you next time." She led me out of the shop.

Outside, she reiterated Quinn's warning. "Make sure you don't get seen with that. We can't risk having you detained." Her wording made me feel oddly important.

I nodded and looked around to see if there were any constables about. There were two across the square and away from us—they always seemed to travel in pairs—loudly questioning a marketplace vendor. I overheard some of it.

"What do you mean you don't know who we're talking about?" one constable barked.

"I've told you time and time again, I used to know him, but I haven't seen him in years," the merchant said.

"So, you don't know where he is?" said the other constable.

"How would I know where he is if I haven't seen him in years?" the man said.

"Don't get snippy with us!" the first constable growled.

The man put his hands up. "I'm just trying to sell my spices in peace. I don't know how long it's been, over five years, I think, since he's been here. The last time I saw him was when we got to the Level Seven warning, and that was a long time ago."

That seemed to pacify the constables a bit. I didn't hear any more of the conversation, and I didn't want to linger in case they turned their attention our way.

As I was about to follow Shasta, I saw the same beggar I had seen before we had entered the store, and he was staring at me with deep, black eyes, a shade so dark that they seemed bottomless. I had never seen anything like it before. Then I heard a kind, resonant voice in my head, *You are the only one who can handle it. His fate rests in your hands.*

His words carried a power that almost knocked me over, a power that made me believe him. I stared at him as he closed his eyes and looked forward. Shasta had already turned the corner, so I broke my gaze with the strange man and hurried to catch up with her, doubting what had just happened. *Had the man actually communicated with me? Does it mean what I think it does? Does he know about the prophecy or the teacher that's coming?* I trailed Shasta down the street, lost in thought that anyone's fate, especially the fate of this supposedly amazing teacher who I had never met, might be in my hands.

I had already felt an inordinate amount of pressure from the talk around the village about my as yet undefined role. With the arrival of the teacher, that pressure had only increased, although it was largely self-imposed. Now, with what this beggar had somehow communicated, I felt that burden increase, and I questioned if I had the determination, resolve, and the skills to be able to fulfill whatever function it was that had been so long foretold.

Nevertheless, at that time, I had no choice but to flow with the circumstances around me, but that was going to change. In due course, I was going to have the ultimate test put before me, one that would entail risk, sacrifice, and death, and my decision would determine not only my future but the future of the entire world.

~

Shasta and I made our way out of the city following a different route than the one we had taken on the way in, finding streets off the main boulevards to avoid the constables. We were successful until we were outside the city and on the forest path back to the Wall. There we came across two constables walking toward us. We were close to the barrier and no one else was around, and even Shasta seemed surprised to see them so far out from the city.

I stiffened, and I think she did too. I tried to remember my training to stay centered and not let external circumstances affect me, but with having lived on the other side of the Wall and having the forbidden trinket in my pocket, fear spread throughout my body.

"What are you two doing so far out of the city?" the larger of the two men demanded.

I left the question for the older and wiser Shasta to answer.

"Just going for an extended walk," she said. "It's good to get out in nature once in a while."

"Have you seen anyone else on your way," the man asked.

I shook my head while Shasta said, "No."

"Where do you live?" the smaller man asked. They were both looking at us suspiciously.

"Over in the apartments by the marketplace," Shasta said. "Hanson Street." Then she added, "Do you know where this trail goes? We don't want to get lost."

Clever, I thought.

The bigger man responded. "It goes to the Wall, but you're not allowed to go that far."

"Oh, why?" she asked. I was thinking the same thing.

"There's a new danger in the area. We can't talk about it," he said.

"I was hoping to get to the Wall to show my daughter," Shasta said, motioning to me. "She's never seen it up close before."

"That's not allowed," the man said.

Playing along, I pouted in fake disappointment.

"Do you think we could come back to see it in a few days?" she asked.

"No." His answer was clipped and firm as his eyes narrowed. "You ask a lot of questions," he added, which triggered his shorter partner to take a few steps around to position himself behind us. Despite my internal attempts to keep calm, my anxiety ramped up as the tension—and danger—of the situation increased. Our window to successfully escape was rapidly closing.

"Oh, I'm just naturally curious, and she really wanted to see the Wall," Shasta said.

I nodded, but I feared it was too late.

The man stared at Shasta for a few seconds before slowly saying, "Roll up your sleeves."

I knew it was over. Internally, I panicked. Externally, I remained calm and waited for her to take the lead, for I had no idea what to do.

Her bearing changed, and I could *feel* her center herself and go deeper within, which expressed as a sudden peaceful shift in her energy. It reminded me that I, too, had the same ability and should do the same. I began to, but the man's sudden lunge at Shasta was too disrupting.

He was quick. He grabbed her arm before she could pull away, and he lifted up her sleeve, revealing her illegal tattoos of the ancient, forbidden symbols. As he tightened his grip, she looked at me and very calmly but intensely said, "Run."

In the second it took for me to register the word and what to do, the smaller man behind us grabbed my arm. I instinctively turned and twisted away, sweeping my arms across my body like when practicing the movements of the slow dance with Naveen but much faster and more forcefully. The move freed my arm and sent the man tumbling to the ground. Without even looking at Shasta or the constables, I began to sprint up the trail as fast as I could.

"Stop!" I heard one of the constables shout, but the energy coursing through my body was too strong to do anything but run. I was in good shape and quite fast, but when I glanced over my shoulder a few seconds later, I could see the man I had thrown to the ground coming after me. It was good that I had a head start because he was gaining ground fast.

Looking up, I saw the Wall ahead towering over the trees, so I knew I was close. I had to get to it, get *through* it, before the man behind caught me. Given the circumstances, not to mention the symbol in my pocket, I feared the worst if I were apprehended.

I kept running, faster than I ever had before, not even feeling my legs. My feet barely contacted the ground as they flew over the fallen sticks and leaves on the path, making me feel as if I were simply gliding above the ground by sheer force of will instead of with any physical effort. But my pounding heart and straining lungs soon brought me back to earth, and I suddenly realized I was in no mental or emotional state to be able to transit the Wall. Fear had too strong a grip on me. If I had trouble going through the Wall before without any external worries, how was I going to do it now? It would be unachievable, especially with someone literally breathing down my neck.

With the constable just a few body lengths away and gaining, I tried to focus on my center. I felt a glimpse of it, but it was elusive. Still, I needed to get into that space before the trail ran out, which would be in mere seconds because the massive barrier was just ahead of me, blocking the trail like an enormous stone sentry.

I could hear the footsteps behind me, more rapid than mine, and the constable's heavy breathing getting closer. I risked a half-glance behind me and saw he was almost within arm's reach. I pushed my legs harder while trying to find the subtle, still space within that would grant me passage through the Grand Wall.

I could not be captured; rather, I would not allow myself to be captured. How could I fulfill my role in the prophecy if I were in the hands of the constables? I would prefer to run hard into the stones and kill myself rather than let myself be taken by the government.

As I neared the end of the trail and the moment of reckoning, I could feel the constable almost on top of me, his fingers scraping my back searching for something to grab. At the same time, I felt something else, an impossibly light and serene energy, opposite from my external circumstances and different from the space of stillness I was searching for within. I could tell it was coming from outside of me, and it quickly built up as I neared the Wall.

Whatever it was, though, it was too late.

I closed my eyes, and with the only breath I had left, I released a primal scream as I ran full speed into the unforgiving stones.

Anna

After their meal, Jillian and Naveen had left Anna to be alone with her writing. Despite their wanting to stay to support and comfort her further, she had insisted they leave. Their presence had been welcome, especially because she could count on them to understand what had really transpired. However, she didn't want to burden them too much with her emotions, as they were hers to bear, a penance for fulfilling such an ill-fated role.

Jillian had asked if Anna wanted her to talk with Promeus instead so Anna could focus on her manuscript, but Anna declined, preferring to hear the old man's words herself. She wanted to make sure she fully understood anything he might say about her writing or anything else he might see with his visionary talents.

Now alone, Anna sat and wrote for several hours, the words once again spilling out onto the pages as if being channeled by an unseen force. Eventually, her hand tired, and she decided to take a break to go to speak with Promeus.

Walking down the path to the village center and then up the hill to the contemplation hall where Promeus spent most of his time, Anna kept her eyes down, looking ahead only a few paces. She didn't want to be on the receiving end of any eye contact. Nevertheless, she couldn't avoid feeling a few sharp stares coming her way.

She climbed the steps to the hall and found the old seer sitting alone on a bench, looking out over the village. He wasn't in contemplation, so his eyes were open, and he had obviously seen her approaching.

"How are you, dear?" he said after she sat down next to him. He reached out and took her hand.

She looked at his wisdom-lined face and could see that he was not like many of the others who were judging her. His energy was like Jillian's and Naveen's: understanding and supportive. Indeed, if she couldn't trust the elders of the community to understand, whom could she trust? With their advanced years and training, they all brought a deeper perspective that infused their understanding and awareness.

"I'm okay," Anna said.

Promeus, seemingly evaluating her like the first time they had met, smiled slightly. "You will be."

They sat in silence for a few minutes looking out over the village. Eventually, Anna spoke.

"Can you tell me anything about what comes next?"

Promeus didn't answer for a few of his very slow breaths. When he did, he sounded sad.

"I have seen what is to happen with Teacher, and I now understand more fully your role, why it was given to you, and why you chose to accept it." He looked at her. "I'm sorry, child. No one should ever have to bear this burden."

"Thank you. It's nice to hear that at least one person understands. Jillian and Naveen do, too, but not like you do. I don't think most will come to that understanding. In fact, if what Teacher says is true, they won't and they shouldn't."

Promeus nodded slowly. "Your sacrifice is not going unnoticed."

Anna looked out over the village while she asked her next question. "What do you see for me?"

"Not much, only that you are doing what you need to be doing."

"Writing?" Anna said.

"Yes," he nodded. "Keep going with it. I feel it will help many people. The next steps will unfold before you at the appropriate time."

"Are you seeing anything else for me besides the writing?"

Promeus shook his head. "I'm not seeing anything beyond the very near future, but I still get a sense of things."

"What do you mean? You always see something," Anna said.

"Yes, usually, but I've never been able to see beyond this point in time."

Anna snapped her head around to face him. "What does that mean?"

Promeus smiled. "I can only assume it means one thing." He looked into her eyes.

"No!" Anna cried. "That's not right!"

"It's okay. I've lived a long life. It's time."

Anna's emotions caught up with her again and she leaned over and hugged her old friend, sobbing.

"I've been fortunate to be here to see the prophecy fulfilled," he said, "and to meet with Teacher many times, which has been the highlight of my life. We've had the most wondrous discussions. He's shown me what's possible—and what *is*—and I will take that understanding with me. It's okay."

Anna continued sobbing, afraid to let go of another one of her mentors. When she finally gathered herself together, she asked a question she didn't want the answer to.

"When?"

"I don't know, but I suspect soon."

They sat together holding hands for some time as the afternoon sun dipped in the sky. People who might have come up to the contemplation hall during that time turned around when they saw Anna outside by the steps. She didn't care what they thought anymore.

As dusk began, Anna said, "You called me 'child' earlier. You know, I'm not a child anymore." She grinned at him.

Promeus smiled, the shadows from the wrinkles on his face shifting in the waning light.

"I know, but you always will be to me."

Teacher

I was still alive, or so I thought. The light energy that had ramped up before I reached the Wall was humming all around me. My legs were still moving fast, but I felt as if I were floating, being borne forward without their help. The words, *I've got you*, rang clearly in my head. There was no tickling on my insides as I had experienced before, as the lightness that encased me filled me to overflowing and took me beyond physical sensations. My mind and emotions were suddenly calm, which allowed me to drop into my center of stillness, guided there by the energy around me.

I emerged on the other side of the Wall, collapsing into the dirt in the center of the trail by the towering red oak, still feeling the lightness. Looking back, I could see the constable who had almost caught me bent over, panting. He seemed so close, yet I knew he couldn't get to me.

He straightened and looked up, and I could see some blood oozing from his forehead. He brought his hand up and felt his wound, then wiped the blood on his uniform. I suppressed a chuckle because I knew he had hit his head on the barrier, something I was glad I hadn't done even though I had been prepared to. His eyes darted around, seemingly looking for whatever secret passage or trigger I had used to get through the stones. Finding none, for there was none to find, he shook his head, grimaced, and turned to walk back down the trail, away from me and the Grand Wall, raising a hand again to touch his bleeding head.

I took a deep breath, my lungs still catching up to my body's needs, and turned around. In front of me stood a solitary man bathed in light, a man from whom all the light energy I had just experienced—was experiencing—emanated. I couldn't tell if my mind was playing tricks on me, but his physicality became apparent when he reached down and offered me a hand, which I took.

Standing, I looked at his face and his implausibly peaceful expression. Instinctively, intuitively, I knew he was the prophesized teacher. There was no question in my mind. In fact, it was such a certainty that any thought to the contrary didn't exist. But there was something else, too, something that made me take a step back in disbelief.

I recognized him.

Before me stood the man I had seen on the street that fateful day on my thirteenth birthday in the city, the man who had picked up the last page of the forbidden manuscript my father had angrily thrown over our second-floor balcony railing. We had connected—me from the terrace and him in the street—a shared moment that had stuck with me ever since. My question of whether he remembered me was answered when he spoke.

"It's good to see you again, Anna."

His voice was as perfect as his calm demeanor—smooth, confident, and resonant. I had no response except to lunge forward and throw my arms around him, giving him a hug so strong it would've hurt an ordinary man.

After a few seconds of that blissful embrace, I stepped back and gazed upon him. His loving smile hadn't wavered. I beheld his sacred presence, a charisma and bearing and power that made all of what I had learned from Shasta and others in the village make sense. All the lessons that had directed me to elevate my energy and find stillness—physically, in contemplation, and otherwise—and all that I had practiced, paled in comparison to their perfect embodiment in this being before me. I could feel those blessed spaces I had struggled to find within firing up, as if the totality of what I had learned was mere kindling and he had just provided the spark from his beacon to light it. I stood in awe.

As my wits slowly returned to me, I recognized it had been his voice that had spoken to me when inside the Wall. *I've got you.* Indeed, I had no doubt that if he hadn't lifted me up, I would have been an injured mess on the other side of the barrier in the hands of the constables, or perhaps still trapped inside it, merged forever with the dense stone.

Realizing I hadn't yet spoken, I said, "Thank you . . . for just now . . . and for before, when I was a child." It was deep and heartfelt.

He gave a slight bow. "You and I have a particular connection," he said, "and it will serve us both well."

I didn't know what he meant, but clearly there was a reason the prophecy included both of us.

"I must go now," he said.

"No! Please don't," I implored. Being in his presence was intoxicating. "Can I go with you?" I wanted to stay with him, wherever he went.

"Not now," he said.

"Wait! What about Shasta?"

He blinked slowly and said, "She will be fine."

"When will I see you again?"

"Soon enough."

And with that, while still gazing at me tenderly, he dissolved into the clear, forest air, leaving a shimmering behind that faded a few seconds later. I was now alone.

I blinked, not trusting what my eyes had just seen. I realized he must have been projecting himself just like Kyna knew how to do, but he was so present and physical with no hint of the strange, hollow energy I felt with Kyna when she projected herself. If he was lessened in any way by doing so, then I couldn't wait to see him in person to feel the full effect of his power and presence. And it now made sense that no one else was with him, as I had assumed someone as important as he was had people around to take care of necessities. I wondered where he really was.

Dusting myself off, I looked back down the trail through the Wall for Shasta, who was probably well on her way to the detainment center by now. Even though my savior had said she would be okay, I was suddenly overcome with guilt that I had left her behind.

All alone and without my trusted companion, I began to briskly walk the long trail back to my village, thinking of my connection with the teacher and how I was going to find and free my friend.

~

I arrived at the village and went directly to Kyna's cabin. She wasn't there, so I tried the contemplation hall where I found her outside discussing the Shasta situation with Promeus and a few other elders in the community. I didn't know how they could have gotten the news so fast.

She saw me approach and welcomed me with a big hug. "So good to see you safe," she said.

"They grabbed Shasta," I said, holding back tears. "I ran and got away. I don't know what happened to her."

"We know," Kyna said. "She got away, too. She's safe . . . for now."

"What? How?" I muttered, trying to understand. When I had left her, she seemed firmly held in the big constable's grasp.

"Well, she knows a thing or two about escaping," Kyna said with a smile.

Surprised but relieved, I took a deep breath and let it out, not realizing I had been breathing shallowly since the experience. Part of me wished I could have stayed and watched how she had gotten away, but that would have undoubtedly made it more difficult for her, as she would have wanted to protect me and ensure my safety before her own. She had done the right thing, as had I.

"Is she here?" I asked.

"No, the last we could envision was her getting away into the woods on the other side of the Wall," Kyna said.

I looked at her, puzzled. How could she know that? I had gone straight to the village, and no one else had seen what had happened. I asked.

"Wait, how do you know that?"

Kyna gestured to Alden, one of the elders listening to us, a small, older man with bright, blue eyes, who bowed slightly. He was known to be able to view happenings from afar, like Kyna with projecting her physical form, but he did it without his body. When I had first heard about his skill, I remember asking Shasta about it because it sounded a little creepy. However, she alleviated my fears by telling me that the ability could only be learned and mastered by those who were well beyond any desire to misuse it in that way. So, it became one of the three most exciting skills I wanted to learn how to do, along with transiting the Wall with ease like Shasta and projecting my bodily form like Kyna.

"The important thing is that you both are out of the hands of the authorities," Kyna said. "And although Shasta may not need it, we're searching for her to make sure she gets back here safely."

"What can I do?" I asked. I felt partly responsible for leaving her, even though she had told me to run.

"Nothing. Just getting back here in one piece is enough." And then she added, "I knew you could transit the Wall."

I shook my head. "I had help."

All in the group looked at me blankly. Clearly, Alden hadn't seen *everything* that had occurred.

"The teacher helped me through it," I said.

"He was there?" Kyna asked, surprised. The others looked at each other, seemingly surprised as well.

"Yes," I said, "on this side of the Wall. He put me in a space to be able to go through it. I wouldn't have been able to transit without his help."

"Mmmm," Kyna said, staring at me with her intense eyes. I could feel her reading me, looking beyond my form. "And what did you think of him?"

"He's amazing. He . . ." I paused, not wanting to offend the elders of my adopted village. I didn't want to say too directly that his energy felt like it was on an entirely different level than even the most skilled and gifted practitioners in the community. "He embodies everything that this village stands for, and more."

Everyone nodded their approval.

"I've met him before," I said, "in the Territories." They all snaped their heads toward me.

Kyna turned her head slightly to one side and asked, "What? When?"

"Just before I first arrived in the village. And I didn't really meet him. It was from a little distance, but we had some kind of connection."

Alden was nodding, looking through me. The others seemed surprised, except Kyna, who just stared at me blankly.

I continued. "It was the first time I felt the types of energies I've learned about here."

Now Kyna nodded.

Just then, we heard a "Hello there!" from some distance away, and Shasta was walking up the hill toward us, smiling. She looked like she had simply gone for a walk. Kyna descended the steps to meet her and give her a big hug, saying nothing. I followed and did the same.

"I'm so glad you got away!" Shasta said to me. "I knew you could do it."

"I had help," I said.

She looked at me puzzlingly.

"I'll tell you later. How did *you* get away? I thought you were done for."

"Some of what we practice has good utility in the Territories," she said with a grin. "Remember your revulsion at the idea of passing through someone's body?"

"You didn't!" I said.

"Well, there's nothing like feeling it for the first time," she said, "especially when you don't know what it is and aren't expecting it. He didn't know what to do with himself, except throw up."

I laughed, both intrigued and horrified at what she had done.

"Then I ran away from him off the trail to a different part of the Wall, and here I am."

I was so relieved to have her back, safely out of the hands of the authorities. I hugged her again.

"Now, tell me what happened to you," she said.

I recounted my escape—twisting away from the constable, running for my life, approaching the Wall that I didn't think I could get through in the state I was in, the uplifting transit, and my experience and brief conversation with the teacher on the other side of the stones. Kyna and the elders listened closely as well, particularly to my description of the teacher. I gathered that most hadn't yet seen him but eagerly anticipated doing so.

When I was finished, Kyna said, "We're glad you're both safe. Why don't you go home and relax before mealtime. I'm sure the travel and experience were tiring."

She was right. I felt it. Now that I was back and I knew Shasta was safe too, I felt weary, mentally and emotionally exhausted from not only the stress of my escape but also from visiting the Territories for the first time in seven years. And the additional information from Quinn about the government's behavior and actions in the city occupied some of my thinking as well.

Shasta and I walked back to our respective homes while Kyna stayed to talk further with the elders. There still seemed to be something they needed to discuss. I wished I could stay to hear it, but I knew it was not my place despite my curiosity and potential future role in the prophecy. It was good for me to leave anyway because I wanted to sit in contemplation to try to understand the day's events. There was a lot to process, and I knew I needed some quiet time to allow everything to come into perspective.

I also looked forward to getting some sleep, which often seemed to have a similar effect of providing context to recent experiences. I almost always woke up refreshed after going to bed with a weight on my mind or with lingering emotions, as if my dreams served as a grand organizing mechanism that purged the unnecessary details and allowed me to see the purpose in all that I had experienced. Despite all I had learned through the teachings and practicing, I had found that time and a good night's rest were among the most powerful ways to heal and understand.

~

Trying to get to sleep that night, I thought of the teacher, or more specifically, of the time I had seen him so long ago. I had anxiously gripped the railing on the balcony of my parents' apartment after having been yelled at by my very religious father, the last pages of the manuscript he had thrown into the street still fluttering down. He was angry at what he saw was a blasphemous story, but it was nothing of the sort. It conveyed the truth, and it marked the beginning of my new life.

The teacher was standing in the street holding one of the tossed pages. He looked up at me, a young, angry, and confused girl whose precious birthday gift was being destroyed under the feet of those walking in the street. When our eyes met, something beyond time clicked and all my swirling emotions faded into the background as he and I connected in a manner impossible to describe at the time. I felt as if there was a world beyond the one I lived in that could carry me from the angst-ridden one I occupied. For the first time I felt hope, and I knew everything was going to be okay . . . no matter what.

His energy at that time was not like what I had experienced with his presence at the Grand Wall but rather an immature version of it, something with great potential but just beginning to be developed. Seeing him so many years later, now in whatever extraordinary energetic state he existed in, I once again felt hope—hope that attaining what he had attained was possible for myself and everyone, both outside and inside the Wall. Indeed, that was what the story in that ill-fated manuscript had imparted when I had read it, the possibility that *all* of us could realize and become such a presence in the world.

I was confused, however, with who wrote the manuscript. The author on its title page was Erich Evepret, which could be a pseudonym, but everything in the story indicated that it was some sort of memoir by the main character, Christopher. How could the author know such intimate thoughts and experiences except by experiencing them himself? And the fact that my father's outburst, the pages raining down into the street, and my connection to the teacher from the balcony was contained *in the story itself* even though it occurred *after* I had read it just didn't make sense. But such was the nature of what was expressed in the manuscript, which took me up and out of the world I knew and transported me to one of far greater magnificence in its time-transcending pages.

But this was real life, and now having recognized the teacher from before, I wondered if there was another copy of the manuscript somewhere I could get my hands on. I had only read it once and was so very young at the time, so I was sure I would understand it more deeply if I could read it again, particularly with having spent so many years studying the finer energetic practices. I resolved to ask when I saw him again.

But beyond these thoughts were the enduring *feelings* from being in his presence, which lingered pleasingly in my body and served as a counterpoint to the stressful emotions from the experience with the constables. Those emotions lessened by the minute, particularly once I focused on their opposite, the teacher and the peace he emanated, the peace he embodied. It was, in one sense, a feeling more real than my thoughts. Although I knew thoughts could affect the body, especially distressing ones when they worked in concert with corresponding emotions, the light feeling of having experienced his presence continued to awaken some aspect within me that was increasingly familiar.

Like my practice of deep contemplation or going to the elevated space within to do the transit, or even when practicing the slow dance with Naveen, this new level of energy felt wonderful, but it was different, deeper, and more profound than the others. It seemed to envelop and hold any remaining worrying thoughts and emotions in its hands to be dissolved, leaving a sacred, loving emptiness that surprised me with its reach. It was so deep and cleansing that I suspected it might have been uncomfortable if I hadn't been preparing for its coming, his coming, for the last seven years.

Eventually, I dozed off, enwrapped in love for this teacher I barely knew but who had already changed my life. Thoughts of the prophecy and any associated responsibilities drifted away, the first time in weeks, and I rested securely in the knowledge that this was the beginning of the next chapter of my life.

~

I bounded out of bed the next morning feeling more refreshed than ever. There was a soft hum of rightness in the air. I was too excited with the recent developments and the feeling coursing through my body to do my usual morning practice with Naveen, so I just waved to him on my way to Shasta's cabin.

She was awake and making tea when I knocked. She welcomed me in and offered me a cup, which I gladly accepted. I always accepted because she made the best and most flavorful tea in the village, and today was no different.

We sat down and shared more details about our experiences the previous day. I didn't have as many questions for her as she had for me: *What exactly did you do to get away from the constable? What were you thinking and feeling right as you approached the Wall? When did you first feel the teacher? Describe what you felt when you laid eyes on him. Tell me all about your experience with him before in the city.*

I dutifully answered each as it was asked, and she listened intently, providing feedback when appropriate. Eventually, I said that the only thing that would really help her understand what it was like was to be in the teacher's presence herself, which she heartily agreed to with a laugh. She said she felt it was going to happen soon, which I enthusiastically hoped as well.

Shasta was right. At breakfast together, we heard that the teacher had stayed overnight nearby and would be coming to our village that afternoon. He traveled with a few followers and preferred to camp outside the villages rather than stay within them. Someone said it had something to do with being away from others to be able to be more in tune with nature. He and his followers had stayed about a half hour's walk away last night.

Apparently, he had been going to the surrounding communities to meet people and give talks, each of which always happened to contain a teaching of some sort. It was said that the lessons took everyone, including the wizened elders, to an understanding far beyond what was already being taught and practiced in their communities. And his presence was said to bring people *into* that sacred place, at least momentarily. Since I had already met him and had experienced some level of his greatness, twice now, I knew better than most what they were talking about, and I couldn't wait.

The village was abuzz with chatter as the sun peaked and then began its descent in the sky. Most of the residents waited restlessly in the clearing, talking about what they thought he would be like and what he would teach. I received more than a few glances in my direction when talk turned to the prophecy, as I was now so intimately tied to it.

Feeling a little overwhelmed by the anticipatory energy of the people waiting and by garnering some of the attention, I walked the path back to my cabin to be alone and center myself. Shasta asked where I was going, and I just said I'd be back soon.

Once inside my house, I sat in my regular contemplation spot in the corner, took a deep breath in, and let it out slowly, letting the excited, sticky energies of others melt out of my personal space. I continued deep breathing, and a few breaths later felt more my customary, contemplative self, bathing in the soft center of my being as I had been taught. However, the feeling was far more light, clear, and peaceful than usual. I assumed it was because I had experienced the presence of the teacher the prior day and it had greatly affected me. But there was another reason.

There was a knock on the door. I rose and answered it and in front of me stood the teacher, who said, "May I come in?"

He was as radiant and shimmering with light as when I had seen him the previous day, and the feeling I had just had while sitting down was still there but now enhanced.

Frozen in place for a moment, I quickly recovered my manners and said, "Of course!" and waved him in. I noticed a number of his followers standing outside, one a beautiful, blonde woman, and I gestured for them to come in as well. They declined, so I shut the door behind me.

The teacher was standing there gazing at me with the kindest smile I had ever seen. He seemed to be looking at me, into me, and beyond me all at the same time, which contrasted to how Kyna and Promeus could switch from looking at me and through me but could not seem to do both at once.

Not knowing what to do, I said, "Please sit . . . if you'd like to." He nodded and sat in one of my chairs. I sat in the other. He observed me in silence for a minute before speaking, which gave me a minute to realize how familiar he felt, and not just because of our past connection.

"Thank you," he said.

I stared at him, feeling a little uncomfortable that this great man was thanking me. "Um, for what?" I asked.

"For being part of my destiny," he said. His eyes continued to take me in on all levels.

I was confused. Was he talking about the past of the future? "What did I do? Or what *will* I do?" I asked. Maybe he'd give me a clue about my predicted role.

"It is not so much what you did or what you will do but who you are," he said, still exuding an exquisite kindness. Or maybe it was thankfulness. Or love. I could no longer tell because different positive energies rose to prominence depending on how I took in his words.

I decided to look for answers, hoping he could define me better than how I defined myself.

"And who am I?" I asked.

"You are," he said, then paused an interminably long time, "more than you know, and you are here to help me, again."

That indicated that I had helped him before, which must have been related to his picking up the page from the manuscript off the street after my father had thrown it.

As if reading my thoughts, he said, "It was our connection that brought us together then, and it has done so once more."

"What connection?" I asked. I was feeling increasingly bold in his company, no longer so intimidated by the otherworldly power of his presence or of the glowing talk about him in the village. Despite his lofty energy and loving demeanor, I was becoming more and more relaxed in his presence.

He just looked at me and smiled, saying nothing, but I could feel it, *see* it, a relationship that transcended time. It powerfully swept over me with scenes of the past, not any past I knew directly from my life but ones familiar to the history I knew of the Territories, and even some from unfamiliar times and places. There were two people in each setting that flashed by, none of whom I recognized, but I *felt* who they were because of their bond. That was the constant throughout the numerous scenes that rapidly played out in my vision, the connection between these two individuals who were inextricably linked. It appeared I was witnessing different people across the moving images, but I wasn't. The characters were different, but underneath it all, he and I were the same.

I became lightheaded for a moment, either from the rapidly changing scenes or from the realization that we *did* have a connection, one that was as deep and as strong as the roots of the grand red oak tree near the Wall. I gazed at him, then sprang out of my chair to smother him with a great, long hug.

When finished, I sat down again, wiping the tears from my eyes. I loved this man, not for what he was or what he had become—although that was reason enough—but because we had loved before and that love was eternal. It was a romantic love at times, but in reality, it was so much more because it ran deeper and longer than any one coupling. It was a union beyond life as I knew it.

Now I understood why he felt familiar, why he gave me the impression of a long-lost family member. It was as if we had lived lifetimes together, had separated, and were just now able to reunite to laugh and reminisce about the past. But I also knew that that wasn't why he was here. There was something bigger and grander at stake, and we both had roles to play.

One enduring question I had struggled with was how any prophecy could be known ahead of time, especially one that included me. Now, however, I could feel the certainty of it, not with any detail but with the feeling that the power and effect of what would transpire had already registered in the ethers of time. It's as if it had already happened and we were just following a path already traveled. I realized that this must be how Promeus and others were able to tune into and access the future, because the ripples of such a potent event were already there, vibrating strongly enough for anyone with a discerning enough vision to perceive them.

I composed myself, then remembered what I had wanted to ask him. "Do you have a copy of the story you wrote, *A Tale of Awakening*? It was destroyed the day we first met." I knew at this point that he was the author.

He reached over and touched my arm. "My dear Anna, it's a story I haven't yet written."

I blinked but was only mildly surprised. Our past connections and my thoughts about how the prophecy was able to be known only confirmed that time was a construct more mysterious than was commonly understood. It defied logic and the laws of this world, but perhaps that was the point of it all. I nodded slowly, trying to wrap my head around it.

He stood up. "We will be seeing a lot more of each other. Now, I believe I am expected in the village center. Will you accompany me?" He held out his hand.

I took it and was reminded of the physical feeling when he helped me when I was inside the Wall, sensing that my physical body was lighter than my surroundings and that I could do anything. We walked to the door—rather, I floated to the door—and we made our way out of the cabin and toward the village clearing, his followers trailing behind us.

Anna

Strengthened by Teacher's and Promeus's validations, Anna wrote voraciously over the next week, consumed by an all-encompassing desire to get her story down on paper before anything else could happen that might distract her. Jillian and Naveen assisted, bringing her food and additional writing supplies when asked. Besides that, she kept to herself, only going outside when necessary or when she knew no one was around.

She kept herself fresh by occasionally heading into the woods behind her cabin to practice the slow dance alone under the trees, which energized her, and sitting in contemplation, which brought her back to her center when her mind began to wander. Now freed from the bindings of her role in the prophecy, it was time for her to explore what her life would be beyond it.

What she wrote helped put into perspective her years outside the Grand Wall, from the beginning with meeting Shasta in the Territories, to village life, to her lessons and experiences with Teacher. Her past tumbled forward into her awareness to be expressed on paper, then vanished just as quickly, leaving her with fond remembrances of the events—even the challenging ones—that had crafted her into who she was. Interestingly, once she had written them down, she seemed to lose some of the details about them but could feel the distinct echo of each experience's energy floating around her, infusing her with the lessons they had brought.

After the week of writing, Anna was walking to the kitchen to retrieve another meal to bring back to her cabin when Kyna approached. She informed Anna that she had been to the city and had heard that Teacher's verdict had been rendered. He was to be put to death in two days.

Anna, already knowing that this would be the case, wasn't surprised, but it still hit her emotionally, especially after being on the receiving end of angry looks from several people on her way back home with her meal.

She stayed in her cabin the rest of the day, occasionally questioning her decision but also knowing that it was for the best. It had to be, she told herself.

She sat in contemplation several times to try to surmount those distracting thoughts. During one sitting, she thought of the Perceiver, and the feeling of being before the wooden sculpture of his form in the cathedral produced an out-of-this-world sense of unity and an acceptance that she wasn't the only one who had been chosen for her role, because *everyone* had been chosen. Whether they were aware of it or not, all were playing out their parts as needed. But it wasn't just that they were chosen— indeed, *had* chosen—to fulfill a particular function in the big picture; rather, they all were walking the same path to awakening—the path of the Ancients, the path of the Perceiver, the path of Teacher—the path Anna continued to tread.

Inspired by this revelation and finding herself once again grounded in the knowledge that she had done the right thing, she knew what she finally wanted to do.

When Jillian visited later that day, Anna asked her how Kamaria, the village's wonderful artist, viewed Anna after learning about what Anna had done. Jillian said that Kamaria was always neutral in these things and usually just focused on her art, and it was the same this time. Anna asked if Jillian could get her to come visit and to bring her tattooing tools. A few hours later, there was a knock on Anna's door.

Anna rose and opened it, and there stood Kamaria holding a small satchel. She was in her thirties, but her hair had turned uncommonly white years before, offering a contrast to her naturally dark skin. Anna had always found it striking.

"Please, come in!" Anna said. "Thank you for coming."

"I was wondering when you were going to call on me," Kamaria said, smiling. "I've been waiting for this."

"Oh, really? Why's that?"

"Everyone's first time is special."

Despite her decade in the village, Anna had been resistant to get a tattoo like so many others around her who sported the various symbols of the Ancients. Her experience with Shasta and the constables on the other side of the Wall had left a sizeable impression that the markings could lead to danger, so she kept delaying the decision. Her hesitation had been positive in one sense because it had allowed her to navigate the Territories with Teacher without needing to worry about a potentially forbidden symbol being seen.

Anna motioned for Kamaria to sit at the table, and Anna took a chair as well.

"So, what would you like?" Kamaria asked.

Anna had thought deeply about it many times, and she was ready.

"I'd like the symbol for the sacred sound, the one that encompasses all others in its truth and unity."

"Ah, one of my favorites. It has a lot of power."

Anna knew that. It was one of the reasons she had chosen it.

She offered up her right forearm, and Kamaria got to work. Before the hour was out, Anna's flesh exhibited the symbol, framed by the typical red irritation from the needling.

"I love it! Thank you," Anna said.

"You're welcome," Kamaria said, as she took out a bandage from her satchel and began to wrap Anna's arm. "Keep the bandage on until tomorrow, then remove it and gently clean your arm twice a day. And keep it out of sunlight."

Anna nodded. "Thank you."

"My pleasure," Kamaria said.

Declining Anna's offer of tea, Kamaria exited the cabin, leaving Anna alone once again.

Although the white bandage covered it up, Anna could almost see the symbol beneath it, what looked like a stylized three connected to a zero with a curved line and dot on top. But she knew the image was so much more than how it appeared or could be described. She closed her eyes and envisioned it and the truth it represented, and she was immediately launched into an awareness within that she had not experienced before.

This is what it's about, she thought. *The sound, the oneness, the unity.* She rested in that space for as long as she could.

Twenty minutes later, she came back into her body, feeling wholly refreshed to continue her writing. She glanced at her arm again, smiled, and picked up her quill.

The First Lessons

Teacher's first lecture in the village was all that everyone had hoped for. It demonstrated his understanding of so much more than what we knew and understood, at least I thought so given what I had so far witnessed and experienced. Even Promeus and the stoic Kyna looked as though they had tears in their eyes as they beheld what had been prophesized so many years before.

Teacher stood in front of the boulder at the edge of the clearing, and the entire village gathered around him and up the grassy hill toward the contemplation hall. I sat near the bottom of the hill, just above the flat area so I could easily see him as he slowly paced back and forth throughout his talk.

It wasn't just Teacher's words that carried the lesson to our minds but his physical presence, his *beingness*, that somehow conveyed the same lesson to our hearts. It was as if what he was trying to tell us came from a place well beyond words, a place that reminded me of the feeling when deep in contemplation or lost in the energy of the slow dance. But even then, what I felt when listening to him went far beyond that. I glanced at Naveen, who was sitting near me, and he, too, seemed mesmerized. Being in Teacher's presence—being in the *feeling* he communicated through his words—almost knocked me over when he looked at me sitting on the hillside with the other residents of the village.

I will do my best to repeat his first lesson here.

"My brothers and sisters," he began, "thank you for the loving welcome to your community. I have long desired to be here with you, for many reasons. I know my coming has been foretold, and many of you have waited a lifetime for my arrival."

He looked at Promeus, who broke out into a huge grin.

"That said, expectations can be a disservice, for they can distract you from being present to what is currently in your environment. So, I ask that you put aside all preconceived notions of what I might say or what you think I am here to do, for even I am not yet fully clear on what those are."

He paused, quickly scanned the group, and smiled.

"Well, at least you tried." A chuckle ran through the crowd. "You're doing your best. I know it can be difficult when excitement has been building for some time."

He stopped his slow pacing and closed his eyes, his hands at his sides with the palms facing forward. Then he opened his eyes, clasped his hands together, and continued.

"Today, I want to talk about the beginning, which is also a talk about the end. You who live in this village have been exposed to some of the deeper understandings that can be known about this world, and many of you have skills that use this knowledge to bend the laws of nature to your will." He again scanned the gathering. "That's okay, for I can see the intent with which you wield those abilities, and they are appropriate," he tilted his head and gave a mischievous smile, "most of the time."

Another chuckle ran through the assembly.

"The majority of you have experienced some level of going within to the peace and tranquility of the internal realm where the sensations of physical world fade in your awareness. Then you finish your exercise or contemplation and go about your day, refreshed yet back to operating as before. I am here to tell you that there is more, so much more, and some of you will realize that in this lifetime. But *all* of you are here now for a reason, and you *all* will make great strides in your practices and help set the stage for what is to come."

He paused.

"So, in the beginning, there was *one*. 'One what?' you might ask. A perfectly reasonable question, but to ask the question is to miss the *one*. There was no what, no who or where, no why or when. There was just the *one*." He paused again. "Now, let us skip ahead to where we are today.

"We all see the world of form." He glanced over at Siya, an older, blind woman, and smiled. "Except for Siya over there. She may not see the world of form, but she can *feel* the world of form, isn't that right?"

"Yes, I can, and I can feel you, Teacher," she said.

Teacher nodded. "Seeing and feeling are but two sides of the same coin, and where we place our intention determines how information comes to us. Siya uses her other senses, and her intuition, to navigate a world she can't physically see. Her focus on *not* seeing allows her to see, only differently than most."

Siya nodded.

"By not having physical sight, she has gained another kind of sight. But what if I told you that by giving up something, you could receive even more than what you relinquish? For example, would you give up the physical sight that you know so that you could see *better*?"

He looked around the gathering. I felt a mild discomfort ripple through the crowd.

"Ah, yes, you want to know what it would be like before renouncing your sight. But what if everything could be revealed to you if you would simply trust, surrender, and allow what is the truth to come forth? And when I say, 'everything,' I mean *everything*."

Teacher said the last word very slowly, then paused. The crowd murmured with excitement, but I could feel an awkward hesitation lurking underneath that conflicted with the energy emanating from him.

His voice then dropped into a more serious tone and said, "What would you risk to discover the truth?"

The question hit me squarely in the chest, as I'm sure it did others, and I felt my initial exhilaration of the idea give way to the fear of what he might ask us to surrender. Those emotions seemed to blend in with similar emotions of others in the crowd. The idea of knowing the truth, having *everything* revealed to me, would be beyond my wildest dreams and likely beyond everything I had learned in this fantastical village. It was certainly far removed from my almost-forgotten life growing up in the Territories.

But what would we, I, have to relinquish? What would I have to trust? What would I have to allow? I assume it would be similar to my practice of going within, just to another depth. That practice, however, didn't ask me to give up anything except to temporarily release my awareness of the world of form to recognize what was within. Was he asking us to make that permanent, to let go of everything we know?

"I can see your fears rising up," he continued. "'What is he going to ask us to give up? Our lives?!'" He smiled. "Yes, in one sense, but what you would gain is beyond anything you can possibly imagine in your current state."

He lightly shook his head. "Well, anyway, I've gotten ahead of myself. I don't want to get too much into that today. Perhaps another time. What I want to talk about today is the beginning, the middle, and the end, I mean the beginning." He gave another playful smile.

"So, I said before that in the beginning, there was the *one*. That's so beautifully nice and simple, isn't it? *One*."

He paused and paced slowly back and forth a few times.

"Now, when you look at the world around you, what do you see? Siya, I'm not talking to you right now, although you know what I mean."

The residents of the village laughed and looked at Siya, who appeared to be enjoying the attention.

"You see differences. You *feel* differences: the grass beneath your body, the breeze in your hair, the firm bark of the tree you lean against, the clay mug that holds your drink. None of these could be distinguished from each other if there were no differences between and among them. But how did these differences come about?"

I thought of my lessons with Shasta and how we hadn't talked about differences like this but rather how things had a fundamental sameness to them. That's how we could practice the transit. This lesson, however, was speaking to something very different.

"There is no shadow without the light, no up without down, no firm without soft, hot without cold, movement without rest, right/left, inside/outside, tall/short, above/below . . ." He trailed off. "A particular characteristic of something cannot exist without the existence of the opposite characteristic somewhere. We cannot know what hot is if we don't know of something cold or less hot. It is in those differences where we find meaning in our descriptions of things."

He paused again, seemingly giving time for his words to sink in. I was noticing that his use of humor, cadence of speech, and pauses were masterfully keeping the crowd engaged, not that we needed any help with that.

"Naveen," Teacher said, looking directly at my friend next to me, whose eyes widened at being called upon. "May I use you for an example?"

Naveen glanced at me with an anxious look, then back at Teacher, and nodded.

"In your practice, what do you feel?"

"Uh," Naveen stammered, "I feel . . . lost in the movement, and the world around me kind of disappears."

Teacher nodded. "And when you finish your practice, what do you feel?"

"Uh, energized and more peaceful."

"So, more energized and more peaceful than before the practice."

"Yes."

"How do you know what feeling energized and peaceful is?"

Naveen looked puzzled, as I was and I'm sure many in the group were.

"Um, it just feels different from before my practice."

"Because you have a comparison to feeling less energized and less peaceful?" Teacher asked.

"Yes," Naveen said more confidently, apparently having found his footing.

"Thank you," Teacher said with a small head bow, and he resumed his slow pacing.

"You see, we say we feel something, but how is that something defined except through a comparison with its opposite? And does that not beg the question of the true definition of what that something is? Certainly, we all see and experience the world differently according to each of our unique perceptions and talents. Naveen is an expert in the movement arts, so he will experience things differently and *feel* things differently than most."

I glanced at Naveen, who looked like he was trying to contain a smile bursting from within. I thought he *should* be proud at being identified as an expert, and I was happy for him.

"So, there must be two sides to something to give it definition and, indeed, meaning, and that meaning is not set in stone; it depends upon the views and experiences of the observer. Why do you think the Grand Wall can only be seen from inside the Territories? It is because the collective perceptions of those who reside within it do not want to see beyond its shadows . . . at least not yet."

I had never been more grateful that I had found a life outside the Territories.

"Look around you. Everything you see, everything you know in your world, is subject to this *two sides* issue of contrasts. We navigate our daily lives this way by evaluating places, objects, people, thoughts, and feelings through differences, whether we are aware of it or not. The thousands of things in our experience *need* the contrasts so we can make sense of our surroundings."

He paced back and forth a few times in silence with his head down. Then he looked up and around the crowd.

"Some of you are thinking that this is like judging others and you don't want to be in a state of continuous judgment. That's an admirable assessment, but it's okay to do this—not judge, for that is a heavier energy—but to recognize differences so that what is around you has meaning and can provide context. There is no shame in existing in the world the way the world has been constructed in the time you are here.

"However, what I am here to tell you—indeed, to *show* you— is that there is so much more than what you see around you in the physical world. Many of you have special abilities or have experienced going beyond the laws of nature. That is one way to reach a mere hint of what I am talking about. Another is to sit in contemplation and find the peace within the center of your being that, in some cases, can help foster such abilities."

Listening to him, I was thinking that's exactly what I had learned, that the more I found my peaceful center, the more I was able to acquire the special abilities I had seen in others and had begun to use myself. But he had said, "in some cases," not "in all cases," which didn't align with those teachings. And if doing the transit or seeing the future like Promeus was just a hint of what he was talking about, then I couldn't wait to experience more.

I glanced at Shasta, who was sitting to my left and a little in front of me, and she seemed rapt with attention, I'm sure hanging on his every word just as I was to take her internal and external practices to another level.

"But even if you have experienced a shadow of what I am talking about, none of you have yet to *fully* and *wholly* accept that other world, which leaves you stuck within this one."

If we were *stuck* in this world, then what would he consider the residents of the Territories to be? I was so liberated compared to my time within the Grand Wall, but if the feeling of freedom I felt in the village was still so limited as to be called *stuck*, I couldn't imagine what being unstuck would feel like, would *be* like. It was a freedom that was inconceivable at that time in my life.

"So, the thousands of things around you each inhabit a duality—or multiple dualities—that you impose on them by your perceptions, which are based upon your experiences and manner of thinking and feeling. This helps you move about the world, and you live your life unintentionally using these contrasts but also living within the greater duality that they represent. This is the *two*, the differentiation that bestows definitions and boundaries."

He stopped and looked into the crowd. I could feel an intensity build up, coming either from him or from the anticipation of what he would say next.

"What if you could go beyond this duality, beyond the *two?* What if you could go beyond the contrasts that characterize your world to a place where only *one* exists? What would you give up for that? What would you be willing to surrender?"

He paused, allowing the questions to sink in.

"The comforts of your house and this village? The wondrous taste of the delicious meals here? What about your partner, your health? Would you give one of those up to understand the *one?* You might give up pain, but would you give up love, joy, happiness? As I asked before, *what would you risk to discover the truth?*"

I sat mesmerized at the questions, not even thinking of how I would answer them but feeling opposing emotions: excitement at the idea of finding out the truth—the *one*—and what it might be like, contrasted with the fear of giving up what I had experienced and worked so hard to accomplish. Could I really relinquish the village, my friends and relationships, my house, and my newfound understanding and abilities for something so abstract and unknown? I didn't know, but I didn't think so.

I believed Teacher, believed *in* him, and knew deep down that he spoke the truth. But I also knew that hearing about the truth and getting to a place to *experience* it were very, very different. Like with many other things I had learned in the village, what at first I had understood mentally—often with difficulty—I then often had trouble bringing down into a tangible experience. That took much time and practice, as evidenced by my years-long study of the slow dance and more recently with my difficulties transiting the Wall. Thinking of feeling—*being*—the *one* he was speaking about seemed an impossible task.

Teacher took his time before speaking again, and I assumed everyone who had heard him was thinking, like me, if they could really give up what they knew in this world based simply on the promise of something more, something that seemed like it couldn't be described but only experienced.

"From the *one*, the *two* cannot exist. That is, contrasts *do* not exist. Everything is perfect and in pure, unadulterated harmony, and when I say pure, I mean flawless—without flaws—as anything less than absolute perfection cannot be of the *one*. And because the *two*—duality, contrasts—do not exist when coming from the perspective of the *one*, the thousands of things in the world around you lose whatever meaning you have ascribed to them because, as I said before, definitions and meaning come as a result of that duality."

He paused again. My head was feeling strange, like I didn't have full control of my logical thinking. It was something I had noticed before when I struggled with new concepts Shasta had taught me. I don't know if it was just me or if everyone went into thinking abstractly when presented with ideas that challenged their normal understandings, but it was happening again now. It felt oddly appropriate given the topic, that we must give up a current understanding in order to find a greater one.

"So, if the things around you have no meaning, what's the point?" He laughed, and the crowd joined in.

"I know that this village, more than most, flows effortlessly with the tasks and needs that present themselves. Well . . . mostly."

A chuckle ran through the group, and I knew I still struggled at times with the flow he was talking about.

"The point is that when you come from the perspective of the *one*, you cannot *not* flow perfectly with your surroundings because you can see that you and everyone and everything around you *are* the *one*. It's not just a perspective; it's fundamentally *who you are*."

Teacher stopped speaking and again closed his eyes with his arms hanging down, palms facing the crowd. Something seemed to shift. I don't know what it was, but whatever abstract thinking space I was in multiplied, and I'm sure others felt it too.

When he opened his eyes a few seconds later, he looked up at the top of the hill, the furthest from him where people were sitting. It took me a minute to realize what he was doing, but it appeared he was gazing directly at each person for a few seconds, then moving on to the person beside them, then continuing to the next. His vision slowly snaked its way across and then down the residents occupying the hill. As it approached my place near the flat area, I felt the energy from earlier increasing in intensity, scrambling any logical thoughts I might have had about what he was doing and why. I felt something—emotions of an unknown quality and origin—begin to come forth.

When his eyes arrived at my row and he looked at Naveen, who was sitting next to me, Naveen expressed an audible sigh, almost like a sigh of relief, but from what, I didn't know.

Then he looked at me.

~

I don't remember much after he held my gaze during that first lecture, and I presumed others were in a similar state, as everyone was fairly quiet and seemingly reflective after the lesson. Not recalling his specific words, what I do remember is as follows:

He repeated that in the beginning there was the *one*, and from the one came the *two*—the duality—and from there came the abundance of what exists in our world. Then he tied it all back to being *one* at the end, a state beyond which the shadows of the world could touch us. We were simply on a path to return to the source that had birthed us, the *one* that continued to animate us, a state of beingness from which we had emerged and into which we would return.

He didn't specifically say it, but I suspected he had somehow communicated or transmitted a small fragment of the experience of being in that state when he looked at each of us in turn. That would explain why everyone seemed so out of sorts afterward, walking around and looking at the world as if they had new eyes that could see beyond the definitions and boundaries he had talked about that related to the *two*. At least that's how I felt as I meandered my way home after the lesson. Just as I had entered another world when I had left the Territories—coming to this village with its incredible people and freedom from the restrictions of my childhood—this felt like I was in yet *another* world beyond even what the village offered and represented. It was a taste of something so much more profound than what I had thus far experienced that I still cannot put it into words.

The next day, Teacher came again to my cabin for a visit, and we talked, alone, his close followers waiting outside. I had noticed he seemed to have a special connection with the beautiful, blonde woman in the small group, who I learned was Ariana, his partner. She and I came to know each other over the ensuing years.

Inside my home, I offered him tea and some fruit, and he accepted just the tea, saying he wasn't hungry. Besides feeling the energy of his oversized presence, I found myself more and more comfortable in his company, like we were two people just having a conversation, even though he was *the* prophesized teacher and I was a willing student. He seemed like a long-lost relative I was getting reacquainted with.

Despite that connection and the visions of it that seemed to span time and different lifetimes, I wondered why I was being singled out for conversation among all others in the village, especially those more knowledgeable or skilled than I was. As if reading my thoughts, he addressed that first.

"Anna, it is wonderful to finally be here with you in this time and place. As I mentioned before, there is something we will be doing together, but even I am not perfectly clear on what that is and when it will come to pass. But there will come a time when I will need you, and I hope you will help me when that time comes."

At that moment, I would do anything for the man.

"Yes, of course," I said without hesitation. After all, we were in the same prophecy, so didn't we *have* to do things for each other? I just wish I knew what it was.

He laughed. "Well, you don't know what it is yet, but I trust all will work out in the end."

I nodded, agreeing with him not because of who he was but because I genuinely believed everything was going to work out. From my experiences with him so far, how could things *not* work out the way they were supposed to and, I should add, the way they were prophesized?

He asked about how I had adjusted to living outside the Grand Wall, and I recounted my first few days after I had run away from home, meeting the people here and getting used to the functioning and habits of the village, as well as my practices with Naveen and lessons from Shasta. He listened carefully, occasionally nodding, taking it all in, although I suspected he already knew most of it.

"Shasta is a fine teacher, and she has been very good for your development. Did you know that she also played a role in my past, just like you? She approached me outside the cathedral in the center of the city one day, and I bought something from her."

I shook my head. I didn't know, but then suddenly, I *did* know. An image of the book cover with the three spirals flashed before me, and I knew that that was what he was talking about. And Shasta's subdued reaction to seeing it in my possession so many years before now made sense.

He smiled and nodded.

I rose and walked to the corner where I had a small wooden box of miscellaneous belongings. Rummaging through them to the bottom, I pulled out the leather book cover I hadn't seen in years, returned to the table, and handed it to him.

He turned it over in his hands, running his fingers across the spirals.

"Yes, this is it."

After gazing at it for a few moments, he handed it back to me.

"You can have it," I said. "I only kept it as a reminder of the story that was within it, your story, but I guess it served its purpose in helping me leave the Territories. And now that you're here, I don't need the reminder."

"No, it is yours now. Besides, you'll need it to put *your* book in." He handed it back to me.

"What? Me? No, I'm not writing a book," I said emphatically, even though I knew there would likely be one in my future. I didn't mention the parables I had written because they were more for my personal growth and understanding than for others' consumption, and I didn't see them becoming a book.

He looked at me, and I could tell he *knew* about the parables despite my efforts to keep them secret, but he just smiled and graciously allowed me my privacy about it.

"There will come a time when you will write it," he said. "You will have clarity about when that will be, and you will also know what to write. Trust in the guidance that is and always will be around you."

I nodded, somewhat reluctantly, but who was I to question his wisdom? How could I not believe him after what I had seen and experienced in his presence?

"And remember, *I* will always be with you as well," he said, his eyes penetrating deeply into me, "when you go within and ask for assistance."

I understood, or at least I thought I did.

"Do you have any questions for me?" he asked.

"Um, yes," I said as a barrage of questions tumbled through my mind, fighting for placement. One loomed larger than the others, perhaps because it had a more physical and practical component compared to some of the abstract ones that were difficult to put into words.

"How did you know I needed help at the Wall the other day, and how did you help me through it?" The fact that he disappeared right in front of me afterward seemed relatively minor in comparison, especially since I knew about Kyna's projection abilities.

He smiled. "Sometimes you don't even have to willfully ask for assistance. Since we have a deep connection, I could feel you were in trouble. You reached out to me even without intending to because of the danger you were in. I also knew that you couldn't be arrested at that time."

"What do you mean?"

"I saw several things happening if you were captured, and it would have gotten in the way of what we need to do together."

I was a little confused but accepted his answer.

"If you weren't there, would I have made it through the Wall?" I asked.

"In the state you were in, it would have been extraordinarily difficult, and I didn't want you to get hurt."

"So, how were you able to help me through it?"

"Because it was a dramatic situation, your energy was mostly in the physical world, and to transit the Wall, your vibration needs to be higher. It was clear you wouldn't have been able to confidently go within as you had practiced, so I connected with you to show you the situation from *my* perspective. But that alone wasn't enough; *you* had to allow yourself to *accept* that experience, and you did. Not everyone can do that."

I nodded slowly.

"This is similar to how healing works at the highest level. I know you've seen some skilled healers here, although there is another village that is more known for it. To heal an ailment or injury, a high-level healer helps bring the person needing treatment out of their *mindset* of illness or injury, which is a belief in the limitation of the physical form. Even though our bodies may be compromised, if we, ourselves, can rise up and see ourselves from the perspective of the *one* I spoke about yesterday, then we can heal whatever it is that ails us. A competent healer sees those they work with *beyond* their bodies, sees them, in a sense, from the *one*, perfect and as they were created from that source. Yet it is fundamentally up to the person desiring healing to *allow* that perspective to take root *more* than their existing perspective of imperfection. Since the physical world is a consequence of what is above it, when we come from the higher context of our source, the *one*, then everything can be perfect and healed on the levels below it."

I was getting it, kind of, but it was a lot to try to make sense of.

"So, like with healing, I helped you with the transit by connecting with you from *my* perspective, and because you accepted that viewpoint, that *experience*—out of necessity, connection, or sheer will—we shared that elevated space, which allowed you to transit the Wall as I would have."

He paused, giving me time to think. Then he continued.

"The more you reduce your doubts about your ability to go within and view the world from that place of peace, harmony, and perfection, the more you will be able to do, the more you will be able to *be*. When you have absolutely *no* doubts about living from the *one*, then anything is possible."

"Anything?" I asked, not really fully believing it.

"*Anything*," he said slowly.

~

I started spending time with Teacher and his followers, and that's when I got to know Ariana.

Apparently, she had known Teacher since before his transformation. They had both lived in the Territories and had had some interactions growing up, but only later did they get together as a couple, just before he went beyond the Grand Wall and had the enlightening experience he was teaching us about. She was thrilled to hear that I was the redheaded girl from the balcony in the city from a story he had told her, someone who had unintentionally helped him on his path.

I had many questions, which she happily answered as best she could.

"What was he like before?" I asked one day.

"Before he found the truth?" she said. "He was like the rest of us, at least like everyone else in the Territories. He had had some struggles, like losing his parents and some difficulties with his farm, but he always managed to smile his way through them. It's tough to remember those times because everything since has been so different."

I nodded. "I'm sure."

She always seemed to have a glow about her. It was a little like Teacher's energy but different, and I could tell they shared a special kind of love.

"He feels very connected to you, you know," she said. "Not everyone gets his attention, but you are often on his mind."

My cheeks may have flushed upon hearing that.

"I'm not trying to . . ." I said but didn't know how to finish. She saved me anyway.

"Oh, I know!" she laughed. "You two *do* have a special connection. That much is apparent, but I know it's not like that."

"And we have this little thing called the prophecy going on as well," I said.

"Yes!" she laughed again. "There's that, too. That'll be what it's going to be. I'm not worried about it. I want to support you both through it however I can."

"Thanks for understanding."

She nodded. "I wasn't always so understanding, but I've grown, as you have and as everyone who comes into contact with him has."

"*That* I believe," I said. "He certainly has a way about him."

"Yes, he does," she said, and I could feel her love for him flowing from her.

"How have *you* changed?" I asked. "What have you learned from him?"

She paused for a few seconds before answering.

"That's tough to answer because it's been many years and many lessons on many levels. I've changed so much that I almost can't remember who I was before. Actually, that's not true. It's more like I'm the same person, only I can now see the world from a much more open, understanding, and forgiving perspective, which has brought innumerable joys to my life. I like to think I was that way before, but I wasn't, as least not nearly to the extent I am now. I owe all that change to him. His way of being inspires that in everyone."

"I've noticed that and I've only just met him," I said.

"Well, you have the past connection with him, too."

"Yes, but it's pretty obvious he has that effect on everyone. His energy is so . . ." I struggled to find a word that fit.

"Loving," she interjected, "not in a romantic love sort of way but in an acceptance of all things in their perfect places in the world."

"Yes, like he's always coming from the *one* he talked about in his lecture."

She nodded, smiled, and gave me a hug.

"I knew I was going to like you," she said.

I hugged her back like the sister I never had.

~

Teacher's second big lecture didn't seem as dramatic as his first, probably because everyone had seen him around the village living like them—eating, drinking, and helping with tasks where he could. I think they began to see him as a regular man instead of, or maybe in addition to, being the master teacher the prophecy foretold.

But even though he appeared to be one of us, he *was* different. We could see that because he usually had several of his close followers nearby who attended to his basic needs, which were few, and simply because his natural presence was so captivating that it was a distraction to ongoing daily activities.

At one point, Teacher asked Naveen to teach him some of the slow dance. Teacher picked up the moves quickly, but his movements paled in comparison to Naveen's smooth and effortless forms. I wondered if that was how awkward I looked the first time I had tried it. Those who witnessed the practice had a good laugh, along with Teacher, who recognized his physical clumsiness next to Naveen's skill. Later, Naveen told me that even though Teacher's movements looked uncoordinated, the power that came through them almost knocked him over. I didn't doubt that.

Through observing situations like this, I had the feeling that Teacher was trying to show us that he was just like us, but also that we could be just like him.

So, when Teacher assembled the residents for another lecture, there seemed to be less a feeling of awe in the crowd than during the first lesson and more a feeling that he was a part of the village, just someone who had happened to have mastered what we wanted to learn.

As before, he stood in the clearing by the boulder, and the rest of us sat on the grassy hillside.

"The other day, I'm glad you all had the experience of the lesson, even though I feel I went a little too far with it, as the concept can sometimes be difficult to take in. You see, even *I* can feel I made a mistake and second-guess my actions."

A chuckle ran through the crowd.

"So, I'm going to go with a basic lesson today, one which you may have already learned about or noticed in your lives."

He looked down and began his slow pacing back and forth before looking up and addressing the assembled.

"I have observed that this village has a wonderful flow to it. You go about your lives taking care of necessary tasks, and most of the time you know what to do and how to do it. Occasionally, though, something doesn't quite go as planned, and you get annoyed or angry, and it throws you off your center. Then what happens?"

He awaited an answer, but none came. He looked at Jamaica.

"Jamaica, may I use you as an example?"

Jamaica gave a slightly uncomfortable nod. I noticed she had a bandage on her hand.

"Yesterday, you didn't get your usual delivery of ingredients in time for the evening meal, right?"

Jamaica nodded.

"How did you feel?"

"I was annoyed," Jamaica said, "because it wasn't the first time a delivery from another village was promised and not delivered."

"Yes, and what did you do?"

"I had to scrounge around and make a meal for everyone with what we had on hand."

"And how did that feel?"

"I was a little bit angry, but we got it done." She glanced at Guri, who was sitting next to her.

"A *little* bit?" Teacher said with a raised eyebrow.

Everyone laughed, including Jamaica.

"Okay, so maybe just a tad more than a little bit," she said.

"How did everyone find the meal last night?" Teacher said, looking around the crowd.

The responses popped out of the group from everywhere: "Delicious," "Wonderful," "As good as ever." He waited for the comments to stop, then looked back at Jamaica.

"And how did you feel later, after mealtime?" Teacher asked.

"I was worried that the meal wasn't up to my usual standards."

"And?"

"And . . . I was still irritated that I didn't have the ingredients I wanted."

"So, you were annoyed, then worried, but the anger lingered."

Jamaica nodded.

"Hearing what people thought of the meal, how do you feel about it now?"

"Better. I'm glad they liked it."

"As you were preparing the meal, what happened?"

She gave him a quizzical look, and he shifted his eyes down to her bandaged hand.

"Oh, I burned my hand on a cooking pot."

"Why do you think you did that?"

"Oh, it happens sometimes. Hazards of the job, I guess."

I was beginning to get an idea of what Teacher was trying to illustrate.

"Do you think burning your hand was related to how you were feeling?"

Jamaica smiled, looked at Guri, who was grinning, and said, "I think I do now!"

Everyone laughed.

"Thinking back, have you ever burned yourself when things were going smoothly, times when you *weren't* irritated?"

Jamaica paused and looked up, then chuckled as she shook her head. "I don't think so."

"Thank you for allowing me to use you as an example," Teacher said, giving her a slight nod before resuming his slow pacing.

"You see, when things are going well, we are in the flow of life around us, naturally listening to and responding to our surroundings. And that flow has a give and take to it in that what we put into it, energetically speaking, is what we get out of it. In other words, what we give—mentally, emotionally, *energetically*—is what we receive.

"This is universal. The vibrations of our thoughts and emotions attract the same level of vibration from our surroundings. This can be difficult to recognize because what we draw to us comes in the form of people, situations, and experiences that may appear *very* different from what our thoughts and emotions express. But make no mistake, there is a direct relationship between what we *have* in our lives and how we *are* in our lives.

"For example, a loving person will have love in their life. They express the sweet, soft, refined energy of love, and that is reflected back to them through their life experience, whether through loving people or situations that express love. On the other hand, an angry person will unintentionally invite situations that foster and reinforce their anger, and then they can justify their anger by pointing to how angry the world is. 'See that terrible experience I was in! I have the right to be angry because I have to deal with that!'

"But it all begins with *us*. *We* initiate the types of vibrations that express out into the world, and then the world reflects *ourselves* energetically back *to* us. This means that *we* have the power to change our world by changing how we perceive it. When we *choose* to see the finer vibrations of love and joy, we *attract* that love and joy into our environment. If we choose other, heavier thoughts and emotions, we will experience *them*.

"For those who think the world is out to get you, think again. The world isn't out to get you, you're out to get yourselves! Take your thoughts, feelings, attitudes, and actions and think about how they are reflected in your experiences."

He looked at Jamaica.

"I know Jamaica is not an angry person, but she had a pocket of irritation that was immediately reflected in her environment through burning her hand. She might say she was distracted by thinking about the missing delivery or rushing because she was frustrated by having to do something different than planned, but whatever the reason, her anger manifested as a burn, which is a typical result of anger."

I saw Jamaica nodding.

"This goes for all of you here, for everyone everywhere. What you experience in your life is a grand lesson in looking in a mirror. If there's something you don't like, look at what your surroundings are showing you through the actions and attitudes of people around you and the circumstances you find yourselves in because *they* are your teachers, *they* can show you *who you are*."

Teacher paused speaking, still pacing back and forth slowly.

"You *are* what you think, feel, and do," he continued, "and you can change *your* world by changing what you think, feel, and do. It's not up to you to change others' worlds, for you don't control them, their perceptions, or what they manifest in *their* lives, but you can make *your* world better and set an example for others to do the same. It starts with each one of you learning from your own environment and changing your behaviors so that you *become* what you truly want to see in the world."

He stopped and surveyed the people on the hillside. I looked around and there were quite a few nods and murmurs of agreement.

"Why do you think those within the Grand Wall live lives full of limitations? There is a certain self-perpetuating energy there that keeps them stuck in old ways of thinking, which can be difficult to emerge from. Often, a dramatic event is needed to inspire and embolden change."

Teacher looked directly at me, and I realized what he said was very true based on my experience. When inside the Territories, I had the dramatic event with my father and the manuscript that enabled me to find the courage to leave the city and come to this wondrous village. I certainly had help from Shasta in doing so, but it was the dramatic event that had triggered the change.

Before he broke his gaze, I suddenly felt a quick twinge of sadness for some reason, and I wondered what it meant.

"Here, outside the Wall, you live with fewer constraints and more freedoms because you, collectively, are a more open society that, for the most part, treats everyone with respect, equality, and kindness. I ask that each of you look at your experiences to see where you can shift how you think and feel so you can attract an even better, more love-filled life."

He smiled playfully and added, "Then imagine if you can think, feel, and do from the *one* I talked about the other day."

The crowd chuckled and nodded, obviously liking the idea. I joined in, because if we could genuinely come from that place of the *one* he had talked about—a place I assume he could be in anytime he wanted—then we would only attract the same thing into our lives, which, I admit, was difficult to conceive of.

Teacher gave a slight bow with his hands together at his chest and slowly walked away. It was clear the lesson was over, at least for now, and he didn't seem to want to take any questions, so we all rose to get back to our daily lives. I, for one, spent the rest of the day thinking about how I could craft my own destiny by changing how I perceived the world, but I also thought that there might be limits to it, because I still had the prophecy to contend with.

~

After our evening meal, Teacher personally invited me to come with him and his close followers to where they were staying outside the village. I enthusiastically agreed, wondering what they did when they weren't out and about in the community. Jillian was excited for me, and I wished she, Naveen, and Shasta had been invited too, but that wasn't the case.

I followed Teacher and his group down a path dappled with the forest's lengthening shadows. After about twenty minutes, we arrived at a campsite with a few lean-tos and tents arranged in a circle around a fire pit. It looked like the group occasionally cooked their own meals, as there were several pots and pans stacked next to the stones that ringed the fire, which was already blazing. Several stumps and logs surrounded the flames.

I sat on one of the logs across from a man and a woman who were already there who seemed to be the caretakers of the fire, and maybe of the campsite, too. They smiled at me and nodded, and I returned the gestures. Eventually, everyone gathered around the blaze in the waning light, most staring silently into the flames. Ariana sat next to me.

Teacher had taken a seat on a prominent stump and was doing the same, but his demeanor was—*felt*—more serene and peaceful than the others. I felt honored to be in his presence once again and thrilled to be part of this presumably special group. After a few minutes, he looked over at me.

"Everyone, this is Anna," he said and motioned to me with his arm. "She's the one you've heard about in the prophecy."

Every face turned to me with eager smiles.

"Anna, you can meet them all individually later. For now, does anyone have any questions for her?"

My face must have registered surprise, because he quickly followed up by saying, "Oh, I apologize for putting you on the spot! I just know that some people here have had questions for you and haven't had the chance to ask them. If you don't want to speak now, you don't have to."

"That's okay," I said. "I don't mind." I didn't know what I could tell them, but I wanted to be a part of the group and answer what I could.

Teacher nodded, which seemed to give a blessing for others to speak. The first question came from a stout, curly-haired man on my right.

"Are you really from inside the Grand Wall? You seem so . . . not like someone from there."

Before I could answer, Ariana said, "Remember, Teacher and I are both from inside the Wall as well."

"Right," the man said. "I guess I'm finding it difficult to understand how or why the prophecy is about *two* people from the Territories when those of us who grew up outside the Wall were raised with beliefs closer to what Teacher is showing us. So, wouldn't we naturally have a better . . . base of understanding?"

"If we went with *your* understanding, we'd be here for a long time," someone said.

The questioner gave a scowl while most in the group laughed. Teacher smiled, then spoke.

"Pekka, that's not how it works."

"Why *not* one of us?" Pekka asked. "Some of us have been with you for years, and we want to help you do whatever it is you need to do."

"You are fulfilling your part," Teacher said. "Believe it, *know* it, whatever it looks like. It may not be exciting or dramatic, but it is important nonetheless. Not only is it important to me, but it will also be important to others."

"But you only just met her. How do you know she's up to the task?" the man asked.

Since Teacher's arrival, I had had similar thoughts, so I was glad the man stated it so bluntly. But I was not prepared for Teacher's answer.

"I don't," Teacher said, triggering nervous looks around the circle, "but she is the only one who can do what needs to be done. As for having just met her, that's not true. I've known her for longer than almost everyone here and, in another sense, for far longer than even that, and I trust her. I trust *in* her. You would do well to do the same."

At one point, before Teacher's arrival in the village, I had begun to get used to the pressure of the expectations around my role in the prophecy, but now that he was here and whatever I was to do seemed imminent, that pressure returned in full force. His stated trust in me, however, lessened its weight. It also seemed to soothe some of the man's agitation.

The man looked at me like he was evaluating my reliability. I could tell he was a bit jealous and resistant to accepting Teacher's recommendation to trust me. I did my best to stay neutral in my expression. I still hadn't yet answered any of the questions, and it seemed I didn't have to because Teacher continued.

"It is *because* Anna is from both worlds that she has been chosen. She, like me and Ariana, knows what it's like here *and* within the Wall, and that is rare. What she has within her cannot be known simply by visiting the Territories. It comes from growing up there, living there, and being infused with the beliefs and happenings of daily life there, which has given her a deeper understanding of the limitations we're trying to tear down and move beyond. She also has other distinctive characteristics that make her uniquely qualified to do what she will need to do. *I* did not choose her. She was destined for this."

Many in the group nodded, accepting Teacher's explanation. The questioner sat stone-faced but eventually gave a slight nod of understanding. I, on the other hand, didn't move a muscle because I could feel everyone's eyes on me and didn't want to indicate my thoughts. Agreeing with Teacher might make me seem arrogant and disagreeing with him might make me seem doubtful, and I didn't want to communicate either in front of the group. And if there was anything I had learned so far in my years in the village, it was that my past doubts were almost always unwarranted.

"Teacher?" a young woman to my left called out softly.

Teacher looked at her and nodded.

"You said today in the village that Jamaica manifested her burn because of her anger. How can we stop manifesting what we *don't* want and start manifesting what we *do* want?"

Teacher took a deep breath before addressing everyone.

"Be aware of the world you find yourselves in, for it reflects your thoughts, emotions, and actions. Your perceptions define your experience, not the other way around. If you don't want something in your life, look at what you might be thinking, feeling, and doing that carries a similar energy to what you don't want and reflect on that. What has a difficult situation come to teach you? It has come into your experience as a lesson, so what can you learn from it? Learn to see that *you* have invited that lesson through the energy you express, and that energy is being reflected back to you. So, to stop manifesting what you don't want, learn from experiences you find uncomfortable or distressing, for they show you aspects of yourselves you may not be aware of. Once aware, you can use that knowledge to *choose* to live differently, which will change what the world mirrors back to you in your experience.

"On the other hand, to manifest what you *do* want, you first must have a framework of knowledge around the desired manifestation because the energy of creation needs some level of understanding within you upon which to be crafted. For example, a cook will not be able to create a perfect kitchen knife from scratch with a forge without some training and understanding of a blacksmith's skills.

"Second, you must have a strong intent, and the stronger and purer the intent, the better the manifesting ability. Know the end result you desire but let go of the outcome. This can be quite difficult, as we all too easily get something in our minds and then hold fast to that particular vision, which can inhibit its creation or the creation of something even better. For example, if you desire a partner, intend on finding a partner with the *qualities* you want instead of a particular person you might fancy or someone with physical traits you find attractive. You would be surprised at what presents itself."

I smiled, because I had seen the woman who had asked the question looking at Naveen in an affectionate manner, so Teacher's example I'm sure was no accident.

"Third, be *excited* about it, *know* it is coming, for your passion for the intended result will power the intent you set. Actually, and more accurately, *feel* the energy of *already having manifested it* and what joys it brings to your life. Your enthusiasm will help spark its creation because you will be expressing the energy you desire and your environment can't help but reflect that.

"And fourth, if possible, don't tell anyone else about what you are trying to manifest. There are two reasons for this: one, because others may dilute your intent or enthusiasm with their reactions, putting doubts or other ideas in your head about it, and two, because sharing what you intend on manifesting can make you feel like you've already accomplished at least a small part of the creation, which also dilutes the intent. This may not make a lot of sense, but it can happen."

"Thank you," the woman said.

It was interesting that this brief lesson on manifesting was quite similar to what Teacher had spoken about in the clearing earlier. Both talks dealt with affecting our surroundings and experiences by choosing how we exist in the world with our thoughts, feelings, and actions. This lesson, however, gave us practical steps to actively direct our energies to not just change ourselves but to *create* something we desired in the world.

I began to imagine the possibilities.

~

Teacher stayed with us for a few months, continuing his lectures to the whole village while also having more intimate discussions in the evenings around the campfire. I was privileged to be extended a standing invitation to join the evening discussions, and I went as much as I could, but I remained mostly silent as I could still feel some jealousy from a few of his followers, even though most had warmed up to me and accepted me into the selected group.

He also continued to come to my home occasionally, sometimes when Shasta, Jillian, and Naveen happened to be there. We talked, joked, and had fun discussing anything and everything, including getting clarifications on some of the lessons he had taught. During these times, I felt like I had truly found the close-knit, loving family I hadn't experienced in my youth.

Teacher seemed more relaxed, too, during these encounters. Once, during one of our discussions with Jillian and Naveen present, I asked him about it.

"Why does it seem that you relax more with us here compared to when with others?"

Teacher looked at me, and I could swear he was hugging me with his eyes.

"For one, it is because I feel close to you, to all of you. Another is that you three can take in the lessons without needing to put me on a pedestal. For many others, including many of my close followers, they cannot do that. They need me to be the teacher, the master, the one *above* them as someone they can aspire to be. If they see me as just like them, they would minimize what I teach because of the doubts about themselves they continue to entertain. You, however, as well as some others, can separate me, the man going about his day in the village, from the teachings. I *am* just like you, and them, and I am something more as well. Some cannot understand that I, and they, can be both, so they need to perceive me *only* as a teacher to look up to because being an ordinary man takes away from that perception. Since that is what they need to see, I give that to them while trying to show them there's more to it.

Jillian, Naveen, and I all nodded. I understood that it has nothing to do with *who* brings a lesson, only that the teaching is true.

"As I have explained," he continued, "the world provides the mirror for the lessons you each need to learn. You don't need a figurehead or leader outside yourselves to guide you, for the answers you seek are in your own contemplation of your perceptions of the world. Unfortunately, most people don't take on the task of looking deeply within because they often don't like what they find. When you have the desire and the will to get to the truth, you *can* manifest it for yourselves, but it may be uncomfortable because it can bring up personal characteristics you may not want to look at. But that's the beauty of it. What may be difficult or painful to view and reflect on is exactly what constitutes the obstacles to a greater understanding. When you address those obstructions with a desire and will to change them, that's when the magic happens, and you find yourselves living a more peaceful, loving, and joyful life, free from the previous burdens of which you were largely unaware."

I wish everyone could have heard this because it tied together his talk in the clearing and his lesson around the campfire about manifesting. If this was true, and I had every reason to believe it to be, then the way to understanding truth, the way to perceiving the world as Teacher did, was to reflect on what we find uncomfortable in our surroundings, because that is what will show us what we find uncomfortable in ourselves. Then, through desire and will, we can manifest the change in ourselves, which results in a change in our environment. It all comes from within us! *We* are the makers of our own environment, our own life, our own fate.

"So, are *we* the *sole* creators of our experiences?" I asked, not quite believing it could be so straightforward and absolute. Perhaps I hadn't taken in his previous lessons as deeply as I thought, or I had some lingering doubts because the prophecy seemed to come from outside of me.

Teacher looked at me with a broad smile, and I could tell that he knew I was really beginning to understand.

"Yes, but it's one thing to understand and yet another to apply that understanding. The way we operate in the world, it's not necessarily easy. If it was, we'd all be able to do this effortlessly."

I nodded and looked at Naveen and Jillian. Both were also nodding, but I wasn't sure they had absorbed what he had said to the level I had. Maybe mentally they did, but I could feel something else bubbling up inside me, the *feeling* of understanding that went beyond my mind, a knowingness that I was taking another step on my path to the truth.

~

When Teacher left after a few months to go back to the surrounding villages, I had hoped he was going to ask me to accompany him and his close followers, but instead he asked me to stay and continue to practice what I had been taught—from him, Shasta, and others. He said he would return soon enough and that I really wouldn't miss anything that he hadn't previously covered in his lectures and discussions here. The other villages, he said, needed more of the basics, and I already had a good understanding of them.

That left me feeling more confident in my abilities but sad that he was leaving. I had been thoroughly enjoying his presence, whether he was speaking to the whole village, leading discussions around the campfire, or relaxing and being himself in my home.

Once Teacher left, life in the village continued as before, with some notable exceptions. Kyna seemed to spend more time in the back of the contemplation hall where I assumed she was projecting herself to his lectures, and Shasta wasn't around because she had been invited to go with him to the other villages. This surprised and annoyed me because he and I were so close, and I had several bouts of jealously that challenged my practices on many days, giving me ample opportunity to practice what he had taught.

Later, I wondered if it was intentional on his part, to do something that he knew would test me to go deeper into his lessons. Indeed, I did start reflecting more on my jealousy as I asked myself why I felt so triggered by his choosing Shasta over me. I eventually began to laugh at the thought, in part because I felt I might have caught him in his ruse and discovered his secret intention, and I wasn't going to let him put one over on me. With that, just as he had taught, my reflections on what my world had presented *did* reduce the jealousy I had initially experienced, and I gained much inner clarity from the process.

He eventually returned, as promised, and the lessons and discussions continued as before. I learned he had been rotating through all the surrounding villages, teaching whatever he saw as needing to be taught based on the level of understanding of his audience. He spent a few months in each place, then proceeded to the next, ultimately finding his way back here.

I also learned that he had asked Shasta to accompany him not because he thought she was better at understanding his teachings or that he liked her more than me but rather because of her teaching skills, which I could attest to. Apparently, she had led many groups in the other villages through practices that clarified Teacher's lessons, and she also integrated some of what she had taught me. Hearing that, I realized how self-sabotaging my jealousy had been, and for no reason, too, as I definitely could not teach as well as she could. Once again, Teacher had provided a valuable lesson, even from afar.

~

He did the village circuit several times over the next two years, usually spending about two months in each place, although sometimes more, sometimes less. There was always a buzz around the community a few days before he returned, as most residents, me included, anticipated being graced by his grand presence and teachings again.

A few days after his last arrival back in my village, he came to my home. I welcomed him in, as always, and we sat at the table with tea I had made. He had a different look about him, one that I couldn't quite read.

"This will be my last time in this village," he said. "I do not plan on returning."

My heart dropped.

"No! What about the prophecy? Don't we need to do something together?" I implored, hoping he would correct his statement.

He smiled. "Oh, Anna, have you learned nothing from your time here? What was the very first teaching you received from Shasta?"

I thought for a moment, and it came right back to me. It was her lesson about appearances right after we had transited the Grand Wall the first time, the day after I had run away from home.

"It was about appearances, that I could understand more of what was happening around me if I took a moment to *feel*."

"That's right. Can you do that now? Tell me what you feel."

I closed my eyes, and a mix of things rapidly flew into my vision. I saw myself going with Teacher to his next destination, which felt new and exciting, and there was a big crowd listening to him that looked different than the one I knew in the village. I thought I was making things up because I saw a flash of my father's red hair in the crowd, which didn't make sense, because if Teacher was speaking, it wasn't the kind of thing my father would listen to. There was also a feeling under the surface that felt sad, but also happy. The contrast almost made me nauseous.

"Am I going with you this time?" I asked.

He nodded, and I jumped up and gave him a big hug, then sat down again.

"Good. What else?" he said.

"It looked like you were speaking to a big crowd, not like in the villages, and I thought I saw my father there, which doesn't make sense."

"And what did you feel?"

"Both happy and sad," I said. "Why is that? Is something bad going to happen?"

"I just need you to remember the teachings. You will need them when the time comes."

"So, the prophecy that foretold us doing something together is finally happening? Do you know any details?"

"Not that I can share at this time."

I had tried many times to get information related to my role out of him, but he was always aware of my intentions and wouldn't answer. Over time, I began to accept that I would learn about it at the appropriate time.

I paused for a moment. "Are we going to the Territories??" It wasn't something I had ever thought would happen, Teacher travelling to the other side of the Wall to speak, because it would be dangerous for him given what he lectured about. The authorities would consider it blasphemy.

He nodded again, and my worry began to increase.

"You said that this is your last time in the village. Are you not coming back?"

He shook his head. "Not likely."

"What's going to happen?"

"I don't yet know exactly."

"But I'll be with you?" I asked.

He nodded. "And I'll *always* be with you," he said.

~

He had asked me to not tell anyone of his plans, although I presumed some people like Kyna, Promeus, and some of his followers knew—certainly Ariana—whether from being told or from other means. And just as he had said, a few months later he assembled the community together for an announcement.

"This is to be our last gathering in your village. The time has come for me to go within the Grand Wall to teach. You have all done well and learned much, and there is still much to learn, but it is time for you to do that without me."

Gasps and murmurs of surprise spread through the crowd, and some started weeping. Even though I knew this was coming, I, too, was moved with emotion. A chapter of my life was ending, and I only had a general idea of what was to come, and certain aspects of it frightened me.

I hadn't been to the Territories since going to the antique shop with Shasta years ago. The traumatic incident with the constables on the way back—and my second assisted transit of the Wall—was seared into my memory, so I worried about what we might encounter. I was sure that Teacher, and what he represented, would be seen as a threat by the Territory Governors. If Shasta and I were almost arrested for Shasta simply having a tattoo that they believed violated the tenets of the Church, then what would happen when Teacher started speaking about energies, manifesting, healing, and reclaiming individual power—things the Governors I'm sure were afraid of? And since I would be with him, would *I* be in danger because of our association?

And then there was the pesky prophecy to contend with. I still knew nothing about what my role might be, only that it was related to Teacher. I began to wonder if he knew much more about what was going to happen then he let on but just hadn't yet decided on the details or decided to tell me.

On the other hand, I was going with Teacher! It was something I had wanted for a long time—to travel with him, be with him, learn more from him. It was a new adventure, which I hadn't had much of since my arrival in the village, except for the adventures in my learning and training and in the landscape of my mind. This would be different, exciting, and potentially hazardous. With what we were taught about learning about ourselves from what we found uncomfortable in our world, this would certainly provide me plenty of opportunities for reflection and, I hoped, for further personal growth and understanding so I could come closer to how Teacher perceived the world.

"There is nothing to be upset about," Teacher continued. "I have loved my time here in your wonderful village, and I have loved you. You are all doing exactly what you need to be doing, and you have prepared well for what is to come. I cannot speak further about that, but you will know soon enough. I only ask that you do not fear change, for change is the one constant in the world you know. Everything is in a state of transience, and once you embrace that, life becomes easier, more flowing, more joyful, and you become more present to what is before you."

I could feel some resistance in the crowd, and I didn't know if it was from people not liking that Teacher was leaving or from an opposition to accepting change. Really, they were the same in this case. I could understand the feeling, as it arose in me, too, because Teacher made it sound as if a *big* change was coming, and that just added to the adventure that lay before me.

"You grow when you learn to adapt to the changes that are *always* around you. You have the tools to view your experiences differently now and to grow in a positive manner from them. Remember those lessons, for they will carry you through shifting sands to a place where you will welcome change with open arms, for every time you allow yourselves to partner with change and flow *with* it, it will become a transformational event, and you will thank the heavens for the experience.

"When you perceive change as a constant in your life, you *become* the flow, like a stream adapting to flow around a rock. The rock exists whether you want it to or not, but *you* can choose to beat your head against it or to flow around it."

He paused and gave a wry smile.

"I think at this point I don't have to tell you that beating your head against a rock is probably *not* the best choice."

The crowd laughed, and I again noticed his placement of humor to shift some of the distressing energy his previous words elicited.

"You have all extended such kindness, gratitude, and love toward me, and I will carry that with me to the end of my days. Indeed, it reflects who you are, individually and collectively. It has been an honor and a privilege to get to know you and be your teacher. I know you will continue with your practices and show the world what you have learned, and you will continue to grow into what you all truly can *be*. I thank you who you *are* and for continuing to represent the absolute best of humanity."

He brought his hands up in a prayer position in front of his chest and gave a bow, and I felt a wave of love wash over the crowd.

Several people wept audibly, and someone shouted out, "How will you teach those inside the Wall? They're not open to these things. In fact, they persecute those of us who have tried to show them our ways."

He looked at the man. "I will teach them as I taught you, although the lessons will be different, more rudimentary, for they don't have the understanding you had here when I arrived. For many, their natural inclination will be to resist what I teach, so I may need to show them the truth in other ways. As for persecution, I trust we will be safe for as long as necessary."

Something about how he said that left me feeling as if he knew what was going to happen, and a flash of worry rippled through my body. I think others felt it, too, or perhaps some were projecting forward and perceiving what was to come. I glanced at Promeus, and he sat stone-faced, showing no emotion. For someone who I thought I could usually read well, as his face was generally emotive, it only reinforced my unease.

Teacher took no further questions from the group but sat down on the edge of the boulder, signifying the end of the lecture. This indicated that people could come up to ask individual questions, which he had allowed on occasion. I never joined in that because I had a different and more personal relationship with him that provided generous time for such activities, so I just sat on the hill and watched, saddened that this would be the last time most would be in his presence.

~

We set out two days later with Teacher and Ariana leading the way, followed by those who usually traveled with him and, thankfully, Shasta. I was thrilled she was coming, not just because she was my friend and mentor, but because she also had at least some familiarity with the Territories—indeed, that is where we had first met—and I might be able to see how she taught groups like in the other villages.

But I was sad that Jillian and Naveen weren't invited. Besides Shasta, they were my closest friends, and my relationship with Jillian had only blossomed further with Teacher's arrival a few years before. When I asked him if they could come, Teacher told me that they were needed in the village because they had different roles to play but that I would see them both again. I was upset for a short time before recognizing that it was yet another example of the lesson of change for me, so after first grudgingly accepting his decision, I then came to smile at the adventure before me.

Before we left, Teacher spoke to our selected group about how to avoid the constable presence that I had heard was now even more sizable than when I had visited before. Apparently, Kyna had traveled for another visit to the antique shop to see Quinn to get an update, and she relayed to Teacher that the

Territory Governors had instituted stricter enforcement of protocols that had left most within the Grand Wall worried about the near future and what might be happening to warrant such a visible use of force. I almost chuckled to myself thinking that they have no idea what's coming, and who.

But hearing that also left me worried, for Teacher, Shasta, and the rest of our group. How were we to avoid the constables? With my last, traumatic experience with them, not to mention knowing that my father was a constable, I didn't know what we were going to do. Thankfully, Teacher shared some thoughts about it.

"I will need all of you to remember your lessons and trust your abilities, for they will help keep us safe while we are inside the Wall. I will help, too, but your feedback will be just as important as mine."

Although I wanted to believe that, I had my doubts.

"I want you to *be* in your internal, contemplative space as much as possible, elevating yourselves and those around you so that when there is something or someone soon to be around us that is *not* resonant to that higher vibration, you will know . . . *we* will know. If any of you see, hear, or feel anything that could compromise us, tell me, even if I'm teaching or in contemplation. This is important at the beginning, because we need the people to spread the word of the teachings without the influence of the government. That will shift later, but that is what is needed now."

I wondered what would happen when it shifted, as I knew the constables were not to be trifled with.

"We already have many friends there, including some who may surprise you, and they will help make straight the way for us. So, let us walk proudly into the Territories *knowing* that what we are here to do is necessary for the ability of the masses to move forward into their future with a fresh start and without the limitations of the bygone age they unwittingly cling to. It is time for *everyone* to reclaim *who they truly are.*"

He paused, then asked, "Is there anyone here who does not want to follow me?"

I looked around and no one even so much as flinched.

"Very well. Let us go forward and change the world."

And with that, we set off down the path toward the big red oak tree, the Grand Wall, and a new and exciting adventure.

Anna

Anna spent the next morning continuing to record her life and experiences with Teacher on the growing stack of handwritten papers on her desk. Shasta stopped by at one point to check in on her but didn't stay long, clearly noticing that Anna wanted to get back to writing. Before Shasta left, though, she complimented Anna on her new tattoo, even though it was still bandaged. By midafternoon, Anna was mentally and physically exhausted, drained from having spent most of the day in deep focus, so, being at a good stopping point, she put down her quill and flopped onto the bed to rest her weary body and mind.

She didn't know how long she slept, but she was awakened by a soft knock on the door. It was Jillian and Naveen, and they, like Shasta, were checking in to see if she needed anything. Anna shook her head, but when Naveen asked if she wanted to practice the slow dance out in the woods, she realized it would be a good idea to revitalize her body after having been seated and relatively still for most of the day.

Jillian joined, and a few minutes later the three of them were moving together as one under the pines behind Anna's cabin, out of sight of the other residents. Naveen led them, as always, and Anna noticed that he had slowed down the forms so that the complete set took much longer than usual. When they had finished and had brought their hands up and then down in front of their bodies, Anna asked about it.

"Naveen, why so much slower this time?"

"I'm not sure," Naveen said. "That speed just felt right. I felt it as soon as we started, to slow it down. I think I was guided to for your benefit. How did you like it?"

"It was amazing," Anna said. "I'm still buzzing. I think I needed it just that way today."

It wasn't just the slower pace that had enhanced the forms for her. She had imagined her new tattoo before starting—it was still bandaged—and a few times during the practice, and it had helped bring her further into an energetic space that was beyond the physicality of her body.

Jillian smiled. "No complaints here. I really liked the slower pace as well. It helped me drop more deeply into it."

"I might have to do that more often," Naveen said. "I think it may have opened me up to another aspect of the practice."

Changing topics, Anna asked, "How's the mood in the village?" She was thinking not just about Teacher's fate but also about how she was being perceived.

"About the same," Jillian said. "I think people are still angry with what's happened, and they're having difficulty accepting other points of view, despite our efforts."

"You two don't have to defend me," Anna said.

"I know," Jillian said. "I'm just telling them that there's always another side to the story, but you know, people can be stubborn in their thinking sometimes."

"Sometimes?" Naveen said, and all three chuckled.

"Thanks," Anna said. "With how I'm feeling now, I think I'll have dinner in the hall tonight. I'm going to have to face everyone at some point anyway."

Jillian and Naveen looked at each other, then at Anna, and nodded.

"We can go together," Naveen said. "It'll be fun."

Anna smiled. "Fun might not be the word I'd use, but I appreciate the thought."

Naveen gave a slight bow. "I try."

"It'll be fine," Jillian said. "Like you said, you'll have to do it at some point. Might as well do it now while we're all together and feeling good from the practice."

Anna and Naveen nodded, and the three went back to Anna's cabin to wait for the dinner bell.

The Territories

Three weeks later, we were in a small clearing in a mostly wooded area southwest of the city. We had come into the Territories from the northeast and had traveled clockwise in a wide circle around the capital, stopping every day so Teacher could present his lessons.

At first, the groups were small, with at most a dozen people gathering in the homes of those who either knew he was coming or had already heard him speak. But within a week, the audiences had grown and we were left with having to hold his talks outside to accommodate the sizeable groups.

We had so far successfully avoided the constables due to our vigilance in noticing when the energies in the ethers shifted from Teacher's wonderful presence to something that was strikingly less loving and peaceful. To me, the feeling was nauseating, so it stuck out prominently compared to what I usually felt.

Early on, we had a close call when Teacher was giving a lesson that I had already heard a few times before, so I was acting as a lookout of sorts outside the home where he spoke. Once before, I had noticed a slow buildup of the stomach-turning feeling of an incoming threat, but this time, it came out of nowhere, and I felt a stab in my gut that almost doubled me over. I immediately knew what it was and knew I had to act quickly. I ran inside and looked at Teacher, who simply nodded and said to his listeners, "I'm sorry, but I must go now," and we proceeded out the door to a predesignated meeting place. Sure enough, a few minutes later, from my vantage point in the nearby woods, I saw a half dozen constables rush down the road and into the house we had just left. They subsequently didn't come after us, so the home's residents had clearly successfully fabricated a convincing enough story for the authorities.

I was fearful that Teacher would be upset with me because I had almost taken too long to recognize the incoming danger, but he just smiled and praised me for my watchfulness. However, some part of me knew that *he* knew that I would be harder on myself than he ever could be. Indeed, I thought about it for days, and from then on, I was much more in tune with my surroundings.

Now, in this small clearing in the woods, there were at least four or five dozen people attending, so word had clearly gotten around about his teachings. The group was a mix of men and women and appeared to span all ages, social classes, and occupations. To me, the crowd *felt* like the previous, smaller crowds but with one notable exception: a man dressed in fine clothes standing at the back of the assembly leaning against a tree. He didn't quite seem like the others, didn't *feel* like the others, so it raised my suspicions, but his presence didn't make me queasy like previous encounters with those from the government. As he was looking about the crowd more as an observer than as a participant, I felt I had to at least inform Teacher.

"Excuse me, Teacher?" I said, approaching Teacher who was sitting on a large rock with his eyes closed as people continued to find places before him to sit.

He opened his eyes and nodded, and I relayed my concerns. He glanced over at the man as I spoke and when I finished, he said, "Thank you, but he's okay. He's just appraising us."

I looked back at the man, who was staring in our direction.

Then Teacher added, "Anna, please go tell him that I'd like to speak with him after my talk."

Even though I shouldn't have been surprised—I had seen so much already that nothing should have surprised me—my face must have registered worry because Teacher said, "It's okay. I need to speak with him."

I nodded my acceptance and quietly walked around to the back of the assembling crowd where the man was. Approaching him, I noticed he sported a thin scar on his right cheek.

"Excuse me, Teacher has asked to have a word with you after his lecture."

The man's dark eyes bored into mine, and I felt a confusing mix of interest in Teacher yet also wariness of him, as well as a sense of responsibility and other feelings that swirled around in such a way that I had trouble distinguishing any one feeling from another. Overall, it gave me the sense that the man was, as Teacher had said, there to observe and was reserving judgment, at least for the time being.

The man looked over at Teacher, who was again sitting with his eyes closed, then back at me, and nodded. I walked briskly back to Teacher and told him that the man had agreed to speak with him after the lesson.

Teacher opened his eyes and smiled at me with a look that told me there was something more to this than what I could yet understand.

As most people had found their seats, Teacher stood up, indicating he was ready to begin. I stepped back and sat where I normally sat during his talks, in front and to Teacher's left, still thinking about who the man was and why Teacher wanted to speak with him.

~

Before I had noticed the man with the scar, I had mingled with and greeted the people arriving to listen to the lecture. There were several reasons for this: one, to show them how friendly and non-threatening we in his group were; two, to do a quick evaluation of their energy and motives for being there; and three, to listen to what they were saying about Teacher and his previous talks, if they had heard them. I found that many had come to listen to him again.

One woman said that her friend had heard one of Teacher's lessons and was so moved by his presence that she could barely remember what he had talked about, which was reason enough to come to see and hear him. Another said that she was excited because she had already heard him once and wanted to again because his first lesson had helped her view her life differently and it was positively transformative. A few people, in hushed tones, wondered if Teacher was one of the Ancients who had come back to show the world the old, pagan beliefs that included otherworldly magic, like the magic that had created the Grand Wall. That seemed to fit, one said, because they had heard that when Teacher had been asked where he had come from, he had responded that he was a traveler from an antique land. I hadn't heard that before from him or about him, but the phrasing felt oddly fitting. And when they mentioned that maybe he had come to break down the Wall, I found myself surprised that I hadn't yet thought of that possibility.

A man, speaking with a friend, said that he was skeptical that *anyone* could be like how Teacher had been described to him, a man with the intelligence, charisma, and power to take on the Governors. This wasn't the first I had heard of that idea, that Teacher was there to challenge and dismantle the government.

With what I knew of him and what he taught, that was never something he endorsed. He simply promoted personal responsibility for bettering our own lives by living with more awareness, love, and compassion. There was never anything political in his teachings. It was clear, however, that many saw what he taught—indeed, what he represented—as direct defiance to the government's laws and the Church's edicts, which made him dangerous to the government but perhaps alluring to the people. It was no wonder we had to be aware of the constables.

"Thank you all for coming," Teacher began. "I know it's not easy with the scrutiny we are under, especially as the group grows in size, but I trust everything will unfold as necessary.

"Some of you have heard me before, and I welcome you back, and to those who are seeing me for the first time, I bid you welcome as well. I trust all your journeys here have gone without incident.

"Today I want to talk about the two voices you hear that are the cause of virtually all your fears and stresses. Actually, just one voice is the source of these distressing thoughts and emotions, but you experience them because of the conflict *between* the two voices: one that seeks drama in your lives, and one that *is* the opposite.

"Now, you may say, 'I don't seek drama in my life. I do my best to avoid it!' Ah, you *think* you do, but there is much operating under the surface of your awareness that holds a power over you that you don't realize. And this is not the type of power you want in your life, for it works to create division, difficulties, and disharmony, which I trust you do *not* want to create for yourselves."

Most in the group nodded and murmured in agreement.

"This one voice does not have your best interests at heart. Quite the contrary, it will ceaselessly work to seize your attention and create circumstances to throw you off balance so that you do not find the peace, joy, and love that you deserve.

"But there is another voice, quite the opposite, that will eternally work to *help* you find that peace, joy, and love. It is not as excitable as the first voice and does not seek your attention, so you do not notice it as much, but it is *infinitely* more powerful. It speaks softly compared to the other voice, which will be shouting in your ears, and you must listen carefully to be able to hear it. Which do you think you would like to influence your life more, the loud, forceful, brash voice that brings you fear, pain, and unease, or the soft, barely-perceptible voice that guides you toward what is best for you?"

The crowd mumbled and indicated the second one, the soft voice.

"Of course. You all want more peace, joy, and love in your lives."

Teacher paused his pacing and gave one of his wry smiles. "Or do you?"

Several people chuckled.

"Think about it. Do you always seek peace, seek joy, seek love, or do you sometimes do things that lead to their opposites? For example, when was the last time you chose to intentionally *lose* an argument so you can have more peace, joy, and love?"

He waited, but no one spoke.

"Anybody? No? Let me rephrase. Would you intentionally lose an argument for more peace, joy, or love?"

A smattering of hands went up.

Someone shouted, "Why would you intentionally lose an argument if you're the one who's right?"

Teacher looked into the crowd and immediately found the man who spoke.

"Thank you for your question. May I ask . . . how do you know, truly know, that you are right and they are wrong?"

"Usually, it's pretty clear when someone's trying to screw you over," the man said.

"Ah," Teacher said, "you've been taken advantage of."

The man nodded.

"Do you know why the other person did what they did?"

The man shrugged his shoulders. "I assume because they're greedy and not very nice."

Teacher paused and closed his eyes for a moment, then opened them. "I know of the situation you are referring to, but I will not address the worldly details of the interaction. I don't want you or others distracted by the particulars of what occurred because they are not important. It is the *lesson* that a situation brings that is important."

The man looked confused for a second before Teacher began speaking again.

"It is understandable to only see your own perspective, but everyone has reasons for their actions, whether they are aware of them or not. And, depending on the character of the person, the actions can be nefarious or noble."

"Um, okay," the man said.

"Sometimes, it's helpful to put yourself in the other person's shoes to try to understand *why* they did what they did, for they may have something in their past that continues to lead them toward certain behaviors. That should not be an excuse, however, but rather one small part of an explanation. And it's possible you won't come to an understanding even if you attempt to. The key, for both parties, is to try to understand what the situation showed you about *yourself*. What did you learn from the experience?"

"I learned not to trust the person."

"What did you learn about *yourself*?"

The man stared at Teacher but didn't seem to have an answer, so Teacher continued.

"Have you been in similar situations before that resulted in the same distrustful feeling?"

The man nodded.

"So, with multiple experiences like this, it is understandable that you feel that way. Do you think this happens to you more than to other people?"

The man laughed. "Yes, I think so!" which drew a few chuckles from the crowd.

"Why do you think that is?"

The man seemed lost in thought for a moment, eventually saying, "I don't know."

Teacher returned his attention to the full group.

"This is what I mean when I ask what you learned from a particular situation, because even though any given interaction may seem different from previous ones, the lesson contained within all of them can be the same. What is external to you comes from what is internal, and what is internal can only be known through reflection. There is *always* a reason why you walk through the experiences you do, and you can discover that by considering the lesson each experience brings, especially if, collectively, they elicit similar emotional reactions from you."

The man nodded slowly, but I didn't feel he was fully understanding what Teacher was saying. Apparently, Teacher also probably noticed this because he switched back to his main topic.

"What I just said is important, but I digress from what I wanted to speak to you about today, so let us get back to the two voices.

"When you are experiencing *any* kind of distressing emotion, such as fear, anger, frustration, anxiety, jealousy, or sadness, know that the false voice is operating and is convincing you that what *it* is saying is true. You will not hear the voice as actual words but rather as one of those disturbing emotions, or even as so-called positive emotions that are overly exciting. Those emotions *are* the voice, or rather an extension of the voice, that you unwittingly embrace because they speak so convincingly through their dramatic expressions. You submit to their influence because you don't know better."

Teacher paused and smiled. "But now you do."

The crowd chuckled.

"Because these intense, theatrical emotions are an obvious calling card of this false voice, it means you have a built-in warning that lets you know when you are under its influence. When you feel one of these emotions, know that this voice is vying for attention, which gives you the opportunity to see it for what it is: the desperate cry of a perpetual victim that needs drama to sustain itself. And once you see it, then it is up to you to *choose* not to heed its call. It is your choice. It's always your choice, only the decision is most frequently made automatically based on habit and without awareness. I am here to provide you with that awareness."

He looked around the group, who sat listening in silence.

"Hmm . . . I see I need to give you a different way of approaching this."

He paused, looked down for a moment, then continued.

"One way to think about this voice is to imagine it as a person, a whiney, manipulative, overly-dramatic, excitable being.

You all probably know someone like this, or someone with shadows of these tendencies, but can you imagine them as a hundred times more dramatic and a hundred times more persuasive, never ceasing in their intense focus on convincing you to do their bidding? You wouldn't want someone like that in your life, would you?"

Many in the crowd shook their heads.

"Indeed, this is the nature of this false voice I am talking about. It is an energy—a substance, a form—beyond what you can see in the physical world but no less real, and it needs *your cooperation* to continue to exist. It will ever work to convince you that what it says, what it thinks, and what it feels is the truth, but it is anything but that.

"Now, let us talk about the other voice, the one that speaks softly, speaks the real truth, speaks with words that lovingly wash over you and lead you to the peace, love, and joy that is possible in your world, something each of you *deserve*, no matter what you may think or feel about yourselves. This true voice will guide you and nurture the best parts of you so that you can be a living embodiment of it here and now, as I am."

Teacher turned his head and looked directly at me for a second, and I realized he had just referenced the last page in the handwritten manuscript I had read before running away from home, the story he had yet to write.

"This voice will not ask anything of you, nor will it try to convince you of its truth, for what is true does not need to explain itself. An apple falling from a tree does not explain why it falls nor try to convince you that it does fall. It simply does what's in its nature, and at the appropriate time, its nature is to fall to the ground. It *is*, with no drama, no apologies, and nothing other than being and doing what it was made to be and do. The true voice's nature is to express itself quietly yet powerfully *through* us, if we but allow it. And it is heard by others through our thoughts, words, and actions that are an extension of that voice.

"So, how do we hear it when it speaks so softly? We do it by quieting our mind and emotions—something the false voice is endlessly fighting against—and then the true voice can be heard. When a normally boisterous crowd quiets down, the gentle, innocent voice of a joyful, loving child can be heard."

Teacher stopped pacing again and looked around the crowd.

"You see, *we* are the extension of which voice we *choose* to express, be it the false voice or the voice of truth. It is *our* choice which to listen to and *our* choice which to express. And, unfortunately, your challenges do not disappear once you become aware and make a single choice to listen to the voice of truth. It's an ongoing process. To manifest permanently moving beyond fears and anxieties requires choosing the soft voice continually. That is, every day when you feel and hear the drama of the false voice, you choose the voice of truth. This is what I had to do to become who I am.

"So, you can start by noticing whenever you have any chaotic thoughts or emotions, for that is an indication that the false voice is raging loudly. If you can come to that awareness, like you are outside yourselves observing the unruly energies swirling about you and within you, then you will have the power of choice. See those thoughts and emotions as not *who you are*; rather, see them as the desperate cries of the annoying false voice looking to be fed by your attention, and then *choose* a quieter path.

"It is that simple, but not necessarily easy. It is a challenge, and once you make headway with it, you will be even more challenged, but any increase in difficulty just tells you that you are on the right path. It tells you that you are more *aware* of the false voice, and you will begin to realize how often it has persuaded you in the past. But even though the going may *appear* difficult, know that you walk the same path as I did, the same path as the Perceiver and the Ancients. You, too, can be like them, like me."

The crowd collectively gasped, and I instantly knew why. Mention of the Ancients was prohibited within the Grand Wall, and tying the Ancients to the Perceiver, the revered founder of the Church and the community that became the Territories, was sure to be blasphemous as well. Not only that, but Teacher had also linked *himself* to the Ancients, essentially claiming to be one of them, and was basically encouraging the group to follow their ways, his way. This would not be received well if the Territory Governors heard about it.

I turned around to look at the man at the back of the crowd, and it appeared he had stiffened and stood up straighter. His eyes drilled into Teacher with an energy that made me uncomfortable. Teacher looked about the surprised crowd, and when his eyes met the eyes of the man in back, Teacher seemed to hold his gaze for longer than he did anyone else.

"Let us take a break," Teacher said. "Talk amongst yourselves and think of examples of when you think you could have chosen better. Some of my followers will roam about to answer any questions you may have."

Shasta, Ariana, and a few others stood up. I wasn't part of what I considered the teaching group, so I remained seated. Teacher looked at me, then looked at the man in back with the scar on his cheek, and I knew it was time for me to fetch him.

I stood up and made my way through the crowd to him. He had made no attempt to speak with others as everyone else was doing. In fact, I saw him wave off a few people who had approached him for conversation.

"Teacher will see you now," I said.

The man nodded, and I led the way back through the small discussion groups that had gathered. I tried to get a sense of the man, tried to *feel* his energies, something I had gradually become better at, but as before, I couldn't get a clear indication of his intentions besides him seeming to be there to evaluate Teacher and the lesson. Teacher watched us approach.

When we arrived, he said, "Thank you, Anna," and he turned and walked away from everyone toward the woods, the man following him. It was clear he wanted to have a private conversation with the stranger.

I observed from a distance. Teacher spoke the most, with the man barely moving a muscle as he listened. Occasionally, the man nodded and spoke a few words, which elicited more talk from Teacher. It was difficult to tell what was being discussed, but the man seemed to understand what was being said.

Eventually, Teacher put both his hands on the man's shoulders—which I had seen him do now and then with his close followers—and said his final words to him.

Then they both turned and looked directly at me.

~

I didn't hear much of Teacher's ensuing lesson, as my mind was occupied thinking about what the two men had talked about and why they had looked at me as they did. What did Teacher tell the stranger about me? Why did the man seem different after the conversation? Why is he now looking at me as much as he is at Teacher? Did they talk about the prophecy? And perhaps most significantly, who is he?

He had the bearing of someone with influence, and Teacher obviously wanted to make his acquaintance for some reason. For what, I didn't yet know, but I would see him at many of Teacher's subsequent lectures.

I asked Teacher about him that night when we—he, myself, his followers, and a few select locals—were sharing a meal a short walk from where he had given his talk.

"Who was the man you spoke with during the break, the one with the scar on his cheek?"

Teacher looked at me blankly, as if his mind was elsewhere. Then his face morphed into the warm smile I knew all too well, and he said, "He's okay. He just needs to figure some things out."

That was a wholly unsatisfying answer, so I prodded. "What did you talk about?"

"Nothing of concern, yet."

"Yet!?"

Teacher laughed. "Oh, Anna, is there anything ever of concern, really?"

"*You're* the one who said it!"

"Ah, yes, I did. I meant it in terms of your perception of what is to come, as I believe you might find it concerning."

"Well, *now* you have to tell me everything," I said.

Teacher said nothing for a moment and just gazed at me with a disarming, loving expression that made me blissfully woozy and almost caused me to forget what we were talking about.

"All in good time," he said with a wink.

He looked around, and a few others nearby were listening to our conversation.

"What I *can* tell you is that some things are going to change soon, and I will need all of you to remember what you've been taught. Do not jump to conclusions but rather take in what happens and discern the roles you will play."

It was clear he was speaking to everyone within earshot. It was, as was often the case, spoken without details, but that was how he challenged us to think and *be* better, to use what we had learned to evaluate things ourselves to move past old concepts and behaviors. I frequently didn't like it, but I had come to appreciate the method.

He looked back at me. "The man with the scar is from the government."

Surprised looks and murmurs went around those listening. I did my best to hide my similar reaction, but of course Teacher saw through all of it and gave a hearty laugh.

"Really? And what did I just say about not jumping to conclusions?" He looked around, dropped into a serious tone, and said, "You all know better." He turned to me. "You know better, Anna."

My heart sunk. I had never been called out like that nor chastised at all by him, and it crushed me. I looked down at my bowl of soup as emotions swirled—guilt for not living up to his expectations, anger at myself for not *living* the lessons better, embarrassment at being singled out by name in front of others. A minute later I felt a hand on my shoulder.

"Anna, I know you can do this," Teacher said quietly enough for others not to hear. "You are here *because* you can do this, and I have the deepest faith in you."

The tears I was barely holding back burst forth, and I leaned over and hugged him.

"I don't know if I can," I said between sobs. "I don't know if I can handle what's coming? Look at me! How can you have faith in me when I can't even handle what you just said?"

He leaned back and again smiled one of his beautiful, enchanting smiles and said, "Because I see you as I am, and I know that when the time comes you will see yourself similarly and operate from that place of peace and strength." He wiped away my tears. "This is not who you are."

I nodded. I believed him. It was difficult not to when in his presence, especially when being spoken to directly.

"It's just that with the prophecy, with whatever *concern* is coming, and the fact that the man with the scar is from the government, which is searching for you, for us, it all scares me. It scares me for *you* because I don't want anything to happen to you."

"Anna, I'm not going to lie to you. What is coming will be your greatest challenge, but it will also be your greatest opportunity." He was still speaking quietly just to me, looking deeply into me, through me. "You are part of the prophecy because you are stronger than anyone else here. It *has* to be you because it would destroy any of them."

I stared at him, not knowing what to say. I had stopped sobbing, and my spinning mind and emotions found some groundedness in his unshakable faith in me. I suppose I was accepting and beginning to feel some of that faith in and for myself.

"Thank you," I whispered.

"Thank *you*," he said.

"I haven't done anything yet," I said, chuckling.

"You will, and it will help change the world."

I nodded. "What was it, again, that I'm going to do?" I asked.

"Nice try," he said, and our joint laughter echoed in the evening air.

~

I came to learn that the man with the scar on his cheek was named Alexander, and I saw him many more times at Teacher's lessons. Sometimes, he was accompanied by one or two other men, but more often he was alone. His demeanor appeared different after that first day, a bit more relaxed and not as intense in his scrutiny of Teacher or the lecture. Interestingly, Teacher continued to ask me to bring him over for private conversations after the lessons or during breaks. What they discussed, Teacher never mentioned, and I didn't ask.

One time, as people were arriving and gathering for another lecture, in the distance I saw Alexander approach the event with another man, someone with red hair. I started to tremble internally, not yet aware of who it was, but it seemed that my body remembered. As they advanced, my eyes finally accepted what my shaking form knew.

It was my father.

I hadn't seen him in close to ten years. He looked older, but more notably, he didn't appear to have the angry edge that seemed to define him when I was growing up. His face expressed a certain measure of weariness, as if he had been beaten down by the recognition that he couldn't exert control over everything and had found a resigned acceptance in it. His red hair, however, hadn't changed at all.

I ducked behind a few people near Teacher to hide my own red hair, which was the exact same color as his. Between bodies, I peered at the two men as they approached.

My eyes then widened as I realized that my father had been a constable and likely still was.

I needed to alert Teacher, so I quickly turned to him, but he was already staring at me from a few paces away, and I couldn't help but feel the same thing I had felt when I had first seen him from my balcony on my thirteenth birthday, that everything was going to be okay. Notwithstanding our ability to communicate in this manner on some level, I had to make sure he understood the danger we were in. I approached him.

"Teacher, that man with the red hair is a constable," I said anxiously, keeping myself out of view of my father.

Teacher nodded calmly. "I know."

He then turned to Ariana, who was standing nearby.

"Ariana, will you bring Alexander and his friend to us?"

"Of course," Ariana said.

"Anna," Teacher said, "come with me," and he began walking away from the gathering crowd toward the woods.

I followed as well as my quivering legs could move me, my mind and emotions spinning wildly. We stopped a good distance from others beneath a large maple tree. I couldn't let myself look again at my father, so I stood facing Teacher and the empty woods in front of me, my back to the approaching men.

"Anna, remember the teachings," Teacher said. "You can choose the other voice."

Whatever I had learned and experienced since running away from home had suddenly become distant and hazy, and I was contracting inside, back to that naïve little girl who cowered before the rules of her upbringing. I took a deep breath and tried to go within to the internal space that held the peace I knew was there, but my false voice spoke more loudly, and I was having difficulty ignoring it.

Hearing the men's footsteps stop right behind me, I took another deep breath, my muscles not yet able to turn me around. Then I heard my father's voice, older and softer than what I knew.

"It's you! I remember you."

I observed Teacher nodding, which confused me. How could my father know him?

"I remember you because you said I would see . . ." My father trailed off, and I could *feel* him staring at the back of my head. Slowly, he finished the sentence, ". . . her again someday."

I didn't know what had transpired between them or why my father said that, but I took another deep breath and turned around.

~

There he was, the same yet drastically different. The lines of age on his face, some new and some deeper, conveyed a different feeling to me from when I had known him. I had expected the same intense, angry expression, only older, but what met my gaze was tired and sad, and now surprised.

"Anna?" he said, his voice shaking.

I nodded. Part of me wanted to give him a hug as a remembrance of the more playful and loving interactions we had had when I was young, and to forgive him for the past, but I was frozen in place. Apparently, I wasn't yet ready to do that.

He took an uncertain step forward, his arms coming up slightly. While I was trying to figure out how to respond, I felt an energy wash over me that softened my hesitancy, and I ran forward and grasped him in a great bear hug.

He hugged me tightly, and tears flowed from both of us, no words being spoken.

I don't know how long we held each other, but eventually we parted, and my father couldn't keep himself from staring at me. When he broke his gaze and his silence, he spoke to Teacher.

"How did you know? How did you know from so long ago?"

"You will come to understand," Teacher said. "And I would like to thank you for your role back then."

"My role? What do you mean?"

"You and Alexander both played important roles in my experience that enabled me to realize what I am, and I thank you for that."

I knew Teacher didn't bestow this kind of thanks to everyone, so I hoped the two men appreciated the depth of it. I could tell this confused my father, but he didn't follow up.

"Anna, how . . . how are you? How have you been?"

I finally found my voice. "I'm . . . good." I couldn't get out more than that.

I think my father didn't know what else to say to me, so he pivoted to Teacher again.

"What is this? What is this gathering? Alexander only said that I needed to hear someone speak."

"I asked him to bring you," Teacher said, "for multiple reasons."

My father looked at Alexander, who nodded, then he looked at me, as obviously I was one of those reasons. Clearly, Teacher had the foresight to know exactly what he was doing. My father turned again to me.

"Where did you go? Where have you been? I looked everywhere for you."

I glanced at Teacher, who gave me a slight nod.

"Did you look outside the Wall?" I said with a hint of a smile.

My father gave a laughing snort, looked at me, then at Teacher, incredulous. His expression turned from stunned to fearful, and I recognized him as he was long ago.

"No!"

He looked at Alexander, who nodded.

"What? We have to tell . . ." he began, but Alexander grabbed him by the elbow, which stopped him from finishing his sentence.

Looking at me and then at Teacher, my father found his voice and said, "So, *you're* the one from the rumors going around?" He turned to Alexander. "Sir, why haven't you . . ."

Alexander shook his head, leaving my father looking confused. There was an awkward silence for a moment, then Teacher spoke.

"You will see that I am a threat to no one. I only ask that you listen to my lecture, then you can decide what to do. Alexander, he must be able to choose, not be ordered."

Alexander let go of my father's elbow and looked at Teacher, who stood unmoving. I realized that Alexander must be above my father in the hierarchy in the constabulary, which meant that they both were potentially dangerous to Teacher and the gatherings. But somehow Teacher had persuaded Alexander not to turn him in and was confident enough to trust that my father wouldn't either.

My father stared at Teacher, seemingly trying to evaluate him as a threat, then turned his attention back to me, and his eyes began to well up again.

"I'm . . . I'm so sorry, Anna!"

I hugged him again, and I could feel how broken and angry at himself he had been. He was baring himself to me and asking for my forgiveness in everything but words. This vulnerability, which I had *never* seen in him, astounded me, and my old love for him as my father began to resurface and envelop him, slowly stitching his shattered spirit together.

~

I sat with him and Alexander at the back of the group while we listened to the lesson, which was about healing. I know my father was listening to Teacher, but he also couldn't stop himself from turning to look at me repeatedly.

"Today, I want to talk about healing," Teacher said before beginning his pacing. "But first, I want to talk about how your environment brings you what you need to experience. There are reasons for this, which I will not go into today, but suffice it to say that everything that you are—the whole of you: physical, mental, and emotional—is reflected back to you by your environment. Because I am here with you today, it means you are ready to hear what I have to say and witness what you need to witness.

"Every situation that you find difficult or challenging contains a lesson, and whatever that experience is, it has come to you specifically to bring you that message. The trick is to be able to discern that lesson among the noise and drama of what is happening in front of you. If you can learn from it and truly understand why you have brought the experience to yourself, then you will no longer call forth similar lessons, for you will have moved past the need to go through it again. Like in school, you don't need to repeat a class unless you haven't learned what that class was trying to teach you."

Although I had heard this lesson before, Teacher was rephrasing it in a way that added clarity to my understanding. I thought of how good I was in school when I was in the Territories, and how I also learned quickly from Shasta, Naveen, and others. I had had my share of difficult situations in my time in the village but hadn't always recognized the lessons in them, so I knew I still had work to do.

I looked at my father, who returned my gaze.

"Many of you are here for this talk because you continue to encounter situations that repeat the same lesson, and it is time to put a stop to that by learning what those experiences are trying to teach you. Can you think of something challenging that seems to happen to you over and over again? Would someone like to share?"

Several hands went up. Teacher zeroed in on a middle-aged woman.

"Abrah, tell us what you've experienced."

"My husband prefers to drink whiskey in town instead of taking care of his chores," Abrah said. "He does some work, but me and the girls have to pick up the slack."

"How does that make you feel?" Teacher asked.

"Angry. Wondering why I married the bastard."

Teacher smiled. "But you have love for him."

Abrah sighed and nodded. The crowd chuckled.

"You have a farm, correct?"

She nodded.

"And he works the land to provide for you and the family?"

"Yes, but there's always more to do."

"Ah, I used to be a farmer as well, so I can understand that the work is never done," Teacher said. "What do you think the lesson is?"

Abrah thought for a moment before answering. "Well, that he needs to step up and do more."

"That is your idea of what *his* lesson is. What is *your* lesson?" Teacher pointed at her.

She looked stunned, like he was asking her to walk on water. She shook her head, seemingly confused. Teacher continued, speaking to the whole group.

"Remember, this is about *you*, not anyone else in the interactions. It's easy to apply your thoughts and judgments to others, but to stop and self-reflect, that is what I'm asking you to do, as difficult as it may be."

He closed his eyes for a moment, then directed his focus back to Abrah.

"You said his actions make you angry. Are you aware of how *your* actions make *him* feel?"

She looked at Teacher blankly.

"Relationships are a dynamic between two people, and how that dynamic expresses comes from both sides, but what this is is different. Your anger is not about him. That's how it may feel, but he is not the source. *You* are the source."

I suppressed a chuckle because Abrah clenched her jaw and started to look angry with Teacher for saying that.

"Aren't there other things that make you angry as well, like when the household isn't in order or you don't get what you want?" He didn't wait for an answer. "And even when you do get what you want, you often have an issue with it and complain about it to your husband or children?"

I hadn't seen Teacher be this harsh with someone, and I could tell Abrah was becoming upset.

"I'm being very direct as you need to hear this directly. The source of your anger is not for any of the reasons I mention, nor is it your husband. It is you. Everyone here wants to look outside themselves to blame others for their own predicaments, but you each are the source of your difficulties.

"Now, there are reasons behind *why* you invite such experiences, and self-reflection can help you uncover the reasons for the drama you face. I will give Abrah a lead, as she needs to hear it from me to begin to understand. Abrah, your anger comes from how you were raised, and I encourage you to look at your upbringing and your parents' relationship dynamic and how that affected you. They did their best based upon how *they* were raised, and it instilled in you a need to control your environment in order to stay safe. That behavior may have been suitable in that family dynamic at the time, but it is no longer necessary. And I will add that *you* can change so that your children don't grow up to repeat what you are going through, which I presume you don't want for them."

Abrah shook her head and looked embarrassed.

"This is about you. Leave your husband out of it for now. He occasionally needs some space and some time conversing with other males, as the energy in your household with you and your two girls is decidedly female, and it unbalances him. Things will get better with you two."

Abrah nodded.

I found it interesting that Teacher chose an example that talked about upbringing, as I was now reconnecting with my father after a difficult childhood dynamic with him. Perhaps this was why Teacher chose her. Again, he seemed to be making connections beyond what his words directly communicated.

"I suppose you're all thinking, what has this to do with healing? Well, many things. The emotions Abrah has felt have affected her physical body. The stress has caused her to feel tightness in her chest and sometimes some jaw pain, isn't that right?"

Abrah nodded.

"But more than the physical, it has caused much mental and emotional strain, which affects everything else in her life. Almost all of you can relate to that. So, one level of her lesson is to try to understand what energy dynamic she is carrying that she adopted from childhood, and by understanding it, correct the misperception that she must act or be a certain way. This is healing."

"Abrah, would you like to experience what it feels like to have this healed?"

A few gasps came from the crowd, and Abrah looked surprised but rose from her place on the ground and stepped forward toward Teacher.

Teacher welcomed her with a hug, then placed one hand on her neck and one on her forehead. She closed her eyes, and he mumbled something I couldn't hear. I sensed a snap of energy in the air and her physical body relaxed so much that she almost fell down. It was only a few seconds, but when she steadied herself and opened her eyes, she seemed like a different person. I, too, was affected somehow and felt a bit dizzy for a moment.

The tension Abrah had held in her face and shoulders had disappeared, and she blinked like she was seeing the world for the first time. Her eyes welled up, and she began sobbing.

Teacher didn't say anything while he slowly walked her back to where she had been sitting and then returned to the front of the group. Most people in the crowd were staring at the woman, who eventually stopped sobbing, but she continued to look about with eyes of wonder.

"What do you think?" Teacher asked her.

"Uh . . . I . . . feel different," Abrah said.

Teacher smiled. "Yes, you should. One thing to note, for all of you: You may recognize and choose to heed the lessons the world presents to you, and you may feel wonderful after doing so, but be aware that many things will try to make you fall back into the ruts that caused the difficulties in the first place. Abrah is seeing and feeling differently now, but she must be careful not to allow old patterns of perception to come back and sabotage where she is. It is the same for everyone. Do not call back to you that which serves only to limit you. Choose to live past those limitations."

Teacher began pacing again.

"So, what is healing? It is the restoration of health, is it not? But what is health? When you can physically perform a task and feel good doing it, you may call yourself healthy, and indeed you are in one sense. But as you know and as you just witnessed, there are often things occurring internally that can compromise your physical, mental, or emotional well-being.

"What did I do with Abrah just now? I showed her that she could see and feel differently. That's all. I brought into her awareness a way of seeing, a way of *being*, that she was previously unaware of. But you don't need me to do this for you. You can do it for yourselves. This is why I am here and why you are listening to me. I am showing you the way, but *you* are the ones to walk your path, you who have the power to heal all conditions that do not serve the best versions of yourselves.

"I see the perfection that you are. I *know* the perfection that you are. I perceive beyond your little cuts and bruises, your illnesses, your petty arguments, your trivial emotional outbursts and see *who you are.* And all of you are perfect as you were created, as *I* was created, for we are the same. The founder of this great land learned this, saw this, became this, and so those around him bestowed upon him the name of the Perceiver, the Grand One, who sees the truth in all things beyond the physical world and beyond time. I am the Perceiver, and you are, too. You just need a little help in getting there. That is why we are here today."

I glanced at my father, who looked like he stiffened upon hearing about the Perceiver, but he also seemed mesmerized by Teacher's words. I wondered how he was absorbing it given his strict religious upbringing. Perhaps those views, too, had softened in him.

"Baron," Teacher said, looking at a man close to the front of the group who I had seen hop forward with a crutch, which now lay beside him. "I see you had a little accident."

"Yes, Teacher," Baron said. "I broke my ankle jumping out of a wagon onto uneven ground."

"I see," Teacher said. "Why don't you come up here?"

Baron used his crutch to help him stand, then hopped forward to Teacher, leaning heavily on his support. His ankle appeared tightly wrapped in cloth.

"Would you like to be healed?" Teacher asked.

Baron nodded, almost looking doubtful. Teacher paused, staring at him, then asked him again more slowly.

"Would you like to be healed?" The words seemed to shift the air around us.

Baron's eyes widened, and he said, "Yes," very clearly. I felt that this time his intention was more aligned to receive the healing. In comparison, his first response felt feeble and uncertain.

Teacher crouched down and put his hands over the wrapped ankle. He then stood and placed one hand behind Baron's neck and the other on his forehead while again mumbling something I couldn't hear. There was an audible *pop* and Baron cried out, but then over the next few seconds his face relaxed, similar to Abrah's. I also felt something shift when it happened. Teacher removed his hands, and Baron looked down at his ankle and gingerly put some weight on it. He gradually leaned onto it more and more until he was standing entirely on what had been the bad ankle. His face lit up with a smile and he jumped up and down a few times, beaming at Teacher before giving him a big hug.

Teacher reciprocated the embrace, then gestured for Baron to sit down. Once seated, Baron began to unwrap his ankle, smiling and shaking his head. The crutch lay to the side where he had dropped it.

This was the first time I had seen Teacher perform such an instant, physical healing, and I was not alone in my astonishment. Most of the crowd seemed to be in a state of awe, including my father and Alexander, although Alexander still retained some of his stoic composure.

"So, what happened there?" Teacher asked.

No one said anything.

"I saw him, and his ankle, as perfect, as perfectly healed. I did not see anything broken but rather saw the break as a fleeting limitation that could be nudged back to its wholeness with the right perception, and I showed *him* that." Looking at Baron, he said, "What did you see and feel?"

Baron shook his head as if still trying to believe what had just happened. "I felt out of my body with a lightness I can't describe, and it was as you say, feeling amazing and whole and perfect, but I don't know how."

"When you can accept that this view, this perception, is possible," Teacher said, "then you can allow it to manifest within you and then express outwardly. I chose both Abrah and Baron for a reason. They are very different and have very different . . . *had* very different ailments, but I knew they both had a particular openness to *allowing* a change in perception, which manifested in their accepting the healings."

"But what is the lesson from my broken ankle?" Baron asked. "Why did I hurt it?" He was rolling his ankle back and forth.

Teacher paused and closed his eyes for a moment, then spoke. "You must think further on this, but ask yourself what you might have received by not being able to walk and work freely."

Baron nodded. "I will. Thank you."

"So, let us talk about *perfect* health," Teacher continued. "It is seeing and knowing that what you may have previously seen as a problem or difficulty is now seen from the context of wholeness and perfection. You all saw Baron with a broken ankle. I didn't. The ankle's defect only registered to me as the most minor of limitations, a temporary, annoying fly that is effortlessly swatted away. You think you need *time* to heal something like that. You don't. You need to *see it differently*. I merely brought him to a place where he could see and believe what I see and *know*.

"You all can do this. I can feel your surprise and wonder at witnessing this so-called miracle, as well as your doubt at hearing me say that you can do this. I am here to tell you that this is not only possible but *normal* for all of us. You all have this ability, if you but listen to my words, study them, and practice. Indeed, these are teachings that have been shared since before the Grand Wall existed, when you had freedom from your belief in limitations. Alas, you will know this soon enough, because when those limiting walls fall, you will see what lies beyond the shadows of the confining beliefs you have adopted as your truth, as your world. And the world you discover beyond those walls is more expansive than you can possibly imagine, just as the whole truth may be incomprehensible at this time."

I swallowed nervously. Teacher seemed to be speaking on different levels again, one symbolically and one that might be interpreted as treasonous: advocating for the Grand Wall to come down. I glanced at Alexander and my father, and Alexander appeared to be clenching his jaw while my father looked as if he was struggling to understand what Teacher had said.

I'm sure Teacher knew exactly what he was doing, giving this lesson knowing that members of the constabulary were present to hear it, and that worried me. What would they do having heard Teacher talk about the Perceiver in such a way and about *walls* falling soon? Talking about the Grand Wall wasn't allowed, at least when I had been here as a child, and advocating for its destruction? That was most certainly forbidden. But at the same time, Teacher was a little abstract with his words and also seemed to have an understanding with Alexander, and perhaps now with my father as well. I had now seen Alexander many times at these lectures with no perceived danger from him or others from the government. So, Alexander was keeping things to himself, or at least keeping information about Teacher and his lessons from those who might be against his presence in the Territories. Alexander's clenched jaw, however, indicated to me that

Teacher's words might be approaching a line where Alexander might find it difficult to ignore his governmental duties. I presumed only the passage of time would reveal the truth.

~

After the lesson, I approached my father, who looked a bit bewildered as he seemed to be trying to understand what he had just heard and witnessed. I wondered how his attitude toward religion and the Church had changed, because if he had the same views from a decade ago, he would have either been flying into a rage or running off to get reinforcements to arrest everyone in the crowd, starting with Teacher. Clearly, his attitude and beliefs had moderated in the intervening years.

Instead, he looked like a few of the others in the group, expressing an almost blank-like stare that told me his mind was struggling with trying to fit what he had seen and heard into his preexisting beliefs about the world. The resulting conflict, as I had seen before, likely took him out of his logical mind and into a higher level of the mind that Shasta had once said was "where difficult concepts can be integrated and understood beyond our limited, concrete minds."

"Father," I said, not having used that word in years, "how did you like Teacher's lecture." It came out a little tentative.

He looked at me, his glossy eyes starting to revert to normal, and said, "It was . . . interesting." His brow furrowed. "I can see why people say he promotes threatening ideas, but meeting him and hearing his words . . . I feel different about it, about him."

He glanced briefly at Alexander, who was watching our interaction.

"But he has to be careful," my father added. "He can't just talk about the Perceiver and the Grand Wall that way. We have laws, and he has to abide by them."

"Even if they're wrong?" I said, finding my voice. "Even if they don't make sense? Father, I've seen and experienced things that you wouldn't believe, things even more implausible than the healings he just did. There's so much more to the world than what's here in the Territories. Teacher's trying to show everyone that. I lived outside the Wall for ten years in a place that everyone in the Territories thinks is full of dangerous and depraved foreigners. As you can see, that's not the case. In fact, I've never seen or felt as much at peace as when I was in my village outside the Wall."

A flash of sadness and regret flashed across my father's face, and I could feel his corresponding emotional pain in my own body. I realized I had inadvertently criticized him.

"I'm sorry, too," I said, "for running away. We both didn't know any better at the time."

He began to tear up. "Oh, how you've grown! I always knew you were smart." He gave me a big hug.

When he released me, I said, "You've changed a lot, too."

He nodded. "I went through a few tough years and learned some things about myself in the process. And I think the day you ran away I may have received a healing like Teacher just talked about, which began my search for understanding."

I gave him a quizzical look.

"A story for another time, but it was when I first met your teacher, before he was your teacher."

Something clicked with a passage in the old manuscript I had read years ago before my time outside the Wall, the words Teacher had yet to write.

"I would like to hear it sometime," I said. Switching topics, I asked, "How's mother?"

"She's okay. She'll be happy to see you."

"Can you bring her to one of these lectures? I think we'll be heading into the city soon, and I think she'd like it."

"I'll bring her, but I'm worried about you being around such sacrilegious speech." He looked at Alexander, then back at me. "There's been talk about arresting this unknown itinerant preacher—who we couldn't find—for exactly the kinds of things he talked about today. Now that we know where he is . . . well, I didn't know what he was like or that you were with him."

"But you heard him," I said, "and you found it interesting and not dangerous." I looked at Alexander. "And you, too, have heard him many times now, so you know he's not a threat to anyone. If anything, he's just what the people need to hear. The only danger is to the old views you all hold."

My father took my hands and looked into my eyes.

"And that's exactly the problem."

Anna

Anna, Jillian, and Naveen didn't have to wait long for mealtime. With the sun dropping in the sky, the dinner bell echoed across the village to Anna's cabin where the three sat chatting after their practice of the slow dance. With the reverberations still lingering in the air, they rose to go to join the rest of the residents in the dining hall.

On their walk there, Anna had some second thoughts about being around others, anticipating sharp looks and criticisms being directed her way again now that Teacher's verdict had been handed down the previous day. Having her two close friends with her, however, took the edge off the emotions that accompanied those thoughts. She also remembered to energetically protect herself as she had been taught, bringing herself up in vibration to feel light and love throughout her body and envisioning a barrier around her that would shield her from anything that wasn't loving, peaceful, or in her best interests. When the three arrived at the door of the building, Anna again felt confident and secure in her own skin.

They entered and sat down together toward one end of the large table. Anna received some glances as others arrived, but the looks seemed more out of curiosity than out of any ill intent. Indeed, she had been largely absent from the goings on in the village due to hibernating in her cabin and working on her writing, so it could have been because she simply hadn't been seen in a while.

Anna saw Kyna, Caedmon, Promeus, and Shasta enter the hall together, and when Shasta saw that Anna was there, she ushered the others over to where Anna and her friends were sitting. Anna was glad to have them close, as she knew they were more aware of the reasons for her actions than most others, and their proximity provided an acceptability to her presence.

Anna felt sad when she looked at Promeus, knowing that his time was soon coming to an end. When he caught her gaze, she experienced a deep connection with him that told her that she was the only one he had divulged his fate to. His look didn't need to ask for her discretion, for the unspoken connection said it all.

During the meal, she did receive a few looks that came with emotional daggers, but being in a protected, energetic space, they didn't bother her. It helped that she and the others engaged in discussion about all sorts of topics—Teacher's lessons, the village since he had gone to the Territories, Shasta's teaching role going forward, Naveen slowing down his practice for an enhanced effect, and the upcoming rainy season. Mercifully, whether intentional or not, Teacher's predicament and Anna's role in the prophecy weren't talked about. It was as if everything was back to normal for Anna, like before Teacher had arrived.

After the meal, she walked back to her cabin with Jillian. Naveen stayed in the hall because he wanted to ask a few others about his different experience with the slow dance.

Once home, Anna flopped onto the bed and let out a deep sigh.

"That wasn't so bad," Jillian said, before laying down next to her.

Anna turned to her side and wrapped her arms around Jillian. "Thank you."

Jillian hugged her back. "For what?"

"For everything. I don't know if I could have made it this far without you."

"Oh, honey, I could say the same."

"Everything felt . . . normal tonight," Anna said, "like it was before Teacher arrived. The only difference is that we know more because of him."

"We know *far* more and have experienced some amazing things because of him. I still wish I could've come with you to the Territories, though."

"Me, too, but I think it was for the best. There was a lot I needed to experience and do, and it was important for me to be alone to understand and work through managing it all. You can read about it, but not yet." She glanced over at the stack of papers on the table. "I still have a lot to write about my time there and I'd rather it be finished first."

"I can't get just a little peek?" Jillian said, snuggling herself closer.

Anna smiled and embraced her more deeply.

"You know, you can *almost* sway me with your presence, but I need to let the rest of the story come out first. But you'll be the first to know when it's finished."

Jillian nodded and nestled her head into Anna's neck. Before darkness had fully descended, they had fallen asleep in each other's arms.

Truths

We continued traveling the countryside with Teacher as he presented his lectures, all while doing our best to avoid the scrutiny of the constables, who we knew were still actively looking for us, at least some of them. The frequent attendance of Alexander and, occasionally, my father, led me to believe that they, or at least Alexander, might have had something to do with us maintaining our concealment from those in the government with bad intentions. However, with the size of the groups growing each day as people heard about Teacher's lessons, healings, and the feeling they had when in his presence, I figured it was just a matter of time before the sheer number of listeners would cause our location to be compromised, regardless of Alexander's interventions, if any.

I maintained my role as an assistant to Teacher and lookout for the group, reporting on anyone I deemed suspicious and communicating anything interesting from what I heard from discussions as I mingled in the crowds. After the incident where we had to escape into the woods before the constables found and searched our meeting place, there really wasn't much that warranted attention, which surprised me. I wondered if Teacher, and perhaps Alexander, were doing something that kept us safe. The extent of Teacher's ability to know and influence his surroundings and the people within it continued to amaze me, so I didn't put it past him.

Before one lecture, I saw Alexander and my father arrive with a woman, who I recognized immediately as my mother. I moved briskly through the gathering crowd to meet them. When my mother saw me, she cried out and ran forward. We embraced, unable to speak through the tears.

"It *is* you!" my mother eventually said, releasing me and looking me up and down. "My, how you've grown."

"Hi, Mom," I said and hugged her again.

I didn't know what else to say, and apparently neither did she, because we just hugged and looked at each other for a minute before my father broke the silence.

"I've told your mother about you and where you've been these past years."

My mother looked at me and placed both hands on my cheeks.

"I still can't believe it. *Outside the Wall?* And with *these* people? Are you okay?"

I nodded but noticed her judgment, something I had faintly discerned when I first saw her arrive.

"I'm great. *These* people are my closest friends." I almost said, "family," but caught myself.

She removed her hands from my face and stepped back.

"Well, just be careful. You never know."

My excitement at seeing my mother after ten years was rapidly diminishing as her words cut more deeply than I would have anticipated. She apparently wasn't as open as my father was to what my life had become. I turned to my father.

"Have you told her about Teacher's lessons?"

He nodded, so I turned back to my mother and asked, "Are you excited to hear what he has to say?"

"Oh, honey, I came to see you and to bring you home."

I looked at her in disbelief and initially couldn't respond, so my father intervened, speaking to his wife.

"I told you that Anna's got her own life now."

"Yes, but it's not her natural life," my mother said. "That's with us. She shouldn't have left us all those years ago."

I found my voice and said, "Mom, this is my life now. I'm not going back."

As I said it, I felt a presence behind me. Teacher had approached.

"You must be Anna's mother," he said, extending his hand. "It's a pleasure to meet you."

It seemed my mother was instantly captivated by his presence, staring into Teacher's eyes like a drunkard while she shook his hand.

"Um, yes, nice to meet you too!" she said.

"I want to tell you that Anna has been a brilliant student and has been a tremendous help to me," Teacher said.

I felt my face flushing.

"Yes, she's very smart," my mother said.

"I must go and teach now. I sincerely hope you enjoy the talk."

My mother nodded and Teacher turned to go back to the front of the crowd.

After he was enough of a distance away, my mother said, "I don't trust him. Why do you spend time with these people when you could be home with us." I cringed again at her words.

It was clear my mother hadn't evolved as much as my father had. She was still steeped in old, limited thinking that related to controlling those around her, even though she had been a positive and somewhat protective counterpoint to my father's domineering nature when I was a child. I found it interesting that my father seemed leagues ahead in being open to new ideas.

"Mom, stay for the lecture and then let me know what you think."

I looked behind me, and it appeared Teacher was almost ready to begin. "I have to go. We can talk afterward."

My mother nodded, and I turned and walked back through the settling crowd to my usual place up front.

~

After the lesson, which was another one about being more aware that our surroundings and experiences mirror our true nature and that we can choose better, I found my mother and father and asked them what they thought.

"Like I said before," my mother said, "I don't trust him. He sounds sneaky, like he's trying to sell you something."

I was surprised, as I thought not just Teacher's words but his energy would have at least shaken her seemingly entrenched judgments.

"He's not trying to sell you anything," I said. "He said that you always have a choice. Did you feel anything during the talk?"

"Feel?" She shook her head. "I feel that it's time for you to come home."

She looked at my father and said, "We should go," then turned back to me. "Anna, it's wonderful to see you, and I hope you can see what the right choice is here."

She leaned in to hug me goodbye and I reciprocated, but it felt distinctively flat compared to the embrace my father gave me moments afterward.

I was crushed. Besides throwing my comment about choice back in my face, my mother clearly had not felt or understood anything about Teacher's lesson, and she didn't seem to care who I was now or what I had been through.

She walked away, but my father lingered for a moment to say quietly to me, "This is all new to her. She'll come around."

I smiled and nodded, feeling that my father wanted to believe what he said, but even he had reservations. I could tell that she wasn't going to come around, at least not in the near future.

I watched them leave, separate from Alexander, who was again having another private talk with Teacher. When they finished, Teacher called me over.

"How did your mother like the lecture?" he asked.

I shook my head. "She didn't understand, and even worse, I don't think she wants to. All she wants is for me to come home, and I don't know how to change her thinking."

He looked at me like I should have known better, and I did, because as soon as I said it, I realized that his lecture about choice included an explanation about how we often try to change others so that *our* circumstances can become better or more comfortable. That, he had said, can compromise *their* lesson as much as our own.

"Okay, I know, I know," I said. "It's just difficult to see her like this, especially when my father seems to be trying so hard."

"Your father is doing very well," Teacher said, "considering his upbringing and profession. I'm very proud of him."

"Thank you for saying that. My mother, on the other hand . . . well, she thinks you're trouble."

Teacher laughed heartily. "And what do you think?"

I smiled. "Well, maybe the good kind of trouble that challenges people to become better versions of themselves."

He reached out and gave me a hug, then released me.

"A parent's love can sometimes express in what we perceive as non-loving ways. This is a lifetime full of lessons for her, and she still has some things she needs to confront in order to learn them. You've discerned her well, Anna. There is little you can do for her at this point."

I nodded.

Changing topics, he said, "Tomorrow, we will go into the city. It's time. I have sent Shasta ahead to make straight the way and announce my coming."

"Where in the city will you speak?" I asked, a little worried because of the constable presence there.

"We will gather in the marketplace, as it is large enough for the expected crowd."

I stared at him uncomfortably because I knew that area was more frequently monitored by the authorities, and I didn't think we'd be able to avoid being seen by them, or worse.

Seeing my reaction, he said, "Some things are going to happen in the city that will be different from out here in the countryside. Whatever happens will need to happen. It will be okay. Trust in the change, for it portends a greater future. You are a part of this, as you have always been, and you still have a role to play."

I knew he was referencing the prophecy again, and it sounded more ominous to me this time. I stared at him, not knowing how to respond. Whatever I was fated to do had been mercifully absent from my mind for most of my time in the Territories with him, but fulfilling it now seemed inescapable, and it was beginning to make me anxious.

He placed his hands on my shoulders. "Remember what you've learned," he said. "Remember there is more at work than what you currently perceive and that what you will do will serve a cause far greater than you can foresee at this time. Remember *who you are*."

I swallowed heavily and nodded. "I'll do my best," I said.

He smiled. "As you always do," he said and gave me another hug.

~

True to Teacher's word, our encampment headed into the city the following day. Our group now numbered in the dozens, far greater than the original few who had crossed the great barrier with him months before. Most were people who had heard him many times and felt strongly enough about his teachings that they had decided to follow him, like me, wherever he led us.

After an hour of walking east, the latter half of the time up the inclined slope toward the city, I saw up ahead several men all clothed in dark blue uniforms that indicated they were constables. They appeared to be waiting for us. My initial reaction was one of panic, but I was doing better remembering the teachings and quickly went beyond it to try to *feel* the situation. What came to me wasn't much, which told me there probably wasn't anything to be anxious about, despite the worried chatter among my traveling companions once they saw the men. I looked at Teacher, who was as calm as ever, and he glanced at me and smiled. I managed to smile back at him, sharing at least a fraction of the peace he radiated.

My father was there, standing next to Alexander and three other men, all in their crisp, official, constable garb. Despite Alexander and my father's occasional presence at Teacher's talks, this was the first time I had seen them in their uniforms. Behind them and to the side I saw Shasta also waiting for us. Something was indeed afoot.

We approached, with Teacher leading the group. I noticed that Alexander wore a more elaborate uniform with more bars on his shoulders and pins on his chest than the others. It seemed

I had been right about his apparent authority over my father in ranking, and he clearly outranked the other men there as well.

Teacher stopped in front of Alexander and smiled, and the rest of us stood motionless as we waited to see what was going to happen next. I caught my father's eye before he glanced at Teacher, and he seemed a little worried, but I wasn't sure whether it was for me, for Teacher, or for whatever might have been planned in the city. Alexander gave a slight nod to Teacher, turned, and walked away, leading my father and the other constables up the road. Teacher followed, as did the rest of us, Shasta fell into step beside me.

"What's happening?" I asked Shasta in a half whisper. "Where are we going?"

"To the cathedral," she said.

The one place I thought Teacher would want to avoid was the cathedral. What could he possibly say to those in the Church who would likely find his teachings in violation of their beliefs? Also, it was dangerous because blasphemy was, as I remembered, illegal. The Church and the government always seemed to be aligned in how they regarded those who spoke out not just in opposition to them but about anything that conflicted with their views of the world.

"So," I said, "are the constables actually *escorting* us?"

Shasta looked at me and smiled, then nodded.

"How did you manage that?" I asked.

"It was Teacher more than me. I just helped prepare for today."

"What's going to happen today?"

"I only know that the plan is to go to the cathedral, then to the marketplace. What will happen at each, I don't know."

The density of the buildings, houses, and shops increased as the group continued up the slope, gathering curious glances from the people we passed. The spire of the cathedral in the distance slowly grew larger, dwarfing the stone buildings in the city center that surrounded it. I hadn't been there in over ten years, but everything seemed the same, although not quite as grand and imposing as I remembered as a child. I chuckled to myself, wondering if that was because I had grown physically or in so many other ways.

When we finally arrived at the plaza—the large, open square with the cathedral on one side and shops and government buildings on the other sides—Alexander, my father, and the other constables climbed the steps and stood by the great door. Teacher paused at the bottom of the steps, and everyone behind him did the same.

He looked up at the impressive façade before him, closed his eyes, and smiled. With Teacher in shadow but the front of the cathedral lit up by the morning sun, the contrast left a profound impression on me. I could now understand why paintings of the Perceiver and other icons could be so revered, like the one that had hung on my childhood bedroom wall that my father had insisted remain there. There was something about Teacher's deeply peaceful energy, the majesty of the cathedral, and the light beyond the shadows I witnessed that day that has stuck with me ever since.

When he opened his eyes, Teacher ascended the steps. One constable remained outside while Alexander, my father, and the other two constables passed through the door. Shasta and I followed Teacher up the steps and entered the cavernous room, trailed by some in the group behind us.

The inside was like I remembered, a massive, open space with many rows of pews that focused attention on the ornate sanctuary up front with the simple, wooden sculpture of the Perceiver in its midst. Besides the constables and those in our group still entering, the rest of the cathedral was empty except for a few chief elders of the Church, including the high priest, who sat in ornate chairs beneath and to the side of the sculpture. It seemed they were waiting for us.

Teacher walked up to the third pew and sat, gazing up at the Perceiver and initially ignoring the Church elders. Shasta, Ariana, and I sat two pews behind him, giving him some space, and others sat behind us. Two constables stood at the back of the church, and Alexander and my father stood together on the left side in front of the first pews.

Once everyone who had entered sat down, the room fell into a hallowed silence that to this day I cannot describe. It was so eerily quiet yet so full of sacred presence that it felt like life itself could spring forth from its center.

I looked at the sculpture of the Perceiver, and it was not as I remembered it from my youth. It was the same physically, but something about it now spoke to me beyond words, connecting me with a knowingness of purpose and a presence that I had only felt shadows of when training in the village outside the Grand Wall. I felt truth and meaning and connection all at once, raising my awareness up and beyond any kind of logical understanding to a place where the trivialities of my physical existence became apparent in contrast to it. Even the thought of whatever role I was to play in the prophecy paled in comparison, and I knew right then that I would do anything I could to fulfill any fated promise to Teacher and to the destiny before me.

After a few minutes basking in that sacred silence, Teacher rose and gestured for Shasta and me to follow him. He approached the elders in the sanctuary, who had been watching him with what I believed was a combination of curiosity and a little bit of suspicion. Shasta and I stayed well behind him.

The high priest rose and stepped forward. He wore a long robe garnished with gold trim and held a jewel-encrusted staff with a small carving of the Perceiver at the top.

"We would like a private meeting with you," the priest said to Teacher, "for we have much to discuss." He glanced at Shasta and I with his dour countenance.

Teacher nodded and said, "I'd be happy to speak with you."

"Let us retire to my chambers for a private discussion. This space is not the place for it."

"Indeed," Teacher said. "Lead the way."

The priest and the two elders walked toward us, then turned and proceeded down a side hallway. Teacher followed and motioned again for Shasta and me to come with him. Partway down the hallway, one of the elders saw us following and stopped, let Teacher pass, then held up his hand and spoke.

"You're not allowed back here."

"They're with me," Teacher said, addressing the high priest. "You have your trusted companions. I have mine."

"Women are not allowed outside of the nave," the priest said.

"Why not?" Teacher asked.

The priest clenched his jaw. "It is the tradition of the Church, and it has been that way since the beginning."

Teacher was quiet for a moment before speaking.

"Since the Perceiver? I believe you are mistaken. Perhaps when we get to your chambers you can point to his teaching that speaks to that. I would love the opportunity to further understand where that view comes from, because women were some of the founders of the Church. Meanwhile, could you make an exception for these two just this one time? I know you've made exceptions before."

The two elders turned and looked at the high priest, whose eyes widened while he swallowed, then they looked indignantly at Teacher. I suspected what Teacher was referring to, and I did my best to suppress expressing my surprise at his boldness and what he might be suggesting. Besides essentially calling the high priest of the Church a hypocrite, he implied worse.

After stewing on the comment for a few seconds, the priest said, "I will allow it this one time," and he turned and continued down the hall to the shock of the two elders.

We followed, and the elder who had initially stopped us allowed us to pass and fell in behind us, saying, "Don't touch anything."

Shasta and I looked at each other, and I could tell that she, too, was stifling a laugh.

I found it interesting that the elders seemed to be more surprised by the priest's allowance of Shasta and I to continue than by what Teacher had said. I assumed they would have heard by this time that Teacher always spoke the truth, so it seemed that they all already knew this information about women and the Church, as well as the priest taking women beyond the nave. The fact that the priest didn't immediately reject Teacher's statements spoke to that.

At the end of the hall, the high priest led us through a doorway on the right into a large room with high ceilings and religious paintings on the walls. He ambled over to sit behind a huge, wooden desk with decorative carvings on the corners and motioned for each of us to sit in one of the many luxuriant, velvet chairs in the room. Teacher sat in front of the desk, the elders sat to each side of the priest, and Shasta and I took chairs along the wall.

I hadn't noticed before, but Alexander and my father had followed us down the hallway and had entered the room. They stood by the door and declined to sit. I wondered if their presence was a condition of having the meeting.

Teacher glanced over at Shasta and me and said, "Why don't you bring your chairs closer to me?" to the horrified look of the elders. The priest's eye twitched but he mostly retained his composure. The men were clearly not used to seeing women as equals to men. Shasta and I stood up and moved our chairs so that we were now on either side of Teacher in front of the desk. I was enjoying how Teacher was challenging the patriarchal culture of the Church and how uncomfortable it seemed to make the priest and elders.

"Thank you for inviting us," Teacher said. "I've been looking forward to this."

"Welcome," the high priest said. "I understand you've been teaching out in the countryside."

Teacher nodded.

"So, what have you been teaching?"

"The truth."

Teacher said it so matter-of-factly that even I was caught off guard.

"Truth," the priest said, pausing. "And what is the truth as you see it?"

"I see truth the same as the Perceiver sees truth."

The priest shifted awkwardly in his seat. "Doesn't the truth depend upon one's perception?"

"Truth can indeed depend upon one's perception, but different perceptions are still governed by higher truths. A lower perception may appear to be the truth on one level yet be inconsistent with a higher truth when seen from a greater context. Do you not tailor your sermons to the understanding of your congregants? Certainly, you know more than they do, but you seek to frame it in a manner they can understand."

The priest didn't answer the question, which to me indicated that he agreed.

"So, what exactly is the truth that you teach?" he asked.

Teacher smiled. "I teach what the Perceiver taught. It is what this Church was built for, isn't it? To expound on the Perceiver's teachings?"

The priest nodded slowly. Teacher continued.

"Perhaps I can best illustrate it by asking a few questions."

Another nod, this time more hesitantly.

"Do you not have sayings like, 'Have faith in the Perceiver' and 'The Perceiver will save you'?"

The priest nodded.

"*How* will the Perceiver save people? *How* does 'faith in the Perceiver' help those in need?"

The priest said nothing at first, and Teacher let the ensuing silence grow uncomfortably. Finally, the priest spoke.

"Faith can move mountains. Faith built this cathedral. Faith can save people from temptations that lead them down a dark path."

"Ah, faith. I agree that faith can indeed be transformational. Why is faith in the Perceiver, specifically, necessary?"

"Who else are they going to have faith in?" the priest said. "As I'm sure you know, most people don't have the will to transform themselves on their own, so they need someone to follow, someone to look to for guidance. The Perceiver fulfills that purpose."

"People don't have the will to transform themselves on their own because they've never been taught." Teacher said. "They need a figurehead because they were never shown *how* to do it. This is what I teach, the simple truths that the Perceiver taught so that people have the tools for self-transformation."

"So, *you* want to be revered like the Perceiver is?"

"Absolutely not! That is the furthest thing from what I desire."

Teacher paused for a moment. When he spoke again, he did so slowly.

"Why use the Perceiver as an intermediary to the truth when everyone can experience the truth directly and change their lives on their own?"

"Because they can't handle it," the priest said.

"Ah, now where is *your* faith?"

Both men let the silence expand for a minute until the priest spoke again.

"The Church is a sanctuary for the masses. We provide guidance in matters of faith, and as such, play an important role in society. Even *if* people learned these ways you talk about, they would still need guidance."

"I agree. I'm not saying the Church doesn't have a role to play or isn't valuable to those who need guidance. I'm saying that when you strip away the hundreds of years of Church doctrine and canon, you're left with the simple teachings of the Perceiver. The people deserve *those* teachings. Don't tell them to follow the Church; empower them and teach them to live and see the world as the Perceiver did. The Church can be there for guidance but not to control their actions or beliefs."

I'm not sure the priest was used to being told what to do, as he sat unmoving with a slight scowl on his face. But something else was happening. I could feel the energy beyond his physical form shifting ever so slightly. There was an openness not previously present, almost like he wanted to agree with Teacher but his responsibilities with the Church forbade him from doing so. Or maybe I was only just now picking up on who he was beyond what he presented on the surface. Teacher continued.

"You ask me what the truth is as I see it. There is no truth as *I* see it; there is only truth, which is universal. Perspectives on it are but shadows compared to the light of truth itself that casts away any misconceptions that serve to bind us to those shadows. Truth is something that is experienced, not taught. It must be lived to be known, not viewed from the mental or emotional parts of our nature and twisted into convenient rationales to help us through our days.

"One may stand on the banks of a river and describe the river as wide and calm, but another on a different section of the river may see it as narrow and turbulent. Both are correct, from their own perspectives. And if someone navigates the river by boat or jumps into it and floats down it through all its stages, that person would have a different and perhaps more comprehensive understanding of the river. But do they know the truth of the river?"

Teacher paused. The priest sat motionless but looked like he was taking in Teacher's words and understanding them. I could feel his mind racing. Mine would be, too, if I was in his position and had to try to reconcile Teacher's lessons with my role in the Church and the Church's role within the Territories.

"So, what is the truth of the river?" Teacher continued. "We can view the river from all these different perspectives, and we can teach people *how* to view the river and how to begin to *understand* the river, but they will not truly *know* the river until they jump in and swim. And even then, until they *become* the river in its wholeness—as a single drop *and* as the entire river—and flow as it naturally flows, a full and complete knowing of the truth of the river will remain out of reach.

"I give people the understanding to *experience* the river for themselves. It is not up to me to guide them beyond bringing them to the water and teaching them how to swim. I cannot be the log they cling to as they float down the river, for that would merely sustain their dependence on that which is not of the river itself, and that only serves to prolong their struggles in learning the truth, as it obstructs the truth itself. To *become* the river, people need an understanding so they can dive in and swim and play and figure out their own path within the flow of the water. This is what I teach. It is not for me to guide them down the river but rather to guide them to trust and guide themselves."

The priest paused, gave a slight nod, then spoke.

"Have you not found that those you teach simply cannot guide themselves, that they need that log to cling to in order to experience the river?"

"Sometimes, but how does one learn to swim by clinging to a log? If a log is always provided and pointed to as necessary to experience the river, it will always be used."

I knew they were talking about far more than the river. Teacher was essentially challenging the Church's edicts as they related to teaching truth.

"Without the log, many drown," the high priest said. "Many need the log just to survive."

"It is impossible to drown in the truth," Teacher said slowly.

As he spoke, I felt him expand his wonderful energy so that it filled the room, something he often did during lectures and healings. In my experience, no one was immune to the bright, open feeling that seemed to vibrate every fiber of the physical bodies present. I observed the elders, and it appeared as if they were trying to contain their reactions to it. The priest, however, eyed Teacher coolly, barely moving a muscle. I was used to it so allowed it to flow over and through me easily. I assume Shasta did the same. Glancing back at my father, still standing by the door, I felt he was struggling like the elders to remain unruffled; his eyes were wide, his jaw clenched, and he shifted uncomfortably on his feet.

This often seemed to be the reactions when Teacher expanded himself like this, and it seemed like the more negative a person was or the more they had heavier thoughts and emotions, the more difficult it was for them to tolerate the energy and retain their composure. Teacher had talked about this to our small group privately at one point, saying that all he does is share of himself, but the effect is that his impossibly light energy encounters the denser energy of others and the resulting internal conflict can cause visible or inner shaking or other physical movement, as well as emotional reactions such as tears.

At that time, Teacher had said, "When a person's body and mind feel the purity of the truth, it resonates to that which is deeply within and calls forth perfection in them, which conflicts with who they *think* they are. The more entrenched they are in their beliefs about themselves and the world, the more difficulty they will have with it. But remember, everyone, whether they are aware of it or not, desires to rediscover this truth within, and this is one way for them to experience it at least briefly on their journey to wholly allowing and accepting it permanently."

"Is this like the healings you do?" I had asked.

"Yes," he had replied. "It is exactly that. It is healing the discordance that people unintentionally express physically, mentally, and emotionally."

I thought of his words during the profound silence we sat in. The elders shifted in their seats while the high priest looked from Teacher to me, Shasta, and then to my father and Alexander. With the priest's relative lack of reaction, I suspected he might have had some familiarity with the feeling, which surprised me. When he again glanced at me, I smiled at him, and he returned a half-smile. In that moment, he and I made a connection, a tenuous one at that, but a connection nonetheless. It felt like we now shared a certain level of understanding.

Teacher observed this and said to the priest, "I would like to speak with you alone if I may."

The priest nodded and looked at the elders on either side of him. They rose as Shasta and I rose, and the four of us filed out of the room. Standing in the hallway, I heard the priest say, "It's okay. I don't need you," and Alexander and my father emerged a few seconds later, closing the door behind them.

We all stood awkwardly outside the door for a moment before Shasta started walking down the hallway toward the nave, followed by the elders. Alexander looked at me, then at my father, and followed. This gave me a chance to linger behind and speak with my father.

"Are you okay," I asked him.

"I should be asking *you* that," he said. "I'm guessing you felt it, too?"

I nodded. "This is normal in my life now. I studied for many years to understand it and allow myself to integrate the energy of it, yet it still sometimes surprises me."

"I felt it before at one of his talks and felt a hint of it years ago when I first saw him in the city, but just now . . . wow. I don't know what to think."

"It's not about thinking," I said, "just allow it to wash over you and you'll take it in."

I paused, then asked, "Is mother going to come to Teacher's lecture today?"

He shook his head, his face expressing disappointment.

"She wants me to tell you that she's home if you want to see her."

I was disappointed, too, because after our first meeting since I had run away, I felt that I might not see her again for many years, if at all. Still, I held onto the sliver of hope that she might learn the lessons Teacher had said she was here to learn.

My father was beginning to tear up. "I'm so proud of you," he said, and he pulled me into a big hug and sobbed.

I realized his sobbing was likely at least partially due to Teacher's energy—really, his *own* internal energy that had been stirred up—which challenged his old, remaining, entrenched views that had heavier vibrations. I did my best to go into the same healing space we had just left, opening up and connecting the expression of the source within me to the same that was within him as we held each other.

It was a moment I could never have imagined a few months ago, and it closed a chapter from my past that I wasn't sure I would have ever moved beyond if not for the presence of Teacher in my life.

~

While Teacher had his private audience with the high priest, Shasta and I sat in the pews and waited. The two elders had disappeared down the corridor opposite the hallway we had emerged from, and Alexander and my father remained standing to the side of the nave. Most of the group that had come into the church with us still occupied the back pews.

Sitting in the quiet of the cathedral gave me the chance to experience it now as an adult. My previous visits when I was a child were family visits, usually at least once a month, and they were always so formal and seemed to occur more out of obligation than for reasons of faith. Now, however, looking up at the wooden sculpture of the Perceiver, I could feel a connection to what I always presumed real faith was.

The center of my chest opened, somewhat like the feeling when practicing the transit, healings, and other exercises, but it was more refined and less physical, a gentle expansion with a lightness like when Teacher expanded himself in the priest's chambers. Interestingly, I felt it only in relation to the Perceiver before me, his open arms inviting me into a direct connection with him rather than me enlarging the feeling to encompass others around me like Teacher seemed to do. I closed my eyes and sat immersed in that relationship, feeling as peaceful as ever and almost falling asleep in the beautiful, blessed landscape of visuals that danced before me.

I wasn't sure how long Teacher and the high priest met, perhaps an hour, but eventually they emerged from the hallway, which pulled me out of my reverie. The priest appeared lighter, his face brighter, and he walked with a less heavy step. He went over to Alexander and my father for a few words while Teacher walked up the aisle between the pews, looked at Shasta and me, and continued to the entrance of the cathedral. I took that to mean it was time to go, so Shasta and I rose and followed him out the large, wooden door.

Outside, the sun was shining brightly on about a dozen of our group that hadn't entered the cathedral. Teacher led the way down the steps, and Shasta, after saying something to Teacher, immediately walked around the corner and disappeared. I wondered where she was going as we waited for the rest of our friends to exit the church. Alexander, my father, and the other constables that were with us before also joined, and together we all began walking out of the plaza down the same street Shasta had taken, led by Alexander, my father, and Teacher. Although I didn't remember the way from my youth, I realized we were heading toward the marketplace.

As we walked, I eventually sidled up next to Teacher and gave him a look, wanting to know what he and the high priest had talked about. He glanced at me, laughed, and said, "It was nothing you haven't already learned. Well, one thing, perhaps. I told him that if the pillars of the Church contain any untruths, then it is not surprising that the Church will see a threat in those living the truth."

I walked a few paces before responding as my mind deciphered the sentence. "What did he say to that?"

"Nothing. In fact, he only asked a few questions throughout our time together. I did most of the talking."

"Since the Church was built on the foundation of the teachings of the Perceiver, how could there be any untruths?"

"When I said that, I wasn't talking about *those* pillars—the Perceiver and his teachings—I was talking about the pillars that make up the rest of the Church: the structure, the doctrine . . . the leadership." He glanced at me.

"Oh!" I said. "Did he understand?"

"Most certainly! He is navigating the fine line between the truth and that which seeks to hide the truth for its own purposes. One must be very intelligent, and shrewd, to be able to do that. He wouldn't be in his position if he didn't understand it. And I'm the only person who can say that to him because I am living from the truth, and he recognizes that."

I was glad to hear that the high priest could see Teacher for who he was, someone who had recognized and was embodying the truths that the Perceiver taught. I thought about the ease at which we had entered the city—with an escort no less!—and realized that the meeting with the high priest was probably set up to be an evaluation of Teacher to see whether or not he was truly a threat. He wasn't, of course, but something remained unsettled in the back of my mind as we continued down the street, and I wondered what we would encounter when we reached the marketplace.

~

The city looked different as we progressed, reminding me that I had seen it through the prism of my stature and understanding at the time, but I also recognized that lots of change could happen in a decade. Once we were close to the market, however, I smiled because I knew we would be passing by the antique shop, which was timeless in its appearance both inside and out, and I also looked forward to seeing the shopkeeper's familiar face.

When we turned the last corner and could see the market square with its shops and many vendors along the walls, it seemed as if I had never left. Like with my recent visit there, everything looked the same with its bustling activity of buyers and sellers haggling over goods. I glanced over at the antique shop and saw Kyna standing next to Quinn just outside the entrance, and I ran over and embraced her before realizing she was likely projecting herself from the safety of the village. Her strong, squeezing hug back, though, made me think that she was really there in person.

"Are you . . . here?" I asked.

She smiled and shook her head. "Someone has to keep an eye on the village while all of you are away."

Her remarkable talent at projecting herself continued to amaze me.

I nodded, turned to Quinn, and gave him a hug as well.

"It's good to see you again, Anna," he said. "I can't believe he's finally here."

"I can't believe we're all here," I said.

I rejoined the group as it began to spread out within the square and caught up to Teacher, who seemed headed to a particular vendor on the far wall. He approached a heavyset spice seller, who looked at him with confusion at first before crying out "Christopher!" and rushing forward from behind his cart to give Teacher a great, big hug.

Teacher embraced him back and said, "I recognized the Martel-shaped shadow on the wall behind you."

Both men released their grasp of each other and laughed.

"It's so good to see you, my friend!" Martel said. "It's been far too long." Stepping back, he said, "You seem . . . different."

"Oh, I am," Teacher said. "A little older, a little wiser."

"Ariana!" Martel yelled.

Ariana had come up behind me and was now standing next to Teacher. She and Martel embraced, and it looked like Martel's eyes were getting misty.

I now remembered that the manuscript I had read the day before I ran away from home so many years ago had these three characters—Christopher, Ariana, and Martel—and that they all had sold goods in the marketplace. Remembering the mystical Lucas character from that story as well, I glanced through the throngs of people, searching for a blind beggar, but didn't see him.

"I can't believe you've come back," Martel said to Teacher and Ariana. "Where have you been all these years?"

Teacher smiled, and I didn't know if he communicated the answer to Martel or not, but Martel's jaw dropped as he stepped back and said, "No! *You're* the teacher everyone's been talking about?"

Teacher nodded.

"You!?"

Teacher just looked at him with his crystal-clear eyes.

"Wow. Actually, for some reason, I'm not surprised. Your strange disappearance, then Ariana's, your obsession with the Wall . . . wait! Did you get to the other side?"

Teacher nodded again.

Martel slapped his forehead. "We have a lot of catching up to do! I want to hear everything."

"We'll catch up later, my friend," Teacher said. "I am happy to see you doing well. Right now, I must prepare for a talk here in the square, which will explain some things."

"Of course, of course," Martel said, backing up. "I look forward to it." He smiled lovingly at Teacher and said, "I can't believe it's really you."

Teacher smiled back and said, "It's always been me, and I am no different than you."

~

It was clear that Shasta had planned ahead for Teacher's lecture, as she had procured a number of wooden boxes that she and a few others helped set up at the end of the marketplace as a platform for Teacher to stand on. The curiosity of the onlookers and the rumors that had spread before we had arrived led people to pause their errands and look toward the impromptu stage. Some, like Martel, had heard that a teacher was coming. Others knew more about Teacher's lectures and had come to the square specifically to hear him. Among the crowd were some with crutches and what looked like injuries and ailments, likely hoping for what they must have heard were miraculous healings.

Even though I didn't expect to see my mother there, I scanned the crowd in case she had decided to attend but found no sign of her.

Teacher approached the platform as the crowd gathered in front of it. Suddenly, the loudspeaker on the corner by the antique shop squealed to life, and three rising tones blared across the market. Everyone but Teacher stopped what they were doing and looked up at the device, including me. I hadn't heard an announcement, or warning, since being in the Territories as an adolescent, but I remembered the same strange quiet in the background because everyone stopped talking when the tones started. I glanced at Teacher, who continued to the stage, stepped up onto it, and turned to face the loudspeaker.

Something I thought he normally would smile at, like he did with most things, instead left him with a clenched jaw and determined expression. He closed his eyes and waved his hand, and the loudspeaker crackled into silence just after the first word, "This," emerged from it.

Some faces in the crowd saw his gesture, and all others soon turned to the platform, as it stood out as the dominant focal point in the market. It seemed that many understood that Teacher might have been the cause of the unexpected stoppage of the announcement. Besides some gasps of surprise and a few whispers, the crowd remained silent and watched for what might come next.

Alexander and my father were standing up front but far to the right, looking like they were trying to blend in with the rest of the crowd near the vendors along the wall. With their uniforms, however, they clearly stood out. The other constables who were with us before were standing toward the back of the crowd, and I noticed a few other pairs of uniforms mingling about. They all had also paused when the announcement began before exchanging puzzled and concerned looks with each other when it stopped. I saw one constable look toward Alexander, who stood unmoving, and I assumed his lack of reaction told the other man to do nothing and to let things play out.

From my vantage point on the side, I also noticed that the high priest and the two elders from the cathedral, along with two constables, stood just around the corner and out of sight from most of the crowd. Their presence made it clear they had an interest in what was about to transpire.

Teacher stood on the platform and surveyed the hundreds in the crowd now looking at him. Once again, his natural ability to garner attention through strategic pauses held their focus, and I wondered during the silence if he was also reading the energy and attitudes of those before him. When he finally spoke, his voice was as clear and as powerful as I had ever heard.

"I want to thank the Territory Governors for announcing this lecture," he jested, giving a wry smile.

I stifled a chuckle as a smattering of nervous laughter swept through the crowd. Many looked at Alexander and my father, both of whom remained still, except for my father pursing his lips and swallowing.

"Whether you are here today," Teacher continued, "because you have heard me before and desire to hear more, have heard of my coming and are curious, or are simply out on this lovely afternoon doing your shopping, it is no accident; you are meant to hear what I have to say. As for myself, I am blessed to be here with you, and you all honor me with your presence."

The crowd was captivated, as I was when I first heard Teacher speak.

"Did you stop the announcement?" someone shouted, piercing Teacher's pause and causing all heads to turn toward the questioner. Teacher's eyes immediately found the speaker.

"Yeah," someone else said while others whispered their surprise at the interruption.

Teacher stared at the questioner. "Yes."

More murmurs spread among the crowd.

"Why?" the questioner asked.

"It was to be a warning, and it was not necessary."

"How do you know?"

Teacher paused, and I could tell it was one of those times he was going to try to communicate not just with words but with his energy, which was starting to hum in my body as it ramped up. Indeed, when he spoke, the current beneath his words left me vibrating.

"Because it was to be a warning about me," he said.

There was a collective inhale as the crowd gasped. If anyone wasn't paying close attention before, they were now. Even the stoic Alexander turned his head from looking forward at the multitudes to looking at Teacher. I wondered if Teacher had strayed from what might have been agreed to beforehand. He continued.

"There are some who fear what I have to say. That's okay. Fear is a normal human emotion to that which is different, and what is different can challenge the reliable, known routines of your lives. It can be frightening when confronted with something that tests your understanding of the world, and the more different an idea is, the more it will cause you to scurry back to perceived safety within the walls that hold the familiar. But note that just because something is familiar and feels safe doesn't mean that it is good for you, or the truth.

"Whether it is in how you think or how you act, routines and habits are like grooves worn in rock, and the deeper the grooves become, the more difficult it is to climb out of them. To adapt to a new way of thinking or acting—in essence, to create a new groove—is hard work, which many do not want to undertake. It is often more comfortable to stick with what you know, to curl up at the bottom of your deep, familiar grooves and look up at the steep walls towering above that seem impossible to climb. There, you can *wish* things were different, but you don't need to *do* anything to change your circumstances because your grooves are comfortable enough or, as the case may be, uncomfortable but *known*.

"But what you can't see from the bottom of your grooves is the verdant landscape above. You know very well the walls of your grooves and the valleys they have created but nothing beyond them. What if you could rise out of your grooves, see that lush landscape above, and choose what you want to create beyond the limits of your grooves? You would truly have the freedom you desire, because what is beyond those walls is infinite."

I looked around the crowd and could tell that most weren't getting the symbolic association with the Grand Wall. Some did, though, and those that did seemed enthralled. But since others had blank or confused looks on their faces, I guessed Teacher would soon recognize he was speaking a bit over people's heads. After a pause, he continued.

"I know most of you worship the Perceiver. Indeed, he is a good man to revere. I must ask, do you live as he did? Do you aspire to see what he saw, to perceive beyond the shadows of the world you live in? Do you wake up in the morning with the first thought being, 'What will I do today to be more like him?' No, you do not, and I will tell you why.

"You do not because you truly don't want to perceive outside your current routines, thinking, emotions, and beliefs—in other words, your static and entrenched grooves. The idea of change from what you are familiar with strikes fear in most of you, and not just a little apprehensive hesitation but a deep, visceral terror that renders you powerless when in its clutches.

"So, how do you begin to climb out of your old and limiting grooves and live as the Perceiver did in the free landscape above, seeing all the valleys but never again being stuck in them? The walls of your grooves are but a self-imposed prison that you are unaware you are living in, so the first thing is to open up to the *possibility* of change. It may *seem* frightening, but it is not. It is that your repeated habits have created a grooved resistance to change. Opening up to the idea that there is something else possible, something other than your current thinking or emotional reactions, is the first step.

"Second, simply *explore* that possibility. Find ways during your day to see the world differently than how you have seen it before and challenge yourselves to bring to your awareness any routine habits and reactions you might be engaging in without reflection. Successfully noticing an entrenched habit and *choosing* to try doing it—thinking about it, reacting to it—differently will provide you with the positive experience that *there is nothing to fear* in doing so. This is how it began for me, and I can tell you from experience that you can climb out of your old grooves if you but open to the possibilities and challenge yourselves to see the world differently in this way.

"As you have successful experiences along this path, you will begin to trust this new way of seeing—of being—more and more, which will help you take it in more deeply until a *knowing* that there is more has replaced your belief in limitations, your belief in your old, entrenched grooves. Then, you will be above the grooves, resting in the fertile landscape and ready to sow the seeds of what you truly desire.

"Following this way is the beginning of how to eliminate fears and difficulties from your life, and it will eventually bring you to a place where you can truly understand and *be* in the flow of the life before you. *This* is the way of the Perceiver, seeing beyond the limitations of the world you know so you can create and live in a world you desire, one of peace, love, and joy."

Teacher paused both his pacing and speaking while the crowd digested his words. Then he resumed both.

"The next time you feel a dramatic emotion or find yourself overthinking something to the extent that it gets in the way of finding peace, I want you to see that emotion or thought as a separate entity. Give it a shape, a color, a smell, a name. *See* it and *feel* it as separate from *who you are*, for *who you are* is decidedly *not* that. In fact, you are the opposite. You are not that emotion. You are not that maddening thought. You are beyond them, for you are the love and joy of the world made manifest, and those fearful thoughts and emotions cannot exist *in you*.

"So, here we have you," Teacher holds out one hand, "and your named entity that contains the thoughts and emotions that give rise to your fears," and he holds out his other hand. "They are different. They cannot occupy the same space. The entity is simply hitching a ride *on* you and directing your life as a rider directs a horse. Throw off the rider, for it is guiding you into aggravating circumstances and it will never stop. It will even try to convince you that the aggravating circumstances it has brought to you *require* its continued direction. No. You are the horse, free to run and roam in the light that you are. Toss aside the rider—the entity, the fears—to allow the horse to climb the steep walls of the old grooves to find the free landscape above and you will find your sight, the sight of the Perceiver."

Teacher stopped and looked out into his rapt audience. I could tell his energy, in addition to his words, were having an effect. Besides a few muffled sobs and shifting of feet, the crowd remained silent.

His speaking reminded me somewhat of sermons I had heard in the cathedral long ago, although those had more emotion attached to them. Teacher's lecture was different. It didn't sound like he was trying to convince people with emotion but rather was speaking truth to them with suggestions on how to proceed. But perhaps that was because I knew him and already understood the topic, even though the naming of the entity representing fears was new to me.

He continued after a long pause.

"The Perceiver saw these entities and chose to rise above them. I did the same. It is not easy. It will challenge you and you will likely fall backward after taking a step forward. However, if you are vigilant and continue to work on identifying and naming those pesky entities that seek to hold you back, you will make progress. And as you do this, the world will open up before you and give you what you *truly* desire, which is freedom from them, and that leads to the freedom that the Perceiver lived, the freedom that I live.

"I know you have heard that the teachings of the Ancients are dangerous. That is not true. I have come here to tell you that the wisdom of the Perceiver is the wisdom of the Ancients. The Ancients were the original Perceivers. To live like the Perceiver is to live like the Ancients, to live like me. And because I am the same as you, you can be just like me, just like the Ancients, just like the Perceiver."

Internally, my jaw dropped. I couldn't believe he had spoken so openly about the Ancients to such a new crowd and with the number of constables present. I wondered if he was intentionally looking for trouble.

The crowd murmurs quickly grew louder, with many exchanging looks of surprise. I doubt anyone had said anything so apparently blasphemous in public in the Territories before, and to equate the teachings of the Ancients to the Perceiver was sure to get the attention of the authorities. Sure enough, although Alexander didn't outwardly show any emotion, I felt his agitation through his stiffened appearance. My father, too, showed his surprise, staring at Teacher with his mouth open. I wondered if Teacher's words put the constables in an untenable position.

Alexander took a deep breath and approached the platform. Stepping up onto it, he whispered a few words to Teacher. The crowd was buzzing more loudly now, and what I heard was a combination of praise for the lesson contrasted with talk of blasphemy.

After Alexander finished saying something to Teacher, Teacher said loudly, "Remember that you, too, can live as the Perceiver lived, free from the limitations of this world. Follow this way, and you will have true freedom. I will see you again soon." And he stepped off the stage.

We, who had come so far with him, followed him as he slowly strolled out of the marketplace amid the increasing volume of chatter and movement as some jostled for position to reach out to touch him. The constables, including Alexander and my father, at that point seemed only concerned with managing the crowd and making sure its actions didn't get out of hand, although I liked to think they were there to protect Teacher from any harassment.

From the midst of the crowd, I heard someone yell, "Are you the Perceiver?" A few shouted "Blasphemer!" A woman nearby cried out, "Please, heal my son!" but Teacher had already walked by. I tried not to look at her as I passed, but just one quick glance provided enough of a picture of desperation that it stuck with me for the rest of the day.

The city was not going to be easy.

~

We stayed out in the countryside like we had done so many times before, the constables deserting us once we were safely outside the city. I had hugged my father goodbye, and he had said, "Anna, please be careful. I don't know what he was thinking, but I'm sure your welcome will not be as accepted next time."

"I understand," I said, "but what did you think of it, the talk? You've heard him several times now."

My father paused, then said, "This time was different. He certainly is an interesting man, even special, but he cannot so openly flaunt the laws without repercussions."

"I worry about that, too. Are you going to try his exercise with the fears and seeing them as a separate entity from you?"

"One thing at a time. Right now, I just want to make sure you stay safe."

"Can you come with us?"

He shook his head. "No, I've been told to stay in the city."

"Why?"

"Orders."

"Have you ever thought about disobeying orders?"

As soon as I asked, I realized I shouldn't have, as my father stared at me like he didn't understand the question. I quickly followed up, "It's okay. I'll be safe with our group."

We hugged again and said our goodbyes, and my father rejoined the constables waiting for him up the road toward the city while I caught up to Teacher and his followers.

We continued south past the blacksmith workshops with Teacher leading the way. It seemed he had a particular destination in mind. Sure enough, after another thirty minutes or so, we turned onto a side road and soon came upon a small farmhouse with fields of apple trees, blueberry bushes, and vegetable gardens in various states of care. Several of Teacher's followers, who I recognized but hadn't seen in weeks, greeted us. It seemed they had been working in the fields and gardens, as they were covered in dirt and there were piles of vegetables and baskets of apples by the covered porch.

I came to learn that this was the farmhouse Teacher had grown up in. It had been in his family for generations, and before he had left the Territories, he used to sell what was grown on the land in the marketplace. Apparently, once he had gone, it had been taken over by a neighboring landowner with ties to the government who continued cultivating and selling the crops. This landowner had been to several of Teacher's talks over the past months and had invited him to come back to the land with his followers. I was told the landowner's generosity was due to having been greatly moved by Teacher's lessons, and he wanted to help in any way he could. I found that allowing Teacher to come back to his ancestral home a poignant gesture of goodwill and perhaps a good omen for what lay ahead.

Our group settled on the land, with everyone helping in the fields and orchards during the day and at night finding sleeping accommodations in the farmhouse, storage shed, and fields. Teacher helped as well, instructing us on his old farming ways that he had used in his earlier life. He didn't do any public teaching during these days, seemingly wanting to take a break from the chaotic ending of his talk in the city. I assumed he was allowing time to pass for things to settle down so there would be less resistance next time. He did, however, take questions and talk some in the evenings.

No constables or new followers came by during this time, which surprised me. I thought the constables would want to keep an eye on him after his last talk, but the land we occupied remained relatively peaceful and uninterrupted by visitors, which I was thankful for. It gave all of us a chance to collectively breathe after the distracting pace of travel and gatherings over the past few months.

Teacher's casual, evening talks took place from the porch of the farmhouse where he liked to sit as the sun went down. Ariana, a few others, and I usually sat on the porch with him, while others sat on the grass at the bottom of the steps or nearby where they could hear the discussion.

It was an intimate time, for we all knew each other fairly well at that point, having traveled and heard the same lessons together, at least most of us. Besides living a simple life off the land during this interval at the farm, the evening sessions provided occasions for us to get answers to any questions we might have had about all that Teacher had taught us.

One evening, I was sitting on the porch next to Teacher, watching the late-day sun slowly descend in the sky above the West Wall, when someone asked Teacher to talk about his life before he had awakened to the truth.

"I was like everyone else," he began, "full of hopes and fears and all that creates and sustains what binds us to the world of appearances. In practical terms, I was a farmer, working the land to serve my role within the only society I knew, but I was also very curious. I spent many evenings here on this porch, unable to let go of the questions that plagued me and incessantly contemplating that which I did not understand, which led me to who I am now. I will not tell you those questions, for you have your own to consider, many of which have brought you to this place with me. Each of you carry unique experiences and ways of thinking and feeling to the pathway before you, and it is not for me to color them with *my* past experiences. I can teach you what I have learned, but to describe anything further about my past would cause many of you to try to replicate it, and you each have your own path to take.

"This is why the Territory Governors feel threatened, because this concept of walking your own path is directly opposed to how they operate, which is to dictate to the citizens that there is only one way to live: *their* way. They fear empowering people because where would that leave them? With no power, of course, which is the reason for their existence in the first place."

"What about the high priest?" I asked. "Is he like the Governors?"

"No, he is not. He has the difficult job of balancing the existing dogma of the Church, the desires of the Governors to use the Church to influence the masses, and the sacred teachings, which he, for the most part, understands, at least intellectually. He has not yet had an experience, however, where he *feels* those lessons with every fiber of his being."

"Will he?" I asked.

Teacher closed his eyes for a moment. When he opened them, he said, "Not in this lifetime. He will carry his acquired wisdom over to his next life, where he will struggle with it as others do. I think it will take . . ."—he paused for a few seconds, again with his eyes closed—". . . three or four more lifetimes for him."

"What?" Someone sitting on the grass said. "That long? Even if he already understands a lot of it?"

"There's a reason I don't talk much about past lives or future lives," Teacher said, "and your reaction is one of those reasons. Focusing on where you are in your growth in relation to multiple lifetimes can be distracting to being in the moment and learning the lessons presented by your current experiences. I say that because you have brought upon yourselves many experiences in this lifetime that repeat the same lessons from previous lives. The circumstances are often different, and the people in your interactions, of course, are different—although you may share interactions with those you've been with in past lives—but the *lessons* are similar because you didn't learn from them when given the opportunity previously. You are here now experiencing many of those lessons again, like repeating a year in school because you didn't fully take in what was presented to you to learn."

He looked at me. "Anna, can I use you as an example?"

I nodded, curious about what would be revealed.

"In a recent past life, Anna worked as a domestic in a wealthy family's home where she cooked, cleaned, and took care of other mundane tasks in the household. In addition to routine tasks, she was at the beck and call of the man and woman of the house to help them with whatever they needed at any time. She did this without fail, even though she yearned for something different, something more exciting. In the little spare time she had, she read books, all sorts of books, as she had been graced with loving parents who had insisted she learn to read as a child, which was less common as it is today. She often thought about writing her own stories, but she needed the income from the work she was doing to help raise her family. In addition, she knew that books written by women were quite rare and not successful, so she thought it would be pointless to even try. Thus, not only did she have no time to write, but her will to write was smothered by this self-defeating attitude.

"In that lifetime, her constitution was, shall I say, a bit meeker," he smiled at me, and I chuckled, "so she spent most of her life raising a family and working and never getting to writing, and she passed away fairly young, still of child-bearing age. So, what lesson or lessons did she not learn? What lesson or lessons might she need to repeat in this lifetime?"

No one, including me, answered. Teacher looked at me, and I shrugged.

"She never spoke up for herself," Teacher said. "She gave herself up to others' needs—her employer's, her husband's, her family's—well before her own. That is admirable, and she raised a loving family, but she had desires for a different life and her sacrifice for others hindered that. So, she decided to come back into this particular life to experience several things.

"One, she was born into a very controlling and at times unsafe household, which limited her personal expression all throughout childhood. Two reasons for this are that she wanted to experience the opposite kind of upbringing she had had in the previous lifetime with the loving parents, and she wanted to finally learn the lesson about listening to the inner desire to express what is within. Her family upbringing gave her both, for she needed to be caged more tightly to be able to find the strength to break the bars of the cage. Her sharp mind and strength of will have been serving her well this time around.

"Two," he looked at me again, "there is something she has wanted to do for a while and has finally started, but she desires to do more."

I looked back at him, puzzled, not sure what he was referring to.

"What has been on your mind these past few years, what you've been doing but haven't told anyone about?"

I looked up, searching my brain for an answer. It took a few seconds before it hit me. I smiled and decided it would be okay to share my secret with the group given the context. "I've been writing," I said.

The group chuckled.

"Indeed," Teacher said. "You retain the unfulfilled desire for self-expression from that past life, and before you started recently it had bothered you that you hadn't pursued it. I can safely tell you that soon you will feel compelled to explore it further. In fact, the world needs to hear what you have to say."

He was staring at me, conveying something beyond his words, but I couldn't quite discern it. He looked back at the group on the grass after a few seconds.

"Any questions?"

Someone spoke up. "You said she decided to experience an unsafe household. First, we decide? We have control over what we come back to? And second, why would anyone *choose* to come back to that kind of environment?"

"To the first question, yes, you have a choice in what you can experience in the next lifetime. To the second, you sometimes want to experience the opposite of what you've already experienced, as it helps you understand the other point of view by being *in* it. This often occurs due to a perceived need to exact revenge or pay someone back with the same energy they brought to you previously, like if someone kills you in one lifetime, then you feel you have to kill them in the next. Note that I said *perceived* need. We don't *need* to go through something like that kind of payback if we learn the lessons that the first event brought. In Anna's case, she saw—before coming into this form—her potential family circumstances as an opportunity to build the strength and resilience she would need to travel outside the Grand Wall and do what she has done, and what she will do. She would not be with us today if she hadn't had these experiences.

"In relation to multiple lives, I'd like to add that many people get enamored with the idea that they were important or had wealth or power in a previous life. This knowledge can come about through receiving a past-life reading from a fortune teller." He paused. "Not one of the ones in the marketplace or central plaza, but there are some genuinely good ones around."

The group chuckled. I thought of Promeus, who could see ahead but would probably cringe at being called a fortune teller.

"Getting information from someone who can see into the past doesn't matter unless it helps point to a missed lesson or a pattern of behavior that is repeating once again in this lifetime. It can arm you with the information to break the pattern and finally learn what you might have overlooked previously.

Whether you were a king, queen, farmer, healer, blacksmith, shopkeeper, vagrant, or all of them . . . *that* doesn't matter, only the lessons that stemmed from what you experienced during those lives."

Someone asked, "How do we make sure we learn the lessons now so we don't have to repeat them later or in another lifetime?"

"Follow my teachings. *Live* them. Be present. See beyond appearances. Understand that everyone struggles with learning and moving forward, so be kind and loving to all, *especially yourselves*. Recognize that *you always* have a choice, in every situation, to learn and grow and rise above the insignificant mental and emotional turmoil of the world, for they are like drops of water in a never-ending river. And one day, you will perceive that *everything* you see in this world—from physical objects, to societal rules, to the people in your life, to your many, many experiences, including everything from your past lives— are also like drops in a river that flows endlessly. And the one inescapable outcome you will find, what everyone is striving toward whether they know it or not, is the recognition that you are one with all things—with each other and with everything around you—from now into the distant past and forward into eternity, and you will realize that everything is in a constant state of transformation, working its way back to the perfection that is the source inherent in all creation. You will find that the one constant that animates the world and connects all things in oneness is love. *That* is what you must live, being in the oneness that is love, and the way to do that is to practice it, even in the most difficult of circumstances, *especially* in the most difficult of circumstances, for that is what the world needs, and that is what will change the world, and your lives, for the better."

The group, including me, sat mesmerized, taking in Teacher's words and the glorious, blessed energy that flowed from them and from him. I could feel myself opening beyond what I normally experienced in my contemplation, transit, and slow dance practices, a more gentle, peaceful, and loving presence that enveloped me in the nurturing embrace of that which held all creation. And I couldn't stop smiling at the feeling of love that surrounded us all.

~

While at the farmstead, I had begun a habit of taking an early morning walk up the hill behind the house past several gravestones by an old basswood tree. I liked that time because few were stirring and the busy energies of the day hadn't yet risen to taint the peace of dawn. There was a large rock I sat on where I could view the fields and orchards below as the sun began to rise over the East Wall. It was my own little sanctuary from being around people most of the time.

One morning, however, was different. Teacher was already sitting on my familiar rock when I climbed the hill. I said nothing and sat down beside him. He seemed different. There was a heaviness about him that I had never felt before. We sat in silence for a few minutes before he spoke.

"Anna, it's time."

I looked at him in the shadowy light, and the heaviness in the air leapt down my throat to the pit of my stomach. I swallowed it, knowing he was talking about the prophecy. My fated role was at hand.

He looked at me. "I need to ask you to do something for me. It is the last thing I will ever ask of you."

I couldn't speak. What had been years in the making, what I apparently had been preparing for since I had first arrived in the village, was upon me. The moment felt as if the world was on my shoulders. I looked away from him and stared down the hill, trying to anchor my focus on the large tree.

"Something is going to happen that will affect everyone, and you are a part of it." He paused, and I found my voice and interrupted him.

"Whatever you ask, I'll do it," I said. I was ready. I would fulfill my role as the prophecy foretold.

"Oh, Anna, I appreciate your enthusiasm, but I need you to understand some things before you answer."

"Okay."

"The government is going to arrest me for speaking out against them, and . . . they will sentence me to death."

I snapped my head around and looked into his eyes. They were clear, but behind them I could feel his pain in telling me, not *his* pain but rather the pain that he knew I would feel.

"No!" I cried out and leaned over to hug him. He embraced me back, and I started to sob. Despite my emotions, I felt like I knew this was coming but had buried any thoughts or signs of it. Now, everything rushed back as my mind tried to make sense of it.

"Do you recall how I told you to remember the lessons, to remember your training? You've spent your whole life preparing for this."

I nodded on his shoulder through my tears. He was right, as always, and I knew it.

"You have a choice. You can do what I ask or not, but you need to understand the ramifications of your decision. I'd like to explain both options to you before you decide."

I finally released him from my grasp and nodded again.

With a glimpse of mental clarity amid the swirling thoughts and emotions, I asked, "But how can I have a choice if it's in the prophecy?"

He smiled. "Prophecies can sometimes be mistaken if there's a focus on something that isn't the primary objective. But that doesn't matter. You *always* have a choice."

"If my actions will help you, then I'll do whatever you ask," I said. If he was going to die for the cause, I would willingly join him.

"I need to fully explain it before you decide."

I nodded. "Okay." My tears were slowing, and I was feeling brave and ready for anything, although my body still felt shaky on the inside.

"You are the only one of my many followers with the understanding, the intelligence, the strength, and the training to be able to handle this, and I want you to fully understand the consequences that will fall upon you. My request is simple: I want you to go into the city and tell your father where we are."

I looked at him. That was it? It did seem simple, despite the likely deadly outcome for him.

"Don't they already know?" I asked. I assumed that after his talk in the marketplace, they would have been keeping an eye on him and the rest of us.

"They have an idea, yes, but you telling your father will trigger a series of events that need to occur. This will result in my death, which is necessary for the long-term impact of my teachings. Unless people witness the drama and conflict of my physical passing, they will continue to exist in the prisons of their own making. I cannot let that stand, so I need to reset the world so that the truth and freedom I know is accessible to everyone.

"Remember my talk about duality? The problem here is that as much as the teachings can stand on their own—encouraging people to rise *above* duality—people need that duality to understand and integrate the lessons into their lives before they can rise above it. They don't have the background, intelligence, and experience to comprehend the teachings like you do. Thus, they need a counterpoint to me."

"What do you mean?" I asked.

He sighed, and I felt a sadness in him.

"If I am to be held up on a pedestal like the Perceiver, then people need someone to serve the opposite role—that of betrayer, fiend, demon—so they can point to them and say, 'Not that!' They need someone to be a vessel for all their negative thoughts and emotions, for only when they package those harmful thoughts and emotions in a container can they begin to be open to the light. Not always, but it is most often the case."

He paused, and I was beginning to understand the heaviness I had swallowed.

"And *I* am to play that role?" I asked, my voice quivering.

"Only if you choose to. Without someone in that role, my teachings will fade over time. However, if you do choose to play the part, know that you will go down in history as the person who betrayed me and was instrumental in causing my death."

"But that's not true!" I shouted.

His voice remained exceedingly calm. "I know, but that is what people will believe, because they need to. You will be the symbol of their own darkness, which they need to see made manifest before eventually seeing it in themselves. Only then can they begin to transform those shadows to reveal the light within."

He turned and put his hands on my shoulders. "And you will forever be associated with the evil of mankind because of it. Your name will be dragged through the mud for generations to come."

I looked at his beautiful face that would soon no longer be of this world, and it exuded the profound peace that I knew he always carried, a peace we all carried but didn't have the understanding or courage to *live* as he did. I began to sob again.

"I cannot ask anyone other than you to do this, for no one else has the strength to handle it, let alone understand it."

I found my voice. "What will you do to 'reset the world'?" I wanted to know what I would be sacrificing for.

His hands still on my shoulders, he said, "I will destroy the Wall . . . for everyone."

And I instantly knew what he meant. The contrast of my life in the city as a child and my experiences outside the Territories made me the perfect candidate for this role. Who else could understand what was needed if not having lived in both? And this wasn't just about destroying the Grand Wall that imprisoned so many; it was about so much more, about breaking down the barriers to perceiving the *whole* world, not just each of our small places in it. His talk in the city said as much, and my time in the village, not to mention Teacher's lessons, had given me the gift of understanding that.

Teacher's role was to break down walls so that others could learn what he did, what the Perceiver did, and what I, to a far lesser extent, did as well, so they could walk the same path to the light within that all his teachings pointed to. My role was to be the entity to blame and curse when they strayed from that path.

"I understand," I said slowly, feeling a sudden sense of calm.

"Do not give me an answer now," he said. "Think about it, and we will speak again. Meanwhile, this must stay between us."

He removed his hands from my shoulders and stood up.

"And I meant it before about the writing. You have much to say about your experiences, and many will learn considerably from them."

I nodded. When he had mentioned writing before, I had felt a flame light up in my chest, sparked by his words on the tinder I had apparently built across lifetimes.

And with that, he walked down the hill, leaving me sitting on the rock contemplating my fate as the sun continued to rise over the East Wall.

Anna

Jillian left early the next morning, leaving Anna alone to continue her writing. A few hours later, there was a knock on her door. She rose to answer it, and there stood Shasta, who immediately stepped in and gave Anna a big hug.

Anna felt an intense sadness with the embrace. Quickly realizing that it wasn't hers, she took a step back and looked at Shasta, who appeared to be on the verge of tears.

"What?" Anna asked, fearing the worst.

"Promeus," Shasta said, her voice cracking.

Anna didn't move or say anything. She just stared at Shasta, not in shock but because Anna was running through Promeus's last, private words to her, knowing that this had been fated to happen around this time. Anna embraced Shasta again, and Shasta began sobbing. Anna felt sad but was not visibly emotional as she normally would have been if she hadn't been forewarned that this was coming.

Shasta let Anna go and walked inside, one hand over her eyes. Anna closed the door, joined her at the table, and they both sat down. Shasta looked up at Anna, having composed herself some after a deep breath.

"I was with him when it happened," she said, "and before he passed, he had the grandest smile I had ever seen."

Anna smiled deeply, knowing that he must have gotten a sense of what was beyond while still here.

"His last words were for you," she continued. "He said to tell you, 'Remember, child, that even that which is foretold can change.' He said to tell you those exact words."

Anna looked down for a moment, searching her mind for any meaning besides the obvious, which she had learned from Teacher, that we always have a choice. Perhaps Promeus hadn't known that Anna knew that, or perhaps there was something else there, something he might have been trying to tell her.

"Thank you," Anna said, looking up.

"Why do you think he wanted you to hear that?" Shasta asked.

"Not sure. I'll have to think about it. I'm glad that at least he was here long enough to experience some of Teacher's lessons."

Shasta nodded, then looked at Anna with her evaluating eyes.

"What are you not telling me?" she asked.

Anna said nothing and just looked back at her.

"You knew," Shasta said after a moment. "You knew his time here was coming to an end."

Anna nodded slowly. "He told me in our last, private conversation a few days ago. He said he had never been able to see beyond this point in time."

"And by extension . . ." Shasta began but stopped. "But that's not right. That ability is not limited to only the person's lifetime. They should be able to see beyond their time of passing regardless, unless . . ." She trailed off.

"Unless what?"

"Well, unless he was so focused on the prophecy that he couldn't see beyond it. Remember, he had spent his entire life preparing for it, so maybe he didn't need to see beyond it because he didn't want to, and that created some kind of block."

"That makes sense," Anna said. "You said he was smiling at the end?"

"Yes."

Anna was beginning to feel something wash over her, a distant, abstract comprehension of what his last words might mean.

"I think he was finally able to see more," she said, "and he liked what he saw."

She could feel that his presence at the end was free from any boundaries, but there was something else there as well that she couldn't quite wrap her head around.

Shasta nodded. "I think you're right. I wish you could have been there to see that smile."

"Me too," Anna said. "He did have a good smile."

"He had a great smile."

"I can feel it like he's here with us."

Anna and Shasta spent the next hour talking about their wonderful friend.

~

After Shasta left, Anna sat in contemplation to try to better understand Promeus's last words for her. With her eyes closed, she fell deeply into the practice, feeling his wise presence in the room communicating to her on a level she hadn't felt before.

Slowly, the previously abstract comprehension began to solidify into a knowingness in her core, and when the understanding reached her awareness, she was jolted back to her surroundings by feeling an enormous weight being lifted off her shoulders.

And when she opened her eyes, she knew what his last words meant.

Transformations

I didn't speak to Teacher for days. In fact, I spent as much time as I could away from everyone else at the farmstead, preferring to be alone with my thoughts and feelings as I contemplated Teacher's upcoming death and my role in making it happen. I disappeared for hours at a time, sitting at the far edge of the apple orchard, walking the nearby roads, and wandering the adjacent fields while considering his request. I even avoided Teacher and his evening talks, instead finding my spot on the rock on the hill where I could view the happenings at the farmhouse from afar.

At first, the idea that my name would be associated with the negativity in the world didn't bother me that much. I was more concerned with losing my friend, mentor, teacher, and the perfect, shining example of what was possible for everyone. Eventually, though, the significance of the symbolism of what my lasting role would be settled in me like a badly-digested meal, which left me on the edge of nausea much of the time.

Three days later, as I made my way up the hill early in the morning, I saw Teacher sitting on the rock where we had had our last conversation. He seemed to know that my ruminating had brought forth questions I needed answers to. I sat next to him, and we looked at each other. For some reason, I laughed, probably to help release the stress I had been under since our previous talk.

"Tell me more," I said, "about what will happen if I do as you ask." I needed to ground myself by knowing the details of the outcomes of my action.

"You will find your father in the city and tell him where we are. He will tell Alexander, who will gather the constables and come to the farm to arrest me for subversion. No one here is to resist my detainment in any way."

He paused, then added, "Alexander comprehends my teachings far more than anyone realizes, and he, like the high priest, also understands the politics of the time and what must be done. This is why I have confided in him, just as I have confided in you. Do not blame him, for he, too, is fulfilling a special role."

I had always found Alexander difficult to read, so I was surprised to hear of his understanding of the lessons. Then again, Teacher had been talking with him over these past few months for a reason.

"After my arrest, you and Shasta must do your best to convince the others to leave immediately to go back to their villages, whether inside or outside the Wall. Some will refuse, as is their choice. I will inform Shasta of this before the constables come. She has an awareness that something significant will be happening soon." He smiled. "Your solitude has not gone unnoticed."

I nodded. "I think she's noticing more than that."

"Yes, many are feeling the solemn weight of the change that is coming. It has put them into a deeper reflective state."

Even with my own relative seclusion from others, I had noticed others also spending more time alone and in reflection, as well as sitting in contemplation for extended periods of time.

"Once you are back in the village, I will visit you."

"How?" I said, then realized he probably would project himself to me like Kyna did to get into the Territories. I felt some comfort in knowing I would see him again after his arrest.

He didn't answer, and I didn't press it.

"Everything else will proceed as necessary," he said. "You don't need to know the details."

"Of your death," I said, annoyed.

"Or of what happens next."

"You said I have a choice," I said, "but that means that you have one, too. You can choose a different path. You don't have to die."

"What is eternal cannot die."

"Yes, that's what you've taught us, but I'm talking about your physical body. You don't *need* to do this." I didn't want to come across as imploring but probably did.

"I have thought long and hard about this, and it is the best way to make a statement that will resonate across generations. *That* is what is most important. In comparison, my body means nothing. I would not have requested you to do what I've asked without knowing the extent of the long-term beneficial effects for mankind. We are in this together, you and I, playing our roles in these transitory physical forms and personalities on the road to awakening the world to the truth. I know what I must do and have made my choice. I don't like the choice before you, but it is not my place to interfere with it, only to present it to you like the choice I have been given. And whatever you choose, know that the love I have for you is boundless."

I thought about asking why he wouldn't resist or fight back against what would clearly be a terrible decision by the Territory Governors, but the answer was obvious. He knew exactly what he was doing, and the repercussions of his actions—my actions—were crystal clear to him and beyond my full understanding. I had no doubt that he could avoid his arrest and death if he wanted to, but he had made his choice.

"You have asked something of me," I said, "so I would like to ask something of you."

He looked at me with his crystal-clear eyes.

"I would like you to reconsider your decision," I said. "That is all. If you do that, if you think about all that has led you to knowing that this is what you want to do and you come to the same decision, I will do what you have asked of me."

He nodded and smiled, and I could feel our connection as strong as ever.

"I will do as you ask and reconsider my choice," he said, and he leaned over and pulled me into his arms. Then he squeezed my hand, stood up, and proceeded to walk down the hill, leaving me once again alone with my thoughts.

~

We met a few more times over the ensuing days by the rock at the top of the hill early in the morning. We didn't speak much, as there wasn't much to say. Instead, most of our time was simply sitting together in that shared space. The mental and emotional turmoil I had experienced when we had first talked about his request and its repercussions gave way to a strange sort of peace over these days, one that cradled me in arms of sadness that seemed to whisper that it would all be okay, whatever I decided. Deep down I knew, however, despite my hesitations, what my answer would be.

I was slowly coming to understand Teacher's perspective and, dare I say, perceiving the circumstances in question the way he did. It was fascinating to witness myself going from my initial emotional reaction, to logically arguing against and then considering the request, to the peaceful feeling of inevitability.

Once that feeling settled upon me, I realized that this, too, contained a lesson. In fulfilling my prophesized role, I would be contributing to the benefit of mankind, and it would only be in others' perceptions where I would be cursed forever. I, the Anna in the flesh, was so much more than this body, this life, these circumstances, and the insignificant misunderstandings of others.

I had spent a decade studying and practicing for just this moment. Teacher knew it, and those who prophesized my role somehow knew it, too. The perfection in which my knowledge and personality fit what the situation demanded was no accident. As Teacher had said, the role could not be played by anyone else. No, it had to be me.

The last time we met together on the rock, I looked at him after we had sat together and watched the sun rise over the East Wall. He turned his head to look at me, and we both knew. The moment was upon us. Even with knowing that what I was doing was the right thing, an incomprehensible sadness swept through me with the knowledge of what was going to happen—to him, to me, to our legacies. I broke our gaze, stood up, and began walking down the hill to make my way into the city, not even able to embrace him or grab his hand for one last touch.

~

I walked up the southern road toward the city with my mind clear but with a heavy heart. This was what it had to be, I told myself.

The deed itself, the action that would consign me to being vilified for generations, was so improbably brief and simple compared to what I knew the resulting effect would be that I questioned for hours whether that was all I needed to do.

I had gone to the Department of Enforcement of Government Operations, the headquarters of the constabulary, and before I even entered, Alexander came outside and wordlessly greeted me with a nod. I asked him where my father was, and he went back inside to fetch him, but not before he and I shared a knowing glance that confirmed to me that he knew exactly what was going to happen, from what I would tell my father all the way through to Teacher's death. If so, that would've made him, me, and Teacher the only ones who knew the truth, as I was determined to keep Teacher's confidence.

My father emerged from the building, and we embraced.

"How are you?" he asked. I must have still carried some emotional remnants of our relationship from over a decade ago because I found myself a bit surprised at his seemingly genuine interest.

"I'm okay," I said. "I need to tell you something."

He leaned in.

"I need to tell you where we're staying."

"Okay."

I gave him directions down the southern road, past the blacksmiths' forges, and onward to the specific farmhouse off the main road where our group was staying.

He listened carefully, saying nothing.

"You got it?" I asked. I wanted to make sure I had done my job.

He nodded. "Anna . . ." he began but stopped as Alexander emerged again from the building and joined us.

"Thank you," I said and turned and walked away. I could feel my emotions rising and I didn't want the two constables to witness them. Before I turned the corner out of sight of them, I looked back, and my father was telling Alexander something, and Alexander was looking down the street at me. I thought his expression might have held a bit of sadness in it.

I scooted around the corner and burst into tears. I had done it, fulfilled my role as prophesized, and now I had to live with the consequences, the loss of my friend and mentor. At that moment, I was not thinking about the resulting impact on me or my legacy at all.

I composed myself after a few minutes and decided to head to the marketplace. I needed some time before going back to the farm and felt that being among regular people would be oddly comforting.

On the way there, I allowed myself to get lost in the sights, sounds, and smells of the city, something I didn't do when our group walked the same path from the cathedral a few weeks ago. Despite noticing some changes in the city that time, this time I perceived far more, feeling the different rhythms of the flow of people and commerce beyond what the buildings and shops presented, and it felt as if the city were like a child I hadn't seen in years and it had noticeably grown up.

It was strange to be past what seemed to be the primary reason of my existence. With the knowledge I held, both of what would happen to Teacher and the wisdom and practices of the teachings, I felt I knew more than everyone I passed, yet at the same time I was simply one of them, making my way down the street as they did. The emotions I had been experiencing dissipated, and I slowly fell into a profound sense of peace, likely because what had been a primary source of stress over the years was now behind me. I realized that everything else I did from this day forward would pale in comparison.

On my walk, on a few poles where the loudspeakers hung, there were government workers looking like they were trying to fix the speakers. I overheard one complaining about how he couldn't figure out why they weren't working.

Turning the corner to the market, I instinctively went directly to the antique shop and entered. The bell above the door rang, and the shopkeeper looked up from behind the counter and smiled.

"Anna! So lovely for you to come by again!" Quinn said.

"Good to see you, too," I said. "I was in the neighborhood."

He came out from behind the counter and gave me a hug.

"How is Teacher? We haven't heard anything since he spoke here, although people are talking."

I looked around the shop to see if anyone else was there, but we were alone.

"What are they saying?" I asked.

"There seems to be two sides to it: one, that he's teaching the truth and that it will be the downfall of the Governors, and two, that he's preparing to lead a revolution, which will be the downfall of the Governors."

I couldn't help but laugh. "So, either way, it sounds like the Governors are in trouble."

He smiled.

"And a revolution?" I added. "Perhaps not the kind of revolution they think."

He winked at me. "I agree."

I began wandering the aisles as I had done as a child, visually perusing the vintage items, some of which were probably the same as I had seen in my youth.

"Looking for any interesting books again?" Quinn asked, undoubtedly remembering his gift to me a decade ago.

"No, just looking," I said, and then something hit me. If Teacher hadn't yet written that book that had changed my life, how could he be put to death? When would he be able to write it? I looked at Quinn, who spotted my surprise.

"What?" he said.

I stared at him as my mind raced, trying to make sense of the impossible timeline. It was confusing enough that I had read a book that, based on the passage of time, had not yet been written from Teacher's perspective but that I had already read. Teacher had even told me this. But now, with his impending death foretold, when would he write it? I knew his lessons contained much talk of timelessness, but still, I believed the book needed to be written and would be written in the world I knew, so he was running out of time. Of course, with his abilities, I had to give him the benefit of the doubt.

"He hasn't yet written the book," I said.

Quinn looked at me blankly, evidently wrestling with the same challenging logic I was struggling with but missing the part about Teacher's upcoming demise. He then stared off into the distance for a moment with a look that told me he was familiar with some of the practices I had studied. He was clearly trying to see or read or prophesize something. I could feel it. In all my interactions with him over the years, as friendly and as unassuming he appeared to be as a shopkeeper, he always seemed to have a far greater understanding of things than most would assume. This would explain it. He took his time before speaking.

"I see," he said slowly, not giving away what he might have discovered.

"What?" It was my turn to ask.

He smiled and said slowly, "He will write it."

I instantly believed him, which began to calm my active mind, with only the lingering knowledge of Teacher's approaching death leaving me questioning *how*. I nodded and turned my attention back to the tables.

I walked the aisles for a few more minutes, looking for something that might grab my attention but found nothing that interested me. Compared to being there when I was younger when I created exciting stories in my head about the origins of the pieces in the shop, I instead felt that the objects were distinctly ordinary, even boring. Perhaps my real-life experiences in the village, time with Teacher, and the understanding of the truth of who we are had given me a standard against which everything else seemed insignificant. It was as if I had lost the attachment to things that would have previously been important to me. Considering my personal experiences that extended beyond appearances in the physical world and knowing the impact of what I had come into the city to do, that made sense. There was so much more to life.

Before I left the shop, I said to Quinn, "Maybe next time I'll try to visit the way Kyna does."

"Yes!" he said. "I believe you have it in you." After a pause, he added, "Will we see Teacher again?"

"I believe you will," I said, trying to cover the sadness that suddenly appeared with his question. I wasn't sure if he picked up on my flash of emotion.

With that, we said our goodbyes, and I left the shop.

I slowly strolled by the other vendors amid the multitudes milling about buying goods. Again, I felt somewhat distant and detached but also incredibly attuned to the happenings around me. Near the end of the market, a man called out to me.

"Hey, weren't you with the man who spoke to us the other day?"

It was the man Teacher had spoken with when we had first entered the market, someone with whom he obviously had a relationship prior to becoming Teacher. I nodded and walked over to his cart, which was selling spices.

"I thought so," he said. "Is he coming back? Will we see him again?"

I gave the same answer I gave to Quinn. "I believe you will."

He smiled and said, "I'm so glad to hear it. Here, take this back to him. He'll know it's from me," and he proceeded to scoop and place a few select spices in a small pouch, which he handed over.

"Thank you," I said. "And thank *you* for whatever role you played in helping him become the person he is."

"Oh, I didn't do anything. We were just good friends."

"Well, that must have been it then," I said.

The man laughed and came out from behind his cart to give me a big bear hug. I embraced him back before turning to walk out of the market toward the southern road that would take me back to the farm.

~

With my self-imposed isolation from others in recent days, my trip to the city went mostly unnoticed. I was back before mid-afternoon. Shasta, however, had observed me coming down the road.

"Hi," she said as I approached the farmhouse.

"Hi," I replied, wanting to avoid talking about where I had been.

She had always been very good at reading me and gauging my moods, and today was no different. She stared at me for a moment and said, "If there's anything you want to talk about, I'm here."

"Thank you," I said. "Not now, but maybe another time," and I passed by her. It was still too fresh and Teacher had asked me not to share, but if anyone would understand, I knew that she would.

I saw Teacher in the distance working in the vegetable gardens as he sometimes liked to do. Passing by the farmhouse,

I decided I didn't need to tell him anything because he probably already knew, so I continued up the hill to the rock where I liked to sit, wanting to be alone. Thankfully, others didn't often go there. As much as I was comfortable being around people in the city, the people here were different because they all knew and loved Teacher, as I did, and I had done something they were sure to find unforgiveable. Teacher had chosen me because I could understand and accept a task that they could not, forgiveness be damned, but I still couldn't yet bear their presence.

I sat alone on the hill for hours, only coming down as the sun dropped in the sky and I became hungry. Because I still wanted my solitude, I descended the hill to the farmhouse kitchen, gathered some bread and vegetables as they were being prepared, and went back to my rock, avoiding people as much as I could. I think those I encountered could tell I was going through something, so they thankfully kept a respectable distance.

Later, as darkness descended, I could hear Teacher speaking on the porch and answering questions, but I couldn't get myself to go down to join the group. Even though I knew this would be the last time he would hold these informal teaching sessions, I couldn't bear to be in his presence, as I felt my betrayal would become apparent. Instead, I looked out beyond the farm to the outlying Grand Wall in the dusky light, wondering what he meant when he said that he would get rid of the Wall for everyone.

The stone barrier was as I remembered it as a child—distant, massive, and mysterious—yet it also now held additional qualities given my experiences doing the transit and my knowledge and experience of what lay beyond it. I could now more fully appreciate the extraordinary limitation it presented, containing a way of life that resisted any challenge to change. But I also knew that that was an artificial way to live, as the limitation wasn't true. There was so much beyond it. Even as a child, I had

had fantasies that there was more to it and more outside it, and those visions didn't just come true, they were true beyond my wildest imaginings.

Teacher was going to do something to the Wall, and I didn't know what or how, but I knew it would be transformational. If everyone had the ability to transit it like I did, or if the Wall was actually demolished somehow, their worlds would open up to the knowledge that there was so much more than what existed in the Territories. Any thoughts of adventure or discovery they may have had in the past would no longer be suppressed by the belief that the rules and regulations they lived under were absolute. And with minds and lands open, anything would be possible.

I sat with these thoughts, slowly finding some peace within the emotional turbulence of this day that had seen my role in the prophecy fulfilled, the day before Teacher would be arrested.

~

I had a restless sleep and was up early as the dawn light began to color the sky. Preparing to walk up the hill to my rock, I heard the crunch of boots on the road echoing in the dewy air. Turning to look, I saw Alexander leading a dozen constables through the morning mist toward the farmhouse, my father among them. I walked toward them, and they stopped in front of me. Alexander said nothing, but he didn't have to. His clenched jaw and sad eyes spoke volumes. He knew exactly what he was doing; he was fulfilling his role as requested.

His eyes left mine and turned to the porch. Teacher had silently stepped out of the house and was standing at the top of the steps. I looked at him, and he exuded the peace I was having trouble finding in the moment. I turned back and looked at my father, who seemed as upset as I was.

The sounds of the constables had awoken a few others, and I heard hushed whispers and movements as those awake went to rouse the rest. Before I knew it, most in our group were standing silently near the porch observing the scene. Ariana had emerged and was holding Teacher's hand. She also looked like she was barely containing her emotions.

Teacher gave her a kiss on the cheek, let go of her hand, and casually descended the steps. As I moved to the side to let him pass, he looked at me with his infinitely wise eyes and embraced me. I hugged him back, not even realizing I was crying. I wasn't alone.

He released me, stepped toward Alexander, and paused. Alexander held his gaze and didn't move a muscle. Teacher then walked around him and through the other constables toward the road. With everyone frozen in place, all eyes were on him until Alexander turned and followed him, trailed by my father and the rest of the uniformed group. They proceeded north up the road toward the city, leaving the rest of us standing alone amid the sounds of sobbing.

No words had been spoken.

~

Breakfast was a somber affair, as most ate in silence on and around the porch. With Teacher gone, my desire to be around people had shifted, probably because everyone seemed to be feeling upset at the turn of events. I suppose I could finally find common ground with others in their expressions of sadness and grief, something I had been hiding during the previous days.

Toward the end of the meal, Shasta stood up and made an announcement.

"Teacher has instructed me to tell you to go back to your villages. There is nothing more you can do here." She looked at me after speaking.

"We have to help him!" someone shouted.

"We can't do anything for him that he can't do himself," she said. "You know this."

"We have to try!"

"No, we don't," I said as I stood up. Everyone turned to me. "He said the same thing to me. We must go back to our villages."

"That's easy for you to say. You're in the prophecy. Tell me, was him being arrested in the prophecy, too?"

I didn't know how to answer, so I just said, "There's more to it than how it appears."

"Well, then tell us!" He was joined by a chorus of others agreeing with him.

Shasta chimed in to save me. "Teacher's instructions are clear. Go back to your villages now. If you want to defy him, that's your choice, but know that you will be risking arrest as well." Her voice was strong and almost scolding.

That quieted the group, but the man who had spoken out turned and marched away angrily, followed by two others. The rest stood staring at me and Shasta, seemingly awaiting further instructions.

We looked at each other, then Shasta said to the group, "There is nothing else to say. Travel well."

Everyone's initial unease at the circumstances slowly morphed into action as people helped clean up from breakfast, gathered their belongings and supplies for their journey home, and prepared to leave the farmstead. I paid particular attention to Ariana, who seemed lost in thought more than the others. Eventually, I approached her.

"Ariana . . ."

Before I could say more, she turned and hugged me in a long, tearful embrace. When she released me, she spoke.

"Anna, you did what you had to do. Thank you."

I didn't know what to say.

"I'll be back in your village at some point," she continued, "but not right away. Save me a seat at the dining table." She smiled.

I nodded, still having difficulty finding my voice.

An hour later, the house was in pristine condition, as if no one had been living in it for weeks. Shasta and I stood on the porch, watching the others leave.

"Are you okay," Shasta asked.

I nodded and took a deep breath. "I'm okay. You?"

She looked at me and said, "Liar."

We both laughed, and she said, "Me too. Me too," and gave me a hug.

We proceeded down the steps and began making our way back to our village, but I stopped when we hit the main road.

"I need to go back to check something," I said. Something had popped into my mind, and I needed to take care of it right then.

Shasta eyed me appraisingly and said, "Okay, I'll wait."

"No, you go ahead. I'll catch up. It shouldn't take long," I said, and I turned and began walking the short distance back to the farmhouse before she could respond.

I could feel her watching me, but when I arrived at the porch and turned back to look at her, she had begun walking up the main road.

I entered the house and looked around, then felt compelled to climb the stairs. Something was drawing me to the bedrooms upstairs, and I suddenly realized what it was. I went up the steps and to the bedroom on the right. Progressing to the bed, I pushed it away from the wall, looking for a loose floorboard by the legs. I didn't find one, but I saw the edge of something sticking out from under the bed after I had moved it. I pulled out the object and let out a gasp.

It was a leather book cover with an embossed image of a crescent moon on the front. I assumed someone from the crescent-shaped village outside the Wall must have accidentally left it there. But that wasn't what had surprised me. What had gotten my heart racing was that I remembered the same image being described in Teacher's book, *A Tale of Awakening*. He had written—or will write—that when he was an adolescent, he had found a book of parables in his room with the same exact cover, and it was one of the first indications to him that monks and the Ancients had really existed. The stories had encouraged him in his seeking and gave context to the lessons he would subsequently walk through.

I turned the worn leather over in my hands and opened it. There was nothing inside. And then it dawned on me.

I scooted the bed back into place, sat on the edge of it, and opened my small pack of personal belongings. Smiling through the tears that were beginning to emerge, I pulled out the pages of parables I had written. They had accompanied me on my journey through the Territories, and I had occasionally added to them when I had had the time and motivation to.

Now, I gently placed the pages inside the leather book cover and held it to my chest, thanking the circumstances that had brought Teacher and me together throughout time.

My original plan in returning to the farmhouse was simply to leave the parables on the table downstairs anonymously. With the role I would be assuming as the representation of people's negativity, I didn't want my writings to be associated with me. I knew, however, that they might benefit others, and I figured someone would eventually find them there.

Now, I could see how it was all coming together. I walked with my pack and the newly-wrapped parables to the slightly larger bedroom on the other side of the staircase and again moved the bed away from the wall. Seeing the edge of a floorboard rise slightly, I scooted the bed further away and lifted the loose plank to reveal a hidden compartment about two hands wide and three hands long. It was empty.

I sat staring at the empty space for a minute before softly laying the book of parables down in its center. Then I put the floorboard back into place and moved the bed to the wall where it had been. Mumbling thanks once again, I descended the stairs and left the farmhouse, walking briskly to catch up to Shasta on the main road.

~

The trip back was uneventful. We eventually caught up to a few others from our village and walked with them around the perimeter of the city to the northeast, ultimately finding the path that Shasta and I took over a decade ago when I first left the city. Oddly, we didn't encounter anyone from the government on our journey.

As we approached the Grand Wall near where Shasta and I had been questioned by the two constables, I remembered how she had taken my hand and walked me through it for the first time. She had been there in the beginning of my new life and was still a guiding force. I also remembered how Teacher had helped me transit the Wall in the same spot when I was being chased by the constable, something I know I couldn't have done without his help.

Shasta and the others went up to the stones and paused, and I could feel their energy shift as they prepared to transit. Shasta turned to look at me and said, "Are you coming?"

"In a minute," I said. "I'll catch up to you."

She nodded, turned, and disappeared into the Wall behind the others, leaving me alone.

I stood quietly in front of the barrier and stared at it, not yet wanting to transit. It gave me a chance to feel the energy of the land I was about to leave, which reminded me of the limitations I felt in my childhood. It made me uncomfortable, and I realized that this was probably how I had always felt when in the Territories and probably how everyone who lived within the Wall felt on some level. It wasn't that I didn't have times of feeling uncomfortable in the village, but there it had a different quality, an openness and lightness that encouraged finding a way out of the feeling. Obstacles or challenges existed to be overcome, compared to the feeling of being constrained and discouraged by them in the Territories.

After a few minutes, I centered myself and reached inward to the light within as I prepared to transit, but it felt different. I could tell something was missing. I tried again and pressed my hand forward to the Wall, and it met the cool, firm stone surface.

Incredulous, I stared at the barrier, then put both hands against it. It was as dense as it could be. I smacked it with my hands a few times, then tried again to go within to get to the place to transit, but it didn't work. I was stuck.

After a moment of panic, I began laughing, not just a chuckle but a full belly laugh that surprised even me. I'm not even sure why I was laughing, but thoughts of my betrayal, what it meant symbolically, and that this might be penance for it ran through my mind. I was laughing so hard that I didn't notice that Shasta had come back through and was staring at me from a few feet away.

"Did I miss a joke?" she said, chuckling in resonance to my laughter.

I stopped for a moment and looked at her, then burst out in giggles again, and she joined in. I walked to her and gave her a big hug, and my laughter quickly turned to tears of sadness over what I had done. She knew—she had to know—and she held me warmly, rocking me slowly back and forth in her embrace.

When I had finally exhausted my tears, she took my hand and said, "Shall we?"

I nodded, and she led the way through the barrier, just as she had done when I was thirteen.

~

The next day, I heard that Teacher would be put on trial for subversion. In addition, it was clear word had gotten out about the role I had played, that I was the one who had told the authorities where Teacher could be found.

The news left me shaking. It was all too real now, and there was no turning back. I returned to my cabin and did my best to go within to calm myself, which helped some.

While practicing contemplation and finding some peace, I remembered Teacher's words about writing. I rose and looked out the window at the magnificent nature that surrounded me, and the desire to tell my story—and his, to some extent— rekindled itself, infusing me with an impatience that drove me to take some blank pages, a quill, and a bottle of ink off the shelf, sit at the table, and begin composing. What seemed to need to be expressed had finally made itself known.

I wrote voraciously over the next week, the words flowing easily from the memories of my wonderful experiences starting the fateful day I ran away from home and found myself in the village with all its remarkable people.

With the village now knowing what role I had played, the information appeared to split the community into those who knew me well, who supported me, and those who didn't know me well, who looked upon me with disappointment and avoided me as best they could. I didn't know how people had learned about it, as I knew Shasta wouldn't have told anyone, but I also knew it was inevitable that they were going to find out, as the point of my deed was to be the face of Teacher's betrayal, and that couldn't happen by keeping it a secret.

Thankfully, I had my good friends around to comfort me when I questioned my decision and found myself emotionally vulnerable. They also helped sustain my writing efforts, fetching food and writing supplies as requested when I couldn't bear to head outside to face the scornful looks of those who didn't fully understand.

I spoke with Promeus during this time to try to get some clarity on what was next for me now that I had completed my prophesized task. He confirmed that what I was doing with the writing was where I needed to be and that the rest would unfold in due time. He also told me that he now fully understood my role and why I had needed to fulfill it. That was comforting to hear, as it helped me feel just a little bit better about what I had done.

He also told me, in confidence, that he would not be in the physical world much longer. He didn't know when, but it would be soon. He said he was thrilled to have lived long enough to see the prophecy fulfilled and to have had the great pleasure of meeting and conversing with Teacher. I was upset but felt better when I took his perspective, someone who had truly *lived* the lessons I had learned and whose life had seen—was seeing—the beginning of what we both believed was to be a great transformation. He was still here, though, and I hoped he was wrong about his fate.

The next day, news of the verdict of Teacher's trial came to the village. The Territory Governors had found him guilty, and he would be put to death in two days. Apparently, Kyna had visited the city and had heard about it as soon as others heard, and she had immediately returned to her body in the contemplation hall to let the village know. If I was getting distrustful looks before, it was doubly so now, which once again caused me to second-guess what I had done.

When Jillian stopped by to check on me, I asked her if she could fetch Kamaria, the village artist, because I was finally ready to acquire my first tattoo. I felt that the symbol I had in mind would help focus my energies and more fully anchor me to the teachings of the village, and to Teacher's lessons, of course, and perhaps help keep me more centered amid the mixed energies directed my way.

Kamaria arrived soon afterward, and when she was finished, my forearm displayed the sacred symbol for the one sound.

I stayed in my cabin the rest of the day, visualizing the symbol and hearing its resonance deep within my body, which helped me rise above the irritating thoughts and emotions—mine and others—that encircled me.

Later the next afternoon, I practiced the slow dance with Jillian and Naveen out behind my cabin, which thoroughly refreshed and energized me, and I decided I wanted to go to dinner with everyone else that evening.

Mealtime was surprisingly normal, despite a few concerned looks thrown my way. I sat with Jillian and Naveen, and Shasta, Kyna, Caedmon, and Promeus joined us for a wonderful discussion as if our beloved teacher was not facing death. It reminded me that life goes on, regardless of my or others' perceptions of the circumstances around us.

Afterward, I fell asleep in Jillian's arms, finding a sense of peace amid the scattered emotions of the previous days and weeks.

The next morning, after Jillian had left, Shasta came by to tell me that Promeus had passed away. I was saddened to hear the news but knew it was coming. She said that she had been there when it happened and that he had some final words for me, which were, "Remember, child, that even that which is foretold can change." I wondered what it meant besides the obvious.

Shasta and I had a long, warm-hearted discussion, reminiscing about Promeus's long life, ability, and teachings as we fondly remembered our time with him. I felt he was there with us, smiling that magnificent smile of his and finally knowing all that he had sought to understand.

Later, I sat in contemplation, trying to go above my mind to comprehend Promeus's last words to me. I felt him there with me, holding my hand and wrapping me in his wise and loving energy. He didn't seem to be trying to get me to understand his words but rather was just sitting with me as we used to sit together in front of the contemplation hall.

As usual, though, being in that wonderfully soft space began to convey the understanding I sought. I stayed with it, and soon a knowingness overcame me that caused me to open my eyes in surprise.

And I knew what his last words meant.

~

The next morning, I awoke to something feeling very different. It snapped me to awareness quickly, and I immediately rose and sat on the edge of my bed to center myself to try to experience it more clearly. At first, I couldn't exactly describe it, but it had a light, refined quality that reminded me of Teacher. I wondered if he was about to visit me.

It was an energy whose power, breadth, and depth built up quickly, and it felt like it pervaded everything, everyone, everywhere. It grew in size and scope to be more powerful than anything I had ever felt with a quality that made it seem unavoidable and inevitable. It rolled over me like a massive thunderstorm over the plains, leaving nothing untouched by the lashing of the wind and rain.

And I knew what it was.

Teacher was destroying the Grand Wall, but it wasn't *only* the Wall that was being smashed to pieces.

A crackle of energy burst forth with the force of lightning, pervading the all-encompassing storm that the world was already immersed in. It infused every crack and crevice of my being, and I at first welcomed it as it surged into me, but as it dug in and scoured at the rust of my perceived faults and imperfections, I could feel myself resisting its cleansing. For some reason, despite working hard over the years to transform myself to come to a better awareness of who I truly was, I still held fast to some obstacles to that awareness, which I could now feel being vigorously scrubbed.

The energy was ruthless in its purging and transformation. I was holding onto things that I felt I needed—doubts about my momentous decision, fear of not being accepted back in the community, and anything and everything I had retained that I had chosen to limit me, whether I was aware of it or not. The energy itself was not harsh and grating—rather, it was soft and loving—but it came across as abrasive because of my continued grasp of what I *believed* I needed to keep close: my attachments and what I felt defined me in this world. *They* were the reason for my discomfort.

And I really didn't need them! In the energies washing over me, I saw that my holding onto past emotions, perceptions, and concepts were exactly the things causing me pain, not just at that moment but throughout my life. I had made great strides to understand myself and had worked to transform what held me back from realizing what Teacher had realized, but I retained views and feelings that were incompatible with that realization. I couldn't step through a portal into a new world while keeping *anything* from the old world, for nothing from the old could exist in the new because the perception from the new would automatically destroy the old.

What a paradox! I wanted to attain the full awareness that Teacher had attained, but in this energy, I knew I had to be willing to let go of the world I was familiar with—every memory and experience, every friendship and relationship, every current perception and understanding—to be able to approach the transformation I knew was possible. The awareness I desired couldn't be found here, in my current life and surroundings that I had worked so hard to improve. The glimpses of truth I had had before were just that, glimpses, and I knew there was no way to finally open my eyes completely to the truth until I trusted that I would receive so much more than what I would give up.

As my imperfections were being unceremoniously scoured out of my being, I also saw that the intensity of my holding onto that which didn't ultimately serve me was directly proportional to the suffering I was experiencing.

So, I said to myself, *No more*.

I relaxed my grasping of the world I knew and trusted that what was washing through me could only help, and through that acceptance and allowing, the discomfort vanished, and I could feel the clean, bare surface of the truth being resurrected within.

While I was trying to understand my personal transformation in that moment, something else was happening around me: the Grand Wall was also being transformed. I could *feel* it in my bones. As my perceived imperfections were being washed away, the Wall was disintegrating, turning back into the dust of the earth, for the Wall and my limitations were one and the same, as they were for everyone.

The destruction of the Wall happened within each of us at that moment. I knew it to be true, the walls of limitation breaking down, the walls of clinging to old ways—old thinking, old feeling, old *being*—dissolving before my eyes in this light of truth. And I could feel it not just in myself but in those around me. The ancient, self-perpetuating shadows in our minds had given way to the eternal source from which all things originated: the light that rested within all.

And I saw that my beloved Teacher was at once the Perceiver, the Ancients, and the light within each of us that is unchanging and ever-present. He, like those who came before him in the light of truth, had taken it upon himself to be a beacon for others on their journey to greater awareness. *He* was doing this, and this moment of cleansing was a resetting of *everyone's* perceptions, whatever their understanding, so that the rocks in the fields of their minds dissolved to reveal fresh and fertile land within which to cultivate this truth.

A few minutes later, the energy subsided, and I was left bewildered but extraordinarily peaceful. Doubts and guilt about my role had vanished, and I felt more present than ever. I stood up and stepped to the door, my body steady but new, like I was using it for the first time.

I walked outside and down the path toward the village clearing. When I arrived, I found others who also looked like they were new owners of their bodies. Their faces all had a peaceful, detached quality and they looked around at their surroundings as a baby might when introduced to a new world. I probably had the same look because that's how I felt.

Slowly, I made my way back to my cabin and lay down. The feeling in and around me gradually dissipated and my rational mind returned, although it felt different from before. I felt a sense of blankness, as if I had lost the context my personality would have normally injected into my thinking and emotions. My inner, sometimes-critical, background voice was remarkably quiet.

Eventually, I drifted off into a deep sleep, dreaming of open fields of wildflowers.

~

That afternoon, as everyone in the village was integrating their newfound perceptions from what we all had experienced, word spread that the Grand Wall had indeed vanished. I wasn't surprised.

I had known when it had happened, perhaps because of my connection to Teacher, my role in the prophecy, or from my diligent practices and openness to his mission. Whatever the case, I had a smile on my face for the rest of the day knowing that Teacher had done what he had said he would do. Even recognizing that his death was imminent couldn't erase the fact that I was finally content with my decision to help him now having seen the results of his actions.

In addition, people abruptly became more welcoming to me, praising me for my brilliant role in having a part in bringing forth the powerful energy we had felt and the destruction of the Wall.

I thanked them, of course, but denied that I knew that any of it was going to happen. What I said didn't seem to matter. Any negative perceptions of me in the village changed within hours.

A few people shared worries about no longer having the Grand Wall to protect us from those in the Territories—namely, the government—but with the shift in awareness we had all experienced, as well as Kyna's reassurances, that kind of talk faded quickly enough.

It was a new age. The Wall was down, and personal failings and constraints had been retuned and returned to a lighter, deeper state more aligned with what was within than what was in the outside world. I was contemplating this and what might come afterward when, in my cabin, I felt an additional lightness fall upon me just before a knock on the door.

I opened it and there stood Teacher, as radiant as ever.

~

"Hello, Anna," he said.

I shrieked in surprise and threw myself into his arms. It took a moment before I realized he was probably projecting himself from his detainment cell in the Territories, as his sentence was to be carried out the following morning. I pulled him across the threshold and closed the door.

"Was that you?" I asked, already knowing the answer.

He smiled. "Yes."

"What was it? What did you do?"

"As you know, it has been difficult to get through to many people, even after they see me, hear the words, and witness the miracles. Collectively, the world was in a difficult place, and it needed something drastic to shift people's perceptions. I simply adjusted what they were unaware of in themselves and removed the heavier, entrenched shadows that prevented their ability to learn and grow."

"I felt it," I said. "It was extraordinary."

"Yes, I can see it in you. Even with where you are with what you have learned, there is always another portal of understanding to pass through while here in the physical world, so you experienced it as everyone else did, just on a higher level. You did well with integrating it, Anna."

I nodded. It was wonderful to be in his presence again, to see and feel him. I suddenly felt sad that I probably wouldn't see him again, that this would be his last visit.

"There's something else I need to tell you," he said.

My heart sunk, but not as much as it would have before the recent event.

"I'm here."

I turned my head slightly and squinted my eyes at him. "What do you mean?"

"You had asked me to reconsider my decision to do what I thought was necessary. I did just that and came to the conclusion that what people experienced this morning and the destruction of the Grand Wall would be enough for them to remember the teachings."

I blinked, not quite believing him.

"Anna, I am here because of you. *You* saved me."

I staggered backwards and sat on the edge of the bed.

"But . . . how did you get away? Won't they be looking for you?"

He shook his head. "They have other things to think about now." He walked to the bed and sat next to me. "The world is changing, and it needs me, and you, as guides to help people understand it."

I was trying to digest what was happening. Teacher was not going to be put to death, he was really here, there was no longer a Grand Wall, and I was going to be teaching what I had learned from him and others. It was a certainly not what I expected when I woke up that morning.

"Wait, what about when you said I needed to fulfill my role so I could represent the opposite of what you represent? If you're really here and that's not needed anymore, who will fill that role?"

He smiled softly. "Upon reflection, I decided I needed to have more faith in people and came to trust that the teachings—through me, you, and others—will be enough for them to realize the truth over time."

"So, who will people point to for their failures?" I asked. "Who will they blame for those times of negativity and bad choices?"

"By not having a figure to represent the darker energies of human nature, I have the sincere hope that it will encourage accountability instead of blame and self-reflection instead of projection."

I nodded, feeling the weight of the world off my shoulders and thankful that I could resume leading what I hoped was a normal life.

"By the way, how's the writing going?" he said.

I looked at him and smiled. "I haven't been able to stop."

"Good. It will go a long way toward helping others understand what has happened."

We chatted for another hour, sharing our respective experiences since parting at the farmhouse and talking about the future. He was going to move back to the farm permanently, and he invited me to do so with him and a few others, but he said my time there would not last more than a year, as I had my own path to follow and different people to teach. I pressed him for more, but he wouldn't provide any additional details.

As he prepared to head out the door, I remembered something I hadn't had a chance to give him. I walked over to a shelf on the wall and grabbed the small pouch of spices that the vendor in the marketplace had given me to give to him.

"From the spice seller in the market," I said as I handed it to him.

"I thought I caught a familiar aroma," he said with a deep, warm smile, accepting the gift. "I am truly blessed to have good friends."

I was almost overcome by his energy in that moment and the profound way he looked at me.

"Everyone in the village will be happy to see that you're out of the Territories and safe," I said.

"There are no Territories anymore," he said. "The walls are down. It is finished."

He winked at me and stepped through the doorway.

And with that, he walked away, leaving me smiling, content with the understanding that the world was going to be okay after all.

Epilogue

Anna reached over her desk, placed her quill in the holder next to the ink bottle, and sat back in her chair. Rubbing her swollen, wrinkled knuckles and looking at the pile of handwritten papers on her right, she felt tired, but she also noticed the beginning of a shift in her energy. Her latest writing project was now complete, and with it came a sense of closure, which often meant that she might be releasing something that no longer served her on her path.

The feeling wasn't unfamiliar, as she had experienced it many times over the decades, but it had a different intensity this time. Previously, she could feel that a certain sense of completeness portended the loss of something she was growing out of, but it always came with an equivalent feeling of something new coming to her, so she knew there would be a progression in her learning and growth. Indeed, that was how everyone learned and grew, letting go of the old to make room for the new. Being accustomed to the feeling, she could allow the process to run its course with a few minutes sitting in contemplation.

With Jillian out of the cabin delivering some clothing she had mended, Anna took the time to do that now, straightening herself after brushing her gray hair away from her lined face and going within to the place of peace she knew so well. It had become far easier over the years, almost to the point of her being able to live from that place consistently, but still she fell short of doing so. She knew it was possible, however, because of Teacher, so she retained a sliver of hope.

Dropping into her center, she found that this time of contemplation was starting off differently than previous times when transition was upon her.

With her eyes closed, she quickly found herself in a peaceful garden surrounded by wildflowers, and Teacher was walking toward her.

She had seen him frequently in person over the years but not in months. When they had seen each other, she had always noticed that he seemed to have resisted aging while those around him wore their years and life experiences like personal decorations. She assumed it was because he was able to live from that space she had become close to but had not yet fully accepted as her own.

Now, in the field of flowers, he looked the same as when she had first met him.

"Hello, Anna," he said as he approached. "Nice setting you've made for yourself here."

Anna smiled, feeling the love and joy she always felt when in his presence. "It's one of my favorites," she said.

"Yes, I can feel it."

He stepped closer to her.

"Anna, I'd like you to do something."

She looked directly into his clear eyes. "A long time ago you said you would never ask me to do anything else for you."

He smiled. "I'm not asking you to do anything for *me*. I'm asking you to do it for *you*."

She gazed at him blankly for a moment before fully comprehending what he wanted her to do, even before he asked, but she needed to hear him say it. He clearly recognized her thoughts and spoke.

"There is only one thing that is keeping you from living as I do, and you know what it is."

"Please, tell me anyway," Anna said.

Teacher smiled. "You love the life you have. You love the village and your friends in the community. You love Jillian and Naveen. You love writing and teaching. You love that you are fulfilling your role in leaving the world a better place, and indeed, the world is a better place because of you."

Anna nodded slowly, knowing what he was going to say next.

"That love has sustained you here, and you will carry it with you. I only ask that you take that love beyond where it is now bound, beyond the world of form."

Anna didn't want to hear more, but she stood tall and continued to listen.

"I know you've had issues with your physical body that the healers could only do so much with. As you are aware, this is because the progression of this world has meaning to you. I understand this, as I was once in the same place. You have lived a long life full of wonder and change, and it is easy to be committed to that which you love about the world, especially as you have gone about making it better for yourself and others."

He paused and put his hands on Anna's shoulders, looking her squarely in the eyes.

"But there comes a time when the last step is before you, and it is just such meaning that is keeping you from the realization you seek."

Anna could feel her emotions rising, but she surprisingly was staying deep in contemplation.

"You have spent most of your life seeking this, and now that final portal beckons, but it requires one last thing: trust. Trust that there is more. Trust that by letting go you will attain more than you can possibly imagine. Trust that those around you will understand and be inspired. Trust that the world will be okay, regardless. Trust that what you must leave behind to go through the portal is something you never needed to carry in the first place. Trust *yourself* to bring you to—"

"To another world," Anna said softly, interrupting him.

Teacher smiled deeply and nodded.

"You've grown from one world inside the Grand Wall to another outside of it, and then to another within. There is but one more that encompasses all of them, in fact *governs* all of them. It is where I reside."

"So, it's possible to live from it while here in physical form?" Anna asked.

"Yes, but for most people, their physical bodies are so intertwined with the world they know that it cannot be done while in the flesh."

"And me?"

Teacher looked lovingly at her. "If you had your current understanding a few decades ago, yes, but now your body is frail and is being sustained by the energy of your practices. Without them, it would have failed years ago."

Anna nodded. Her physicality had certainly diminished over the last few years to the point where most movements caused some aches and pains.

"*You* have to be willing to take the step through the portal, knowing that you are forever connected to those you've loved. You, and they, will be okay."

Anna looked down, knowing the moment was here. After all Teacher had talked about having a choice, she knew she had to make one now, and she did.

"What do I have to do?"

Teacher put two fingers under her chin and lifted it so he could look into her eyes. She felt an energy building up with a power that could consume worlds.

"Accept *who you are*."

Immediately, the power that had built up released around and through her, blinding her with a brightness that made the flowery landscape seem quaint in comparison. The dazzling light had a clarity that heightened every one of her senses, including non-physical ones she had spent so many years cultivating, which left her seeing and feeling beyond anything she could have ever anticipated. And she did what he said and surrendered to it, accepting and allowing it to engulf her on all levels.

She felt it through her entire body, a relinquishing of the last vestiges of the life she loved, and any physical aches she had had just moments before instantly vanished as she was held in the shimmering, refined arms that seemed to extend outward from her as far as she could see.

Those arms brought a sacred connection to everything they encountered, and she could finally understand what she had been missing, what Teacher had been trying to get people to understand through his countless lessons. She had been caught up in the world, enticed and enthralled by encounters that produced glamours and distractions simply by living her life. She knew this, but now, feeling the oneness of the connection to the people, places, and things in her life's experiences, she could see how shallow her understanding really was, despite all of what she knew. It had to be *felt* to be known, not just mentally understood. Even her past feeling of it seemed to pale in comparison to the fullness of the experience that was occurring.

It all made sense now, everything Teacher had ever said, from his beginning lessons, to the lectures in the Territories, to the private talks on the porch of the farmhouse. She could understand the full context from which he taught and lived to a depth she never had before. It was a knowing beyond all shadows of physical existence, and it was just those shadows she had to let go of to realize it.

She recognized that the pang of sadness that rose briefly was exactly what he had said it was: her attachment to the world of form. In the feeling, she rested in the understanding that it was all impermanent anyway, that she and others were simply playing their roles while in bodies that could interact in the way they did, and it all seemed so minor in relation to the all-encompassing feeling of oneness that surrounded her.

But it wasn't just surrounding her; it was emanating *from* her. *She* was the body of oneness from which the arms of light extended, and she recognized it as the source from which all things originated. Her life and the lives of everyone she had ever encountered were but shadowy specters in a world of illusion built upon the permanence of the oneness she shared with them. *She* was the source, just as everyone else was as well.

And suddenly, she realized that Teacher had *not* come to visit her in contemplation. It was her own projection of what he represented—something innate in all people—that had brought her to this state. She had achieved it herself from the depths of the clear, inner wellspring of peace and harmony she was finally wholly, completely, and *unconditionally* submerging herself in. And she knew that it wasn't something to be achieved because it was already there and had been for eternity.

She understood—fully, finally—the whole of what Teacher had experienced and what he had become, from his challenges as a farmer struggling with his life and the questions he grappled with to his awakening and teaching. It was all there, in her experience, too, and in everyone's, if they dared to look and take the steps to challenge how they viewed the physical world.

She didn't know how long she sat in contemplation, but she was roused out of it when she heard Jillian come back from her errands and close the door behind her.

"Oh, I'm sorry!" Jillian said. "I didn't mean to disturb you. Do you want me to leave?"

"No," Anna said softly, seeing beyond her partner's white hair and beautifully aged features. She stood up and took a step forward, still looking at Jillian with a depth she hadn't known was possible when she had sat down and closed her eyes.

Jillian watched her approach. "Um, are you okay?

Anna smiled with a knowingness that transcended anything she had ever experienced, an understanding of life and love pouring out of her to enwrap Jillian and fill the room.

And she took Jillian's face in her hands, looked into her eyes and through her physical body into that which made them both the same, and she spoke the timeless words she had read on the last page of a story from long ago, words that she now finally, truly understood the way Teacher had intended.

"I am."

Acknowledgements

I would like to acknowledge and thank my beta readers and editors for their feedback and editorial contributions, including Ruth Santos, Brandon Jopko, and Tere Gade, among others. I would also like to acknowledge and thank those too numerous to list here who have touched me in any way as we connected beyond time mentally, emotionally, and/or physically, for it is through those connections that I have found what makes us all the same. The concepts in this book come from that place.

About the Author

Peter Santos has been studying spirituality and healing for over three decades while balancing a varied and successful career using his left brain. His extensive travel to sacred sites around the world, including walking the Camino de Santiago in Spain and trekking to sacred Mt. Kailash in Tibet, has grounded the spiritual wisdom he has received, and he is happy to be able to share what he has learned through his writing and teaching. He lives in Vermont.

If you enjoyed this book, please consider leaving a review, as reviews can meaningfully support independent authors like Peter. In addition, you can stay updated on Peter's writings, events, and other projects at www.peter-santos.com and on Facebook at www.facebook.com/petersantosauthor.